God's Angels Devil's Demons

Final Frontier

Jered Abrams

Copyright © [2023] by [Jered Micah Abrams]

All rights reserved.

No portion of this book may be reproduced in any form without written permission from the publisher or author, except as permitted by U.S. copyright law.

Contents

1. From The Shadows — 1
2. Ring Of Sorrow — 24
3. Walk Of The Stranger — 47
4. Lost At Home — 57
5. Old Invaders — 71
6. A New Purpose — 85
7. Long Way from Home — 96
8. The New Hunt — 105
9. The Most Dangerous Game — 115
10. Path of Destiny — 125
11. Deceit and Dispair — 135
12. Unlikely Pair — 146
13. Spectre — 157
14. The Warning — 167
15. Daughters Of Eve — 174
16. Queen's Return — 185
17. The Good Guys — 197

18.	War in the Heaven's	205
19.	Unexpected Return	213
20.	Itching Iniquity	221
21.	Flock to Battle	230
22.	7 Lights	241
23.	Bellicose Avenger	247
24.	Final Call	255
25.	Transitions	265
26.	Homeward Bound	270
27.	Second Chance	278
28.	For All To See	287
29.	Time Like No Other	290
30.	A New Beginning	295

Chapter One

From The Shadows

There are places beyond the cosmos of human understating. These are the places where spirits move and dwell. However, these spirits don't always agree with one another. You may know them as angels and demons—each side being diametrically opposed to the other. Their issues seem simple to understand, but the intricacies of their interactions may be more complex than you realize. For example, fallen angels are former servants of Heaven that rebelled and are now instruments of evil. They live and fight to see the destruction of any kingdom that stands against their own dark agenda.

Then, somewhere in the heavens lies a room encased by a great hall. In this room is an ancient scribe standing and writing on a kind of scroll. He turns his head and catches your gaze. His skin is like living silver and the pupil of his purple iris is live with fire. There are no sign of wings nor is there any indication that this is an angel.

"Thank you, narrator. I can speak for myself. Welcome to the hall of Ancients, dear reader. My name is unimportant at the moment, but I do the work of a scribe. Think of me as a Curator, Maven, or even a Connoisseur of knowledge."

The scribe pauses briefly then shifts his attention back to you. "You may call me CMC for now."

His gaze is off you yet again. He places the scroll on what appears to be a desk. It quickly fades away. "Recording the events, stories, and works of believers is my specialty. Today we shall do just that. This tale is from a believer from the strange land of Texas. It is based on the final book of biblical canon: the Book of Revelation. A very important yet cryptic account of the end times. This tale is not meant to substitute the reading of scripture nor is it a prediction of dates of biblical events. This tale exists merely as a visual aid of what could be. Farewell for now, dear reader, for you have not seen the last of me."

Far from the hall of ancients lies a land designed to train heavenly warriors for battle. This area in the heavens is known as Milhama. Some of Heaven's mightiest angels gather here to coordinate and plan their attacks on their enemies. Here, a high-ranking angel known as Ignas stood before a class of Zimrats, lower warrior class of angel.

Ignas was larger than most angels and had an ego to match his size. His skin was light purple and there were five eyes on his body. Two where eyes normally are, one in the back of his head, and the other two on each of the backs of his hands. He wore a black and gold robe with a large train. An elegant sword hilt known as Alypto hovered behind him and kept the robe train from touching the ground.

"Strike true when you engage with your enemy. Demons may be weak but they are dangerous in large number," Ignas said.

The Zimrat angels under his command obeyed every word that came out of Ignas's mouth without question. While they trained, another large angel walked toward Ignas. Ignas recognized the angel immediately and excused himself from his subordinates.

"Master Michael, what brings you to Milhama?" Ignas asked.

Michael shook his head. "Please don't address me as your superior. We all know what you've done. You've done more for this kingdom than I ever have."

"Very well," Ignas said. "How can I be of service."

Michael took a moment to observe the Zimrat angels. He smiled at them fondly. "The great battle with the dragon is nearly upon us," Michael said. "Your orders are to immediately deliver the Infernal Arms to the four horsemen."

Ignas processed the order. Internally he was annoyed, but he was cool and calm externally. "Michael, I fail to understand why one of my Zimrats can't deliver those accursed weapons? I'm an Oze just like you. Is it right for us to deliver tools of death to the enemy? Especially since the great battle is upon us."

"These orders are not from me," Michael said. "You know this to be true. Deliver the arms then do as you like."

Ignas folded his arms. "Is there anything else?"

"There is one more thing," Michael said. "The Lord of Host has also authorized you to dispatch a Nava angel into the first quadrant. Make sure you dispatch your Nava angel after you have delivered the weapons to the horseman. It is of great importance. You may call him what you want."

Michael briefly paused and rested his chin in his hand. He scrunched his brow and focused deeply. "This mission may prove too much for a Nava. Nevertheless, orders are orders. One of your favorite games is Flash. I believe humans the humans call it chess. How about we name the Nava after the human variant of the game."

Ignas nodded and kept quiet.

Michael turned around as if he heard something. "I must be going, old friend. We are settled on a name for this Nava, and you have your orders. Maybe we can play a game together after we crush hells angels. Just you and me."

Michael departed. Ignas wasted no time with his new mission. It filled him with dread but also purpose. He left heaven immediately and descended into the depths of hell to retrieve the Infernal Arms.

Hell wasn't designed for heavens angels. They only came here if they were under strict orders. High ranking angels like Ignas loathed this place. He wanted to leave as soon as he arrived. Ignas reached his destination and searched for the weapons. Many serpents gathered together. Ignas forced them away, but his search continued to be futile.

"Where are they?" A familiar voice echoed in the distance. "The great Ignas has been reduced to an errand boy. I'd never thought I would see the day."

Ignas was angry but remained calm. There were no emotions to process. Only logic and strategy.

"Hello, Mamba," Ignas said. "Of all the snakes in the garden I loathe you the most. Now where are the weapons? I have no time to chat."

The snakes twisted and wound together. Fire engulfed the snakes, and they broke apart and formed four items: two great swords, a pair of spiked balls connected with chains, and a silver crown. Ignas stretched his hand out, broke the will of the weapons, and had them follow behind Alypto. Ignas quickly left Hell and headed for earth. He hoped never to return to the great pit again.

The city of San Diego rested in the darkness of the early morning. It looked nothing like it did in the past. A massive wall encircled the city, and its growing population struggled to sustain itself.

One woman who lived within this city paced back and forth in her room and checked her Cobber, a two-inch-wide silver bracelet that housed an AI companion.

"When is my package getting here Molo?" she spoke at the device on her right wrist.

The AI responded quickly: "Your package should arrive in less than five minutes."

The woman walked into her kitchen and sifted through the mail. She stared at the big manilla envelope addressed to her from something called Zohar for a moment then placed it down and sat next to the door. Her focus was more on the package than the envelope. She began to do push ups then retreated to her cold cup of coffee. The woman checked her Cobber and stood up. "Great, its here," she said.

She opened the door and watched as the drone dropped off a large box.

"Thank you for choosing Jopa," it said. "It is recommended that you receive assistance. Do you need assistance with this case?"

Th woman grabbed the case and maneuvered it inside the apartment.

"I got this, tin can," she said.

The drone buzzed away and the woman dragged the heavy case in her living room. "Molo, scan for malware or any defects," she said. "I paid good money for this thing."

The AI scanned the box as ordered. "There are no malware or defects detected."

The woman took opened up the first layer of the brown box. She read the bold golden letters: *Life Egalitarian Organism*. "So that's why everyone calls them Leo's," she said.

The woman opened the second layer and a machine-like being slowly shuttered and shifted out the box. It made strange noises and began to glow. In its black and white alloy suit, it looked human, though its gold, glowing triangle on its left temple distinguished it from humanity. The woman waited for it to respond to her. Seconds later, it was fully functional.

"Hello, my default name is Leo. I require a name. What shall you call me?"

The woman pondered the question. "I need you for a very particular task. So, I will name you after my dad. He was good at completing task. Both decisive and pragmatic. Your name from this point on is Westin."

Westin processed the info and moved on. "All Leo's require a DNA sample to register in the database. How will I extract this DNA?"

The woman began to pluck her hair, but Westin stopped her. "A blood sample will suffice."

"Good grief, Westin, you could have just said that."

The woman stuck out her hand while Westin pricked her finger and took a small sample of blood.

"Thank you for your cooperation. Registration is complete. I'm yours to command."

The woman wasted no time in asking questions. "Are all Leo's operated by Organic Intelligence? If so, that would mean that you're under the jurisdiction of the super robot Persephone. Am I correct?"

"That is correct," Westin said. "Most Leo's are manufactured by the company known as Jopa and are ruled by Persephone. However, I am a Chinese model, and I am currently not under her guidance."

The woman scoffed. "You're telling me I spent one hundred thousand dollars on a Chinese trinket? The box says made in America. However, I suppose it's good you're not under OI control yet. Remind me again what tier you are."

"I am a mid-tier Leo model superior to lower tier models and inferior to higher tier models. However, I will not obey the OI known as Persephone unless overridden."

The woman became ecstatic. "That's perfect. I can tell my story without being silenced. Molo, bring up my notes."

Westin approached the woman. He was careful to maintain at least three feet from her.

"May I see that primitive AI you call Molo?" Westin asked.

The woman raised her eyebrow. "Sure, why not."

Westin observed the AI and took it over. "The primitive AI is gone. I am now connected to your Cobber device. You may now use my name when addressing it."

The woman didn't seem phased.

"Look Westin," she said, "we don't have much time. I need you to listen and record everything I tell you."

"Very well, I'm listening."

Westin moved to the corner of the room while the woman stood in the center. She set up artificial lighting to enhance her presentation. Clearly much thought went into this. She took a deep breath and began to speak.

"This is a message for both young and old. For posterity and antiquity. My name is Yessica Cali Hoffman. I am a Lieutenant Commander in the US Navy. Welcome to the last day of America. Three months ago, the war we all feared finally came to an end. Some call it the Last Straw. Others call it World War Three or simply the Great War. I regret to say that this story doesn't have a happy ending. Ultimately, we lost. This nation is now a nuclear wasteland, but somehow the West Coast was spared. California, Oregon, Washington, and Alaska are all that's left of the States. The rest of America is either gone or plunged into civil war."

Yessica used her Cobber to create digital augmented map. She analyzed it closely as she continued.

"America's real problems started two years into the great World War. This is when the Great Catalyst occurred. Over the course of three days, the US president, vice president, and Speaker of the House were all killed in coordinated attacks supposedly carried out by Christian radicals. Its widely believed that these radicals had the help of Christian members of government. This event caused this nation to quickly spiral into civil war. 3-D printers only made things worse. Today they are as common as bread lines. Cheap and deadly plastic-printed pistols and rifles flooded the streets when civil war broke out.

"China was our main adversary during the Great War. They took advantage of the chaos and had their drones drop tons of ammo boxes across the nation to keep the civil war going. America may have survived had this not happened. Democrats and Republicans formed new pseudo states among the American wasteland. Today, they still fight over what little resources are left."

Yessica tapped her Cobber. It pulled up a massive map of California.

"Things are different in the states. The military protects the innocent and the remnants of America—such as the Constitution and other important documents. Today we have our first female African-American president. Los Angeles, California, has become the capital of the United States. It is five times its original size and is also encased with a great wall that's quality rivals China's. It kept the rebels out at first, but the city grew too quickly with refugees. Now Los Angeles is a sophisticated slum."

Yessica created a visual display of the world nations with her Cobber. She shook her head when she looked at it then continued.

"Today there are no more superpowers. Nations like China, Russia, America, and India are gone. All victims of nuclear weapon attacks. There is one silver lining. Most of the nukes used were EMPs. Only twenty thermonuclear bombs were used to destroy major cities. Thus, the world was spared from a nuclear winter. All that is left is a bevy of nations formerly known as NATO. Today they are called Pangaia. An alliance of nations, this group claims to rule the world. Their sphere of influence looks very similar to the old Roman empire. Led by their overlord Supreme Queen Elizabeth III. They will take over what's left of America in eight hours. When the clock strikes twelve pm, I will no longer be a free citizen. I'll be a citizen of Pangaia. Forced to take an oath to serve the goddess Gaia and her prophetess the Supreme Queen. US dollars will become the Pangaia currency known as bract, and the wealthy will possess power like no other generation before it."

Yessica took away the augmented displays and closed her eyes.

"It seems like I'm destined to be a part of this strange empire. They are ruled by queens, kings, merchants, and a religious cult known as the Conglomerate. This one world religion blends all faiths into one. You're able to believe in whatever god you want, but you must acknowledge Gaia as the supreme being of everything. We're also dealing with another CAVA 31 virus outbreak. Currently on the Echo variant."

Yessica sighed and opened her eyes. She looked into Westin's eyes and finished her address.

"The last ember of this war was in the middle east. The fighting between Israel and Iran finally ended two weeks ago. The man responsible for brokering peace between these two nations is a former US Navy Admiral. We called him 'Five Star Freddie.' The fifth ever fleet admiral of the Navy. He hung up the uniform and became an ambassador of Pangaia two months ago. Somehow, he managed to broker peace between Israel and Iran. This peace treaty should be a definitive end of this awful war. There is one bright side to this story: Africa is now a paradise for both rich and poor from around world. Like most of Europe, it has been spared any nuclear fallout. Okay, Westin, that's enough for now. We'll speak more later."

Westin walked to the window with human grace and saw the morning sun rise over the horizon. He looked at the great wall surrounding the city and marveled. "That's an impressive wall, Yessica."

Yessica looked out the window but wasn't impressed.

"We spent billions on the walls in San Diego and Los Angeles," she said. "It was supposed to stop crime, but this place has become more of a favela than a fortress."

Yessica began to walk away but stopped and turned around when a thought came to her. "Can you grant me access to Sedah?"

Westin nodded. "Yes, I can but I can't access Sedah without Persephone. Doing so would corrupt your data."

Yessica still had questions, but her Cobber began to alert her.

"Do you want to keep my combat abilities operational?" Westin asked.

Yessica quickly answered, "Yeah, keep 'em. Why not."

She focused on the call. It came from the local naval base. Westin patched the call through. Yessica answered, but Weston was unable to hear her voice or the callers. She hung up the phone and headed for her room.

"Are you in distress Yessica?" Weston asked.

"No, my Command called. They need me at the base. I have to go, but you can't stay here."

An idea popped in her head that seemed brilliant at the time. "I'm taking you to my storage facility," she said. "No one can find you there, and you'll be safe from Pangaia."

"Whatever you think is best will do just fine," Weston said.

Coronado Naval Base trained some of the US military's most elite fighting forces: the Navy SEALs. US Navy SEALs do some of the most daring, urgent, and dangerous missions for their country on a regular basis. The most elite of Navy SEALs, arguably the greatest fighting force on the planet, are known as Seal Team Six.

At this base a small group of Navy SEALs lifted weights prior to morning quarters. The weight room was outside, and the cool breeze from the Pacific embraced them as they enjoyed the clear blue sky. Yessica walked by as they trained. One of the SEALs took notice and got the attention of another SEAL close by.

"Is that Artemis?"

The other SEAL continued to curl heavy weights. "Yup, sure is."

"Why does everybody call her that?"

The SEAL put down the weights and wiped the sweat from his brow.

"She has never failed a hunt," the SEAL said. "And her beauty is divine. Let me tell you a fabled legend about her: One day Artemis was on mission and was separated from her team. A cobra appeared and bit her arm. The snake died two minutes later. Artemis was unharmed. You must know that no one has risen up through our ranks like her. She made SEAL Team Six after only two missions on record. It's truly remarkable what she's accomplished. Now do you see?"

The SEAL's jaw nearly dropped. "Crystal clear. I guess I'm a believer now."

The mood was jovial on the base. This was the Navy SEALs last time together, so they did a 5K fun run and an obstacle course to lift their spirits. The SEALs then hit the showers and got ready for quarters.

Yessica left her office and ran into Commander James Baker down the hallway. He smiled at her as they did their secret handshake.

"Remind me again how a toothpick like yourself made SEAL Team Six."

Yessica laughed but quickly returned to her usual serious demeaner. "Remind me how a meathead like yourself made it out your mothers'..."

A nearby sailor yelled with great enthusiasm. "Attention on deck!"

Yessica and James stood at attention and watched as the base Captain and a three-star admiral walked past them. When the admiral was several feet away, they relaxed.

James took notice. "What's that all about?"

Yessica shrugged. "Who cares. I heard you made it to Zohar. Congrats and good luck."

At this time, most SEALs were transferring to Zohar, the most powerful intelligence agency in world. They often hired US special forces to serve as consultants or mercenaries.

"Thanks," James said. "Will you join me? I know they want you."

"We'll know by the end of today. Hooyah."

A large number of SEAL Team Six gathered and waited patiently. Leading the formation was Senior Chief Hapily. He was given the code name "Hope" for his no-nonsense attitude and adherence to Christian doctrine. When the officer in charge approached, he took command. "Certified Roughnecks, attention!"

The Senior Chief turned and saluted the officer. "All Roughnecks are here and accounted for ma'am."

Yessica held her salute. "How's your daughter, Senior?"

"Safe and finally back in my custody ma'am."

Yessica dropped the salute and turned toward her men. "At ease, Roughnecks." She gave a stirring speech that greatly lifted their spirits. This was likely their last time seeing each other, and she made sure to personally address all of those under her command.

When she was finished, she dismissed the sailors. A yeoman approached her urgently. "Sorry to bother you ma'am but the captain wishes to speak with you."

Captain Magnetta was a far above average Navy SEAL. He quickly rose through the ranks for his bravery and audacity and for always looking out for the wellbeing of those under him.

He sat in his uncomfortable chair and smoked a cigar. He granted access when there was a knock at the door. Yessica entered and gave all her formalities. Captain Magnetta put his feet on his desk while Yessica maintained an alert posture.

"Before I continue, lieutenant, I must know. How in the world does a woman of your weight and build become the leader of SEAL Team Six? It defies the very laws of nature."

Yessica had dealt with this question her whole career. It simply wasn't enough to be special. She had to be otherworldly.

"SEALs are born not formed sir."

The captain smiled. "Excellent answer, LTC, or should I say, TOT? At ease."

Most SEALs called Yessica Artemis. She also had another title called Terror of Tehran. Hearing it brought back dark memories. It was part of a past she often tried to forget. The captain puffed his cigar and explained himself.

"I'm sure you're wondering why a three-star brass monkey had the audacity to show his face in our house. Well, it turns out it was for good reason. You've got orders to sixth fleet. The admiral wanted the best for this mission, and I told him that was you and your men."

Yessica scrunched her eyebrows. "May I speak freely, sir?"

The captain nodded. "Of course, lieutenant."

"America is about to become Pangaia, and we have no legal authority to do anything."

"Duly noted, lieutenant. However, technically I still have three hours before that happens. Until then you and your men still belong to me. Any other questions?"

"My boys can handle whatever. A full SEAL team should do just nice."

Captain Magnetta rose to his feet and held a piece of paper in his hand.

"I can't give you a full team," he said. "You'll have to choose your three best men. Go ahead and name them."

Yessica looked as the captain held up the piece of paper. It read "Execute Tehran Protocol." Yessica knew that this meant to use codenames. Her guard was up. She knew she was being monitored.

"I'll need Hope for leadership and marksmanship," she said. "Blade for linguistics and weapons. And, I'll need Joker for comms."

The captain was pleased with the selection. "This mission will be your last, Artemis. Briefing will be in ten minutes, officers only. Just me, you, and the three star of honor. It's that sensitive. Your transport is old faithful. The USS Adams. It leaves in two hours."

"Sir," Yessica said, "that's a Zumwalt class Destroyer. We're trained to respond immediately. It will take weeks to get to sixth fleet on a surface ship. Why can't we catch a ride on a submarine or use air transport?" "Everything will be explained in the briefing LT. I'll also have a yeoman inform and gather your team."

Then the proud Captain did something he never did: he reached his hand out to a subordinate. "It was an honor being your Captain."

Yessica shook his hand and prepared herself mentally.

Captain Magnetta then gave her some cryptic final words: "A deadly beast has no bite when a huntress has its head in sight."

Yessica thought he was referring to one of her legendary feats of the past. However, only those under her command referenced these feats. "I don't understand sir."

The captain continued. "Happy head-hunting Artemis. I know I can count on you. You're dismissed."

Yessica left the office and attended the briefing. When it was finished, she returned to her locker room and found a top-secret file on former five-star admiral Freddie Samson. This was a blatant disregard of Operational Security, but she knew this file was left here for her eyes only. She figured it came from none other than Captain Magnetta.

The seas were calm and the mood was jovial aboard DDG 1003. The USS Adams was a relic of the past. It was slim, deceptive, yet also deadly. Yessica and her team gathered on the aft flight deck to discuss the mission. The area was cut off from the rest of the crew, which allowed them to speak freely about their sensitive mission. Senior Chief Hapily tried to gather the men in formal ranks, but Yessica forbade it. They huddled instead.

"Before I give details on the mission," she said, "I need to know if you're with me. We'll start with you, Blade."

Petty Officer Leif "Blade" Orrell was a brilliant mind and a consummate quiet professional. Yessica had no doubts about his abilities as a warrior. His focus was another story. Leif was a bit of a party animal.

"O money stands for old money, ma'am," Blade said. "I'm with you."

Yessica was pleased. "The Leif of the party speaks. What about you, Joker?"

Petty Officer Steve "Joker" Manelski was a serious sailor but only during the mission. Joker liked to think of himself as a social caretaker as well as a comedian.

"Saltwater shots are on me, ma'am," Joker said.

Yessica maintained her serious demeaner. "Just keep your head on a swivel, Joker. What about you, Hope?"

The large Senior Chief smiled. "Where you lead, we'll follow, ma'am."

Yessica thanked her team and got straight to business. "We're on route to Israel to provide overwatch for our former five-star admiral Freddie Samson. The same five star who defeated China with the power of the world's greatest Navy. Hooyah!"

Yessica's men hollered "Hooyah" right back. It was an old US Navy term of endearment meant to bolster sailors' confidence when spoken.

Yessica smiled proudly and continued her speech. "Though his strategic genius was no match for the civil war at home. We all know that this civil desperation led to our nation's nuclear demise. He became a diplomat after the conflict between China and US ended. The admiral was both Jewish and a master strategist. Pangaia put

17

his talents to work quickly. He was put in charge of brokering peace between Israel and Iran. Our mission is to ensure this peace process happens smoothy. We have three weeks to prepare."

Joker looked at the others. They all thought similarly, but only Joker said it. "This isn't a mission for SEALs, ma'am. What gives?"

Yessica kept quiet until saying, "That's all for now. Dismissed."

Yessica read the file on Freddie Samson for the second time. She didn't notice anything different at first, but she did find something of interest. There was some sort of land deed. Her focus was taken when a hand knocked on the door. Yessica wondered who it could be this late at night. She hid the file and opened the door. It was Joker.

"What is it, Joker?"

"We're just wondering what you're not telling us, ma'am."

Yessica became agitated. "Stop calling me *ma'am*. I've always hated that."

"How about LT?" Joker said.

"Getting warmer."

"How about boss?"

"Yes, Joker, that will do."

"I'll inform the others, boss. May I speak freely?"

Yessica wanted to finish reading the file but gave in. "Yes, Joker."

"I was thinking that this may be our last time together. I wanted to know where you stand."

Yessica was confused. "What are you talking about Joker? Are you talking about Hawaii?"

Joker nerves were clear. He was an easy tell. His hands shook when he was scared. But so was Yessica. Her face reddened, and tears filled her eyes.

"It was one night, Joker. We were drunk, and my husband just left me. It won't ever happen again, so stop bringing it up."

Joker had been holding on to this memory for quite some time. "You know how I get nervous around beautiful women, but I'm here anyway. I just want you to know that I love you, boss. No matter what."

Yessica felt pity for Joker and tried not to wound him further. "Sorry, I know you care for me. We'll talk again when we finish our mission. I promise."

Joker left the room, which gave the space back to Yessica. She immediately combed through the file. The file described that Pangaia worked with Freddie Samson to divide up what was left of America's West Coast. This would divide America into sections. Ambassador Samson had apparently agreed to get a large sum of land in Washington. About forty thousand acres. Reading the file put a pit in Yessica's stomach. This file was proof that during the Ambassador's two-month reign he used his influence to sell out America for personal gain and territory.

The purpose of their final mission was now revealed. They were to kill this American traitor. However, the intel reports inside the file reminded them that the USA and its military were no more. They were now rouge mercenaries. After the mission, they could choose to be a part of Pangaia or walk away into the sunset. America would be a land divided up by Pangaia.

The last part of the file revealed that a ranger unit would also be helping out with the operation. Yessica wondered about their role, when she heard another knock at the door. Yessica put away the file and opened the door. A woman with red hair barged in and put her bags on the other bed. Yessica was used to having her own space. Now she would have to share it with someone else.

"Who might you be?" Yessica asked.

The woman reached her hand out. "Lieutenant Colonel Ruth Hopkins. I'm a doctor assigned to the Ranger unit that will be helping you."

Yessica shook her hand and introduced herself. "Lieutenant Commander Hoffman. Thanks for the help, I guess. How many Rangers are helping out?"

"There are three, if you're including me. Don't worry. Pronto and Sinkular will brief you."

Yessica's arrogance swelled within her. She wanted to make sure the Colonel knew what she was getting herself into.

"Look I know that Rangers do some mean push, but we're not just Navy SEALs. We're SEAL Team Six. Think you and your boys can keep up?"

The Colonel flopped onto the bed and stared at the celling. "I have no doubt Lieutenant Commander Hoffman."

"Call me Yessica."

"Very well, call me Ruth."

Yessica checked Ruth's credentials via her Cobber to make sure she wasn't a spy. After a thorough check, she relaxed and shared the details of the intel file with her. Ruth considered the evidence.

"I wonder why he chose to betray his countrymen," Ruth said. "We all thought that he would lead America into independence from Pangaia. This is troubling news. What are you going to do?"

Yessica polished her combat knife. "I'm going to send this Judas thirty pieces of lead to the brain."

Ruth reached in her bag and tossed a package to Yessica. "They told me to give this to you."

Yessica opened the package and found small cube. She didn't know what it was but put in in her pocket for safe keeping.

Weeks later the Navy SEAL and Army Ranger units arrived in Tel Aviv, Israel. They disguised themselves as Pangaia security and worked closely with them to provide overwatch for the Ambassador. Hope was normally the designated sniper, but Yessica insisted she be behind the trigger. They all had comms but kept the line clean. No one spoke unless they had to. Yessica held a 50-caliber rifle and was just shy of a mile away. "I need more distance," she said.

Suddenly the cube in her pocket came alive. It transformed into the Leo known as Westin. Yessica's jaw dropped.

"What are you doing here?"

"I'm here to help," Weston said. "It was easy to find you. Apparently, the USS Adams was the only US military vessel at sea."

Westin transformed into a massive sniper rifle capable of carrying 90 caliber rounds. "Will this help?" Weston asked.

Yessica tossed the 50 caliber and got comfortable with the Westin sniper.

"Had you disabled my combat abilities, this moment would not be possible," Weston said.

Yessica hated idle talk when on mission. "Yay, me. Now shut up and just spot me already. I need to focus."

Westin guided her shot accordingly but had one last piece of advice. "Yessica, I've found something extraordinary in your blood. Your blood is so toxic that it can prevent normal blood cells from ever clotting again. It's the ultimate killing machine."

Yessica knew Westin was being polite. "You don't think the shot alone will kill him? It is true that I rarely bleed."

Westin became proud. "This can only be found using state of the art tech. Lucky for you my model has such tech."

Yessica cut herself on the finger. She doused a single 90 caliber bullet in blood. Moments later, the ambassador's car arrived and he made his way onto the stage. Yessica decided this was the time to come clean about what she knew. She explained all the details of the file and what was their final mission. Their secure comms remained silent as Yessica explained the treachery of their former leader.

"Captain Magnetta told me that our arrival had to be unassuming," Yessica said. "So no subs or planes. Pangaia intelligence would expect that. This is a highly delicate mission. Which is why we're not in uniform and its why it took three weeks to arrive here. The USS Adams was a gift to Pangaia as a peace offering. Let's make it a gift that keeps giving. Five-star Freddie Samson has to go. Only a handful of people will ever know the truth about this mission. I've tested every one of you. You are wolves and not sheep. Shredders and not shepherds. I know that you are all with me. For that I thank you."

The ambassador began his speech in front of a sea of people. While he spoke, both teams answered in unison. "We're with you, boss."

Yessica controlled her breathing. She lined up her target and slowly pulled the trigger.

Chapter Two

Ring Of Sorrow

Three women walked toward a skyscraper. They entered the tall shining tower and rode the elevator to the twenty-third floor. They stepped off the elevator and entered an executive suite. A large, muscular man lifted weights in the center of the office. His name was William Calig, the CEO and owner of Jopa, the world's most successful company. Jopa's net worth was believed to be valued well into the trillions of dollars. No other company came close to Jopa's wealth, reach, and influence. William noticed the three women but continued his workout.

"Hello ladies," William said. "Nice of you to join me."

The three women approached William but stopped a few feet away. On the left was his assistant Cynthia. To her left was his publicist Lisa. On her left was Carrol, the Chief Operations Officer at Jopa.

Lisa spoke first. "William, the Geo-Ball will be a great opportunity to measure your favor with the citizens of Pangaia. I do hope you will take this opportunity seriously."

William dropped the weights to the floor and grabbed a towel.

"Thank you," William said. "I'm aware of the ball's importance. I'm ninety-three years old, not fifteen. There is no need to chide me."

He sat down in his chair and took a deep breath. "Tell me something good, Carrol."

William spun around in his chair like a child. Most people were intimidated by his large presence but not these three women. They were his chosen advisers due to their loyalty and ruthlessness.

"We're doing good in all areas," Carrol said. "Manufacturing can't keep Leos on the shelf, and our peace-keeping weaponry is still bought by Pangaia in bulk. There is a slight problem with our business with young people. They are rejecting our SIGIL tracking devices. Apparently it's not what the planet intended for them."

William scoffed. "That's no surprise. This is what happens when you put a bunch of tree-hugging liberals in high office." He turned to his assistant. "Is my outfit for the ball ready?"

Cynthia bowed slightly. "Yes. I've procured an outfit for you," she said.

William leaned back in his chair. "Well then, let's see it."

A high-end model Leo bot walked into the room, wearing an outfit similar to what Henry VIII wore. However, it had a modern flare.

William loved it.

"It's perfect," he said. "Now get back to work."

The three women turned and headed for the door.

"Not you, Cynthia."

Cynthia turned around and approached. "Yes?"

"I'm heading for the shower. The ball starts in an hour. Care to join me?" William asked.

Cynthia turned him down playfully. "You truly are the man William." She gently touched his massive chest. "The problem is you're not my man."

"Well, it was worth a shot, but that's not why you're here right now. I need you to gather my birds and have them meet me at the hotel after the ball."

Cynthia nodded. "Right away," she said. "Is this for business or pleasure?"

"Pleasure, of course."

Cynthia looked down, concern drawn across her face.

"What is it?" William asked. "Don't you think this type of behavior is dangerous? If the public ever found out that the great father William acted like this. It could destroy you."

William sat up in his chair and smiled. "I haven't been called father for a very long time," he said. "Did you not know that the man was not made for the woman but the woman was made for the man. It's actually biblical."

William reached out and took Cynthia's face in his palms.

"I like it when you play hard to get," William said. "Your resistance only fuels my passion. It doesn't quench it"

Cynthia tried to get a word in, but William stopped her. "Just make the arrangements Cynthia. Now leave me be and get back to work."

Pangaia's third annual Geo-Ball was being held in the island nation of Cyprus. All the kings, queens, celebrities, and merchants of Pangaia gathered to celebrate their dominance over the earth. It started out as a noble cause for maintaining world peace. However, the formal event devolved into a publicity stunt. The leaders of Pangaia were required to have Neo-Tudor era style clothing. These were the orders of the Supreme Queen, a woman obsessed with the period of time between the fifteenth and seventeenth century. For this was the era of her hero: the great Elizabeth the First, arguably England's mightiest queen.

William arrived in great flare to the ball. Thousands of adoring fans cheered as he walked the green carpet toward the entrance. The press at the event did all they could to get his attention. William gracefully declined their advances. However, one person with the press caught his eye. It was a young man in great physical shape. He wore a sleeveless vest, had sunglasses on, and donned a pink mohawk. William beckoned Cynthia to his side. "Who is that man and why isn't he dressed appropriately?" he asked.

Cynthia whispered in his ear. William raised his eyebrows when she unmasked his identity.

"Bring him to me," he said.

Cynthia brought the young man over to William. "May I introduce DJ Pauly E," she said.

William sized him up quickly. "Do you know who I am?" he asked.

The young man slapped William's shoulder. "Of course, dude!" he said. "Everybody knows who you are."

William became agitated but hid his emotions well. "You certainly lack decorum," William said. "But I may have use for you. If you'll excuse me."

William entered into the grand building and took his assigned seat. The lavish event flaunted the wealth of Pangaia. The host of the ball sang on the main stage. Cory Abraham who was a living legend. After the song Cory paid tribute to an even bigger legend. "I would like to just honor a titan that passed away last week. None other than my big sister Beth Abraham. Who passed away at the age of 113. May you rest in peace."

A round of applause occurred, but William barely put his hands together. Something about this woman didn't sit well with him.

"Now let's welcome to the stage our Potentate, Supreme Queen Elizabeth the Third," Abraham said.

The entire room stood and welcomed the magnificently dressed woman.

"Thank you, Cory," the Queen said. "We all mourn the passing of your sister. One of our greatest minds. I remember when Gaia first spoke to me in a dream. I was just the prime minister of England back then."

The Supreme Queen took a moment to search the crowd. "Where are all the former prime ministers?" she asked. "Stand up please."

The Supreme Queen looked into the dark crowd and saw dozens of people stand up. "Isn't it good that we are kings and queens now?" the Queen said. "Gaia spoke to you also during that time. It's the only reason Pangaia became a reality. She may have chosen me as her prophet, but it was not because of my brilliance or my wealth. It wasn't because of my power. She chose me because her divine will allowed it. Today, I share this responsibility with you all as equals. Let us celebrate this journey together tonight. Our amazing world has been entrusted to us. Here's to an eternity of Pangaia. It won't be long before our wounded world heals itself from the ashes of war."

The audience erupted in applause. William maintained a sour look on his face, but he applauded as well.

"Three years ago, we destroyed our greatest foe—the great Red Army," the Queen continued. "We did so with precision. With the grace of mankind's greatest creation, Persephone, and with the guidance of Gaia. I'm asking you all to keep your faith in me knowing that there is nothing that we can't accomplish. Enjoy the ball everyone."

The Supreme Queen ended her speech and walked on the dance floor, which cued Cory to sing one of his famous slow dance songs. She looked in the crowd and saw William staring at her. She used her finger to indicate his presence was requested. William walked onto the floor and began to dance with the Supreme Queen. Their relationship was rocky at best, but they did need each other more often than not.

"Hello, my Prince William," the Queen said.

William tried not to roll his eyes. "My grandfather fled England in disgrace before settling in America. I'm no more a Prince than he is. I was born and raised in Dallas. You do realize that at my heart I'm a Southerner through and through. I also was a savage priest but you know all this already. Forgive my foolish chatter." William said.

The Supreme Queen dropped her gentle façade and whispered into his ear. "I know everything about you William. You need not lecture me." Her eyes darted across the room. She schemed and plotted as she danced. "I'll get to the point. War is coming and I'll need your help and resources. If you do as I say, I will make it worth your while."

William looked around and saw all eyes were on them. He flashed a smile to his competition and pretended to be enjoying himself.

"Very well, Potentate," William said. "You have it. Is that all?"

The Supreme Queen also looked around the room but with much more style and grace. She loved attention and basked in all it had to offer.

"I need you to deal with the savages quickly," she said. "There are reports of them destroying Conglomerate temples and shrines across our empire. As you know, these same savages destroyed the American empire, which cost us tremendously. The loss of wealth caused by them is unforgivable."

The Supreme Queen stepped away from William, and her servants immediately escorted her off the dance floor. William returned to his seat and watched the others dance. A Leo waiter came up to him with a bowl of what looked like cooked ground beef and asked, "Would you like some delicious flock, Tera Merchant William?"

William declined. "No thank you. I'm not that kind of people person."

Days later, the leaders of Pangaia came together to discuss a matter of great importance. The Supreme Queen sat on her throne as the Tera king of France reported to her.

"My Queen, the Cava virus is spiraling out of control. We should put resources into developing another vaccine."

The Supreme Queen listened intently to all her subordinates. She held up her hand to indicate that she was about to speak. "What does Zohar have to say?"

A man with curly red hair appeared as an augmented hologram before her and said, "My Queen, we have intelligence that the nation of Israel has the only known vaccine for this virus. Yet they refuse to share it. As Deputy Director, I recommend sending a peace-keeping force to retrieve this vaccine."

The Supreme Queen was pleased. "Then we have no choice," she said. "Pangaia's Peace Force will retrieve this vaccine."

Persephone stood next to the Supreme Queen. As General of Pangaia's Peace Force, Persephone was widely regarded as humanities' greatest creation. She had prosthetic skin, apparel inspired by technological fantasy, and a face with low glowing symmetrical lines to distinguish her from mortals. Persephone coordinated and executed the attack against the great Red Army in years past. The Supreme Queen glanced at her and gave her orders.

"Persephone," the Queen said, "arrest the Prime Minister of Israel immediately. I hereby declare that from this day forth, Tera Merchant William Calig, the leader of Joint Path will take the Prime Minister's place as king. Israel's territory is now under the control of Pangaia."

The elegant machine bowed. "It will be done, Potentate. Our resources should increase considerably with Israel under our control. It's a land with great wealth and resources. This is even more true since Jopa moved its headquarters there four years ago. Making William Calig Tera king of Israel will move him to fourth in line to the Supreme throne. Are you sure that you wish to proceed?"

The Supreme Queen acknowledged the clever machine. "Yes, I wish to proceed."

William wasted no time with his new position. He gathered his assistants in his office and went through a flurry of reports.

"How will I be received in Israel, Lisa?"

The publicist created a virtual display and said, "All reports say you'll be welcomed since we have multiple sites in Israel."

William was pleased.

"Very good," he said. "Who will be leading this invasion force, Cynthia?"

"Turkey will be the dominant force," Cynthia said. "The other forces are also Arabic. They all have a serious grudge against Israel. Iran has been ordered not to attack Israel. Unlike Israel they chose to be part of Pangaia. Israel is the last nation to resist Pangaia."

William was pleased with the reports. "Carrol, how will this affect profits?"

Carrol looked at her devices and computed the numbers. "It's estimated that our profits will go up sixty seven percent over the next five years," Carrol said.

William had a Leo help put his coat on and said, "Thank you, ladies. I'm off to speak with the Conglomerate."

The Conglomerate—Congo for short—was the official religion of Pangaia. This religion merged all faiths into one. The people of Pangaia were free to believe in whatever religion they wanted to so long as they acknowledged Gaia as the supreme God.

William entered a virtual room with various priest, monks, and faith leaders from all over Pangaia. There was no official leader of the Conglomerate, unlike the government of Pangaia. Therefore, William asked general questions and any member of the Conglomerate could answer.

He asked, "What do you suppose is Gaia's will toward this upcoming invasion?"

An Iman answered, "Gaia would not want war. We should reason with Israel. However, that's not our main concern. We need to address the savages attacking our temples. Were you not a former savage yourself, William?"

"Yes I was," William said. "I'll deal with them later. Listen to me. The people hear your voices. I need to know where the citizens of Pangaia stand. Are they for this invasion?"

A pastor chimed in: "We all know the influence you have with Zohar. Why are you wasting time asking us? Ask them."

William agreed. "It's true there was a time when Jopa and Zohar were under the same roof. That was ages ago. Jopa is just a business now. Zohar, on the other hand, is global intelligence, but they are not omnipotent. Just give me a yea or nay already."

An unknown priest answered William. "I am a Taoist priest. This is my first day here, but I think I know the problem. It is said that Gaia only appears to those that have access to Sedah. Why not ask those whom she has spoken to recently? You are a king now. Surely you can ask your co-rulers what they think."

William was pleased. "So you're the brave priest from the east. I'm glad that the people of your great nation are coming on board to Pangaia. I'll have my servants get in contact with you so we can properly introduce you here." William waved goodbye to the gathering crowds and made a quick exit. Thanks, everyone. I have my answers."

Within days, a massive force of both machines and men gathered at the northern and southern borders of Israel. Persephone showed herself to the world by a phenomenon called Echo Vision, a technology created during the Great War that was originally intended to reveal intentions to enemy and to avoid unnecessary casualties. Persephone led this force, hoping to bring Israel to its knees. At first, the Peace Forces faced no resistance. However, soon after the army splintered and became annihilated by all types of natural disasters. Many nations withdrew from the invasion, with the exception of Turkey and handful of other Arab nations. William watched every minute of the war with his own small army of secret drones. All the reports he read signaled that this would be a long and drawn-out conflict. He didn't want this and tried to think of a way to end this invasion quicky. William's ultimate goal was to have an Israel free from all Muslim's and foreigners.

Two Israeli prison guards entered a high-tech prison facility. They were assigned to the Beast section, which housed the worst offenders. The cells here were all small cube-like boxes with little room to stand or move around. The door on these cells was a blue holographic laser that could cut through human bone if one touched it. The two guards came to a prison cube and looked in awe on one of their prisoners.

"She's been like this for days," one guard said. "I don't think she's eaten or drank anything."

The other guard tried to get her attention. "Hey you wake up!"

The prisoner kept her eyes closed and maintained a tranquil presence.

"Hit the switch," the first guard said. "That will wake her up."

A gust of high wind began to push the prisoner toward the hot laser door. The prisoner immediately snapped out the trance and tried to keep from being shredded.

"Okay, I yield!" she said.

The guards were pleased. "That's what I thought," one said. "You're about to die anyway. Might as well be with your friends."

The guards escorted the prisoner outside. There were six other prisoners all blindfolded and tied to large wooden poles.

"Hey boss, glad you could join us."

Yessica stopped and marveled. "How can you see me, Joker? You're blindfolded."

"It was just a guess. Do you think they have steaks in SEAL heaven? I could use a steak right about now."

Yessica refused to answer. She was too busy being tied to a wooden pole and having a blindfold put over her eyes. One of the guards pulled out a small thick stick and hovered it over her mouth.

"Open your mouth!" he said.

Yessica spat on the ground, looked her captor in the eye, and said crassly, "Say pretty please, and I'll consider it."

The man forced the stick in her mouth and punched her in the gut. A firing squad of ten men loaded their rifles and aimed at the captives.

"Ready, aim,..."

A sharp loud whistle sounded. The executioners paused and searched for an explanation. A large man wearing cowboy boots walked toward them.

"Hold your fire, morons, and untie these colts," the man said. "I need them."

The guards all recognized him. "You're Tera King William Calig? What are you doing here?"

Unbeknown to them, several lethal small drones the size of insects flew above them. They were almost invisible to the eye. William whistled again, causing the air to pop with small gunfire. The guards now all lay dead where they stood. A Leo next to William unbound Yessica and her team. When William saw Yessica's face, he ran to her.

"My God, you look just like her," William said.

Yessica was confused.

"Do we know each other?" she asked.

William quickly changed the subject. "I'll be brief since we don't have much time. I have a mission for you all. The mission is to force the Pangaia Peace Force out of Israel."

"You just killed ten men," Ruth said. "Aren't you worried you'll get caught?"

William laughed. "Only the weak get caught! However, you sure are beautiful. I could use a nurse like you in my stable."

"I'm a doctor, actually."

William scoffed. "Yeah, right, and I'm a Democrat. Of course, I'm not worried about these guards. I've already framed you all for it anyway. Do you want the mission or not?"

The team all looked at each other and conferred.

"We're in," they said.

William hooted and hollered.

"That's the spirit," he said. "I need you to test out a new weapon for me. However, I'm a businessman not a slave master. I will reward you should you succeed."

Yessica answered, "What's the reward? We don't come cheap."

"I've worked with enough mercenaries to know that your loyalty is bought rather than earned," William said. "How about I give you all a blank check of freedom. You'll get new identities to keep Pangaia off your trail. I'll also arrange for safe passage anywhere in the world. What do you say, Yessica?"

"How do you know my name?"

William ignored her question.

"Fine," Yessica said. "We already said we're in. What else do you want?"

William began to pace back and forth. He looked deep in thought. "According to the Bible, there is to be a great invasion into the nation of Israel by a kingdom called Gog. I believe we are in this battle. Your prime target will be the second in command. We shall call him Meshech. The third in command shall be called Tubal."

William signaled his Leo, who in turn gave to Yessica and her teams their Cobber's back.

"I will speak to you by Echo Vision," William said. "It uses triangulated sound waves plus cobber encryption to form digital entities. Early on, it was used at first as an alarm system against the Red Army. Good thing is that it doesn't need satellites."

Will looked at his Cobber and excused himself. "I really must be going. The Leo here will get you what you need and answer any questions. Good luck on the mission."

William headed to Egypt to meet the Taoist priest he spoke with earlier. They met and greeted each other in a secret location.

"Hello, William," the priest said. "My people in China are very curious to know about how Sedah works. I know that after today they will be most pleased to hear my report."

William pondered what he would say next and settled on asking, "What do you think Sedah is? Is it a dream world or some grand illusion? It's actually a bit of both. So now the question is, how do you get there?"

The priest looked confused. "Aren't we supposed to connect to some sort of device or machine?" the priest asked.

William chuckled. "My friend you are the machine."

In an instant they were in the organic reality of Sedah. The priest looked at his clothes. He was dressed as a peasant. He searched for William but couldn't find him. He heard a voice above.

"Look up, priest."

The priest looked up and saw William seated on a golden throne dressed like a Roman emperor. There were digital personas kissing his feet as he smoked a bronze pipe.

"I know you're wondering how you got here," William said. "The truth is that all citizens of Pangaia have access to Sedah. This is because we require all citizens to have SIGIL. It's a tracking system that lives in the bloodstream. You were granted a SIGIL chip when you became a Pangaia priest, were you not?"

The priest asked, "The chip put in my Cobber gets in my blood?"

"I know it's a lot, but just trust me. It works. People like me are called Whales. We can grant or deny access to Sedah anytime we want. Sedah was once just an application of the teraverse. We don't give unlimited access all the time. That's bad business. We create a need and provide the solution for a price of course. Do you understand?"

The priest was amazed.

"Can I see more?" he asked.

"Certainly, but I heard you still have questions about Persephone," William said. "I admit she's an enigma to many. She is Jopa's prized creation and runs police, jailers, first responders, Cobber's, hospitals, health insurance, social credit scores, Leos, and more."

The priest looked concerned. "Is it wise to give a creation that much power?" he asked.

William thought little of the question. "Persephone is the ultimate property. She is not the ultimate power. Enough questions, priest. Let us travel deeper into Sedah. Where all your fantasies come true."

Yessica and her team were flying above Israel in a military transport plane seventy thousand feet in the air. They wore special breathing apparatus and had state of the art rifles and equipment. Their targets were a few miles apart. Ruth and the two Rangers would be going after Tubal. Yessica and the other SEALs were after Meshech. Their flight was brief but that didn't stop Joker and Blade from falling asleep. Yessica looked at her watch.

"Ten minutes to jump, Hope," Yessica said. "Wake the boys up."

Hope did as ordered and gently shoved the back of their heads to the cold steel frame behind them. Yessica looked comfortable as did the other SEALs. The Rangers were a different story, so Yessica asked, "What's wrong soldiers? Never did a HALO jump before."

Ruth, Pronto, and Sinkular shook their heads.

"HALO is an acronym for High Altitude Low Opening," Yessica said. "You'll be fine. Just check your altimeters like any other jump. I hope you and your boys can swim, Ruth. I forgot to bring floaties."

A loud buzzer sounded and was met with a flashing red light.

"Five minutes to jump. Joker, do what you do best," Yessica said. "Lighten up the mood."

Joker sprung into dialogue. "What grades do you need to join the Navy?"

"Just tell us," Hope said.

"Seven C's."

Joker looked at Yessica, who had a stone cold face as usual. However, Ruth became hysterical.

"Good grief," Yessica said. "It wasn't that funny. Keep going, Joker. Like always, the jig is up if you can make me smile."

Joker relished the challenge and continued: "What do you call a Ranger who can read and write?"

"This better be good," Hope said.

"Sir, yes, sir or Ma'am, yes, ma'am."

Once again, Ruth nearly fell out her seat laughing. Pronto and Sinkular didn't find it funny at all. Yessica looked annoyed.

"One more, Joker," Yessica said. "Make it good."

Joker thought for a second then went for it. "Two Airmen are walking down the street. The first Airmen speaks. 'Look a dead bird.' The second Airmen looks up in the sky. 'Where? I don't see it.'"

A small smile crept upon Yessica's face. Joker was ecstatic.

"Yes, I won," he said.

Blade looked disappointed and said, "Hey, my little brother's in the Air Force."

The Cargo doors flew open sending a rush of cold air through the plane. There was nothing visible save the dark red lights. Ruth and her men walked to the edge of the ramp and jumped into the darkness. Yessica stood up next and walked to the edge of the ramp. She boldly jumped into the darkness as her men trailed behind her.

The infiltration of the enemy camp was a breeze for the SEALs. They had done missions like these their entire careers. They easily made their way to their target without anyone knowing of their presence. There were small threats, but they were quickly neutralized with deadly precision. It only took them seven minutes to find their targets tent from the ice cold Mediterranean waters. Upon arrival they donned special black mask that hid their identity and changed their voices. Yessica gave her orders. Blade and Joker took action and neutralized the guards around the target's tent. Yessica and her team entered the tent and bound a sleeping Meshech. He tried to scream but Blade put a special device on his mouth that allowed only their team to hear his voice. Blade calmed the man by speaking perfect Arabic: "Calm down, my friend. This will be over soon."

Yessica left the tent and contacted William via Echo Vision.

"We have the target captured," she said.

"Good job," William said. "I expected nothing less from SEAL team Six. Show me why they call you the Terror of Tehran. Do what you do best and contact me afterward. Remember that we had a deal."

Yessica reentered the tent and gave her commands through Blade: "Withdraw your forces or face punishment."

The man was terrified.

"Okay, okay," he said. "I'll do whatever you want. Just use this code on my Cobber."

Joker did as commanded, and the order to withdraw began.

"That's it, boss," Joker said. "We should go."

Yessica took command.

"Give me the weapon, Blade," she said.

Blade hesitated, which caused Hope to chastise him: "That wasn't a request, Blade."

Blade took out a strange device that looked like a collar and put it on the enemy's neck. Yessica bent down and explained.

"This is no dog collar," Yessica said. "It houses a seven thousand degree Fahrenheit heated laser that starts at back of neck and works way all the way forward to your throat. Its main target is cervical area of central nervous system. Once the laser starts it will stop after six seconds when it reaches the outer cervical area. If you choose to relent the collar will release med gel which will heal the damaged tissue. You'll be scarred but still alive. If you continue to refuse, the laser will start again and stop after six seconds. Resting at the center of your neck. Med gel can be released but the major damage is done. If you make it this far, you'll be alive but paralyzed from the neck down forever. The next six seconds will end your life if you refuse to relent. Your head will fall to the floor, and you won't have to worry about us anymore. Thankfully, the laser is hot enough to cauterize your flesh so we don't have to worry about your blood splattering over us through this process. Therefore, this collar gives you three six second opportunities to submit."

Yessica continued to give orders: "Press the button, Blade." Blade did as ordered and watched the man scream.

"I relent! I relent!"

Yessica paused for a moment from her madness. She saw what looked like a woman standing in the tent with them. She shook her head thinking she was just seeing things. Next to this woman was a fiendish looking demon with two massive horns in its head. It kept calling her "Velovia."

Yessica ignored them and continued to press on. "Start phase two, Blade," she said. "Hit the button."

Blade did as ordered without questioning. However, Hope had seen enough.

"That's enough, boss," Hope said. "He has relented. We should go."

Yessica refused and said, "We need to fully test the weapon or there is no deal. I don't like this anymore than you do. Hit the button, Blade."

Blade pressed the button and walked away. He stopped for a moment when he heard a soft thump. He rationalized Meshech's death as just another horror of war then exfiltrated with his team.

William brought Yessica to a secret military base deep in the desert of Israel to thank her and her team on a job well done.

"You and your boys did great," William said. "I wish I could say the same for the Rangers. They got cold feet when it was time to test the weapon."

Yessica groaned and asked. "What is that thing by the way?"

"It's called a halo," William said. "You had a prototype, but I will use your data and make it more efficient. You've done Pangaia a huge favor."

William brought Yessica to a low level of the base. It was miles underground and massive in size. Yessica's mouth nearly hit the floor when they walked in the center of it.

"What is this thing?" she asked.

William began to strut. "This is a Harbinger gate," he said. "But you can call it a teleporter. One of the first models. I've tried to get it to work but I can't find a power source suitable for it. If it worked properly, it could probably send you to the moon. I tried nuclear and other sources but no luck. However, that's not why I brought you here."

Two Leo's appeared and surrounded Yessica and grabbed her. William put on two special gauntlets. He then took out two large orbs and held them in front of him.

"I call these Icarus orbs," William said. "You're smart so I hope you get the meaning."

William smashed the orbs together, which created an artificial atmosphere.

"The positive and negative charges in these orbs creates an artificial atmosphere that can be manipulated with these gauntlets."

Yessica struggled to move and asked, "What are you going to do? Strike me with lightning? You've got to be kidding me."

William nodded and said, "Yes, in fact that's exactly what I'm going to do. You see lightning is about fifty thousand degrees Fahrenheit. These orbs will make it twice that. It's probably the only thing that can kill you."

Yessica still didn't understand.

"Why me and not all my team?" she asked.

William moved his hands, heated the artificial environment, and said, "I'm afraid you'll never get to know. Sorry, but it's time to die."

Yessica felt the heat surge through her body. In an instant, the demon she saw in the enemy tent appeared. She tried speak but became mute when she felt the heat of lightning strike the top of her head.

Her body lay lifeless on the ground. As William ordered the Leos to dispose of the body, a woman appeared on his Echo Vision.

"Incoming call from..."

Annoyed, William said, "Yeah, yeah, put her through."

A woman sitting at a desk appeared.

"Is it done?" she asked.

"Come on honey, have a little faith," William said.

The woman seemed displeased and berated William. William didn't seem to mind, but one thing bothered him.

"When are you going to stop wearing those ugly pearl earrings?" William asked.

The conversation ended moments later, and William departed from the scene. He was overjoyed. The invasion of Pangaia's Peace Force turned out to be a terrible failure, and Israel was now free from all foreigners. William was proud his plan had worked. Though there was still much to be done.

He spoke next with Cynthia on a secure line. "Tell the contractors that it's time to begin building the temple. Make sure you destroy the dreaded rock dome before they start building. I want a clean slate."

Yessica gasped as she awoke from her slumber. With fury she clawed her way out of a giant trash heap. Finally, she relaxed when she was atop the massive trash pile. Yessica felt a pull from her body. A spirit separated from her. It was the same terrifying demon from before.

"I guess I have you to thank," Yessica said.

The demon turned around and hovered over the trash heap. The other being, the man that dressed as a woman, was there as well.

"What are you?" said Yessica.

The man dressed as a woman looked displeased.

"I'm disappointed in you," the man said. "You don't recognize your old pal? I guess I shouldn't blame you. I am what's called a Depth Lord. This handsome demon floating to my left belongs to me."

The strange being stared at Yessica in silence for a moment then realized his error.

"I'm called Quintopolas," the man said. "I'm here to help. What a shame that William. He offered you freedom but didn't keep his end of the bargain. Typical human royalty."

Quintopolas realized that Yessica wasn't in the most receptive state of mind. Her focus was clearly elsewhere.

"Sorry, my dear, I'm starting to babble. Where would you like to go? Anywhere but this dreadful Gehenna trasheap I hope."

Yessica didn't hesitate to answer. "I want to go home."

Quintopolas looked at her funny.

"And where would that be?" he asked. "Reading minds is not one of my primary abilities."

Chapter Three

Walk Of The Stranger

Three friends rode in an old recreational vehicle down the highway. Atop the vehicle was a white mountain bike and two kayaks. Alice drove, while her friends Shawn and Lindsey enjoyed their dinner.

"Hey Alice, pull this thing over and have some food. It's not good to drive on an empty stomach," Shawn said.

Shawn considered himself the leader of the group, though Alice and Lindsey knew this to be a farce.

"Just let her drive, Shawn," Lindsey said. "Unlike you, she at least volunteered."

Alice checked her navigational display. They were about thirty minutes away from their destination. She struggled to keep her eyes open but was determined to make it to their destination. On this same road was a lightly dressed man wearing thin shoes that were molded like feet. He walked slowly down the middle of the dark highway. Alice was driving nearly eighty miles an hour when she saw the man. She panicked and turned the wheel to the right. The recreational vehicle swerved and crashed off the side of the road. The vehicle was wrecked, but Alice and her friends were unharmed. They made their way out the vehicle and noticed the strange man. He slowly made his way toward them.

"What is wrong with you? We could have been killed," said Shawn.

"He might not be in the right state of mind," Lindsey said. "Be calm."

The sun was nearly set on the horizon causing the darkness to get more intense. Around them, wolves howled. Alice and her friends began to panic. Alice crawled back into the decimated RV and pulled out her bow and arrows, a pistol, and a rifle. She and her friends armed themselves and focused their attention on the strange man. Alice again tried to reason with him.

"How about you not just stand there and help us fight," Alice said. "It's the least you can do."

The mysterious man stood still as the howls of wolves grew louder and closer. Alice could now sense several of them behind her. She turned around, hoping to find one of the beasts, but it was too dark for her to see. The wolves inched closer, and the three friends used various lights to illuminate the area. Suddenly, the mystery man snapped his fingers. The wolves became silent and obedient upon the completion of this action. Moments later he spoke.

"Besera, come to me."

Alice and her friends heard heavy steps heading toward their way. They were all skilled hunters and knew what was approaching. Their fears were confirmed when a massive grizzly bear appeared and stood on its hind feet directly next to the mysterious man. He made a sharp whistle and the wolves inched closer and closer to Alice and her friends. He gave a final verbal command to his deadly beasts.

"Eat the loudmouth and the blonde but spare the other girl."

The man watched as the wolves and bear both feasted on their prey. The lone survivor couldn't stand to see such chaos. She fainted as soon as the wolves began eating her friends. The mysterious man took the bow and arrows from her and towed her on the back of the bear. He then removed the white mountain bike from the vehicle, placed it on the highway, and began to ride it.

"Besera, take her home to Arkamedes and watch her. I'll be there soon."

Arkamedes sat on one acre of land, far away from civilization. The mystery man waited patiently around a fire in the pitch-black darkness. A man on a red all-terrain vehicle approached the fire. The small man dressed in the armor of War got off the vehicle and stood around the fire. Moments later, a man riding a black flying drone approached the fire. He looked sickly and wore rags for clothing. After this, a man on a pale hover craft also gathered around the fire. He looked like Death and wore the armor of a dark knight. Behind him was a very large demon with two massive horns in its head. The mystery man took charge when they were all settled around the fire.

"I will give you all your orders once the angels give us our armament," he said. "Are there any questions before we get started?" The one that looked like Death spoke first.

"Will you aid us in our endeavors Damiano?" he said.

The mystery man pondered the question then answered, "Not exactly, Death. I will remain here. Please, call me Simeon."

The one that looked like War became annoyed. "The angels are late," he said. "What's keeping them so long?"

Simeon and the other horseman decided to talk about the glory days of the past while they waited. They spoke of strange ancient kingdoms and massive reptilian beast. A time when giants ruled and roamed the earth. Their focus shifted when a large purple angel with five eyes appeared and stood in the fire. He had three weapons and a silver crown in tow.

The one that looked like Death spoke to the angel. "They sent the great Ignas to run such a simple errand? Why am I not surprised? You might not be so special after all."

Ignas caused a great sword of vitality to rest before his accuser.

"You would do well to simply obey Samyaza," he said. "I will eradicate your existence should we meet in battle again."

The great angel sent a slaughterous sword to the one that looked like War.

"I never did like you Azrael," he said. "Your infernal arm seems fitting. A very big sword for a very little angel."

Ignas sent the last weapon to the one that looked like Pestilence. This weapon was linked with spiked balls, ropes, and chains. At the center of these balls were scales and sand clocks.

"Here are your sequence wings Ramiel," Ignas said. "I trust you to be the adult in this party."

The great angel turned toward Simeon, folded his arms, looked down on him, and said, "Come get your crown of lasciviousness, you disgusting beast. Don't think for a second that you have any real power."

Simeon smiled and put on his elegant silver crown.

"Aww Ignas. Really, you shouldn't have," Simeon said. "I'm so thankful that heaven sent us humble horsemen their greatest vacuum cleaner."

The horsemen laughed, but Ignas didn't seem to mind.

"My part is done," Ignas said. "Beware lest I see any of you on the battlefield."

The great angel vanished before them, which gave the horseman a feeling of satisfaction. Simeon was glad to be rid of him.

"I'm glad that's over but I can't help but wonder. We're you once family with Ignas?" Simeon said.

Samyaza answered, "Yes, in a matter of speaking. We were once like kin."

Simeon gave his orders. He started first with Azrael the horseman of War.

"I want you to focus on Israel," Simeon said. "After that get our forces ready for heaven. Finally, I want you to finish with the savages."

Azrael bowed and said, "It will be done, Simeon."

Simeon then spoke with Samyaza the horsemen of Death. "You're going to be busy Samyaza. It will be difficult but keep our forces out of Tartarus. The reapers will be in your way so you must be clever when dealing with them. We'll need every blade we can muster for our battle with Michael. Work with War and kill our enemies with through blade, famine, and the beast of the earth. You'll also be working with Pestilence from time to time."

Samyaza understood but had another question. "What about my son?" he asked.

Simeon raised his eyebrow. He looked at the demon then back at Samyaza. Then he answered sarcastically, "Of course, I can see the resemblance. What is your name, dog?"

The demon cowered but spoke. "Me called Ifrit."

Samyaza came to his son's defense. "Please excuse him. He has trouble with speech."

Simeon didn't seem to care.

"Do what you want Samyaza," he said. "Just keep your dog on a leash. I desire the company of serpents not scoundrels."

Simeon gave his final orders to Ramiel, the horseman of Pestilence.

"Keep up the good work, Ramiel," Simeon said. "This cava variant is effective and not to overburdening to humans. Just be ready use your ultima attack when the time comes."

Simeon began to dismiss the horsemen, but a voice echoed in the darkness.

"What about me?"

A man dressed as a woman stood around the fire.

Simeon was repulsed by his appearance. He began to mock him.

"Samyaza, you old scoundrel," Simeon said. "I see you brought your maid."

The other horseman laughed at the strange visitor's expense. The man became defiant.

"You would do well to mind your tongue," the man said. "For I am the Depth Lord Quintopolas."

Simeon wasn't impressed.

"So, you are my demon wing," he said. "Which means Ifrit here and his kin are under your leadership. Though I do require warriors, not women."

"I am your most loyal servant and your left hand," the man said.

Simeon scoffed. "If you are my left hand then it is time for an amputation."

Quintopolas used his ability to get into Simeon's thoughts—an ability he rarely told anyone about. He used his talents and spoke with him secretly with his mind.

"We both know you're not him, and you're not ready."

Simeon acted ignorant. "What are you talking about?" Simeon said.

Quintopolas spoke again. "You are no Damiano. I've known him since the beginning. I fell with him. If I tell the others what I know, they may not follow you."

Simeon felt cornered.

"Very well, maid," he said. "What do you want."

"I want an infernal arm like the others. I will tell them what you are lacking if my demands are not met.

"Very well, maid," Simeon said. "I will play your game for now. I have no power to create infernal arms, but you can have a weapon given to me by a close friend. However, once they are released there is no putting them back."

Quintopolas agreed and understood. "Very well, just tell me where to find them."

Simeon dismissed the horseman and went to the far side of his base. He approached a large cage guarded by his pet bear Besera. Inside it

53

was a young woman. Simeon knelt down and peered into the cage and said, "I've got big plans for you, Alice."

The morning sun began to rise upon Arkamedes. Simeon lay upon a bed made of wood. He tried to close his eyes and sleep like Alice but was unable. His last memory of sleep was long ago. It was as if an entire chapter of his life was missing. He decided to forgo sleeping and went to work on his own mock tabernacle—a large dirty white tent that he had collected. It took him a while, but eventually he got it set up by himself. He had a meticulous mind and organized the inside of the tent like he would an actual tabernacle. He placed a wooden chair where he wanted his throne to be. When it was all set up, he sat upon it completely still, not moving an inch, for hours and meditated.

Simeon then got off his throne and approached Alice's cage. She didn't look pleased to see him.

"Would you like some breakfast?" Simeon asked her.

Alice turned her nose up in defiance but her belly growled loudly. Simeon smiled. "I'll take that as a yes."

Simeon stretched out his hands, looked around the cool and quiet land, and said, "I don't have pigs and chickens, so I hope you're not wanting eggs and bacon."

He turned to his pet bear and asked her opinion. "What shall we provide her with?"

The bear lay on the ground and growled.

"No, that won't work. She's not like us. Alice doesn't eat all flesh."

Simeon had an epiphany. "I'll have to hunt then. Moose shall suffice."

Simeon kept Alice's bow around his body at nearly all times. His quiver of arrows were also always close by. He got up to hunt but Alice spoke. "I heard a voice calling you a beast. What's that about?"

Simeon sat next to the cage with his legs crossed. He seemed to be in the mood for chatter.

"Think of me as Nimrod," Simeon said. "Do you know of him?"

Alice nodded. "Of course," she said. "He had something to do with Babylon."

Simeon was impressed. "Very good, Alice. The Torah says Nimrod was a mighty one in the earth. A mighty hunter before the Lord. He helped unite the earth by his dominant and primal way of living."

Alice didn't see where he was going with this. "So are you like Nimrod's descendant or something?"

Simeon began to draw in the dirt. "Not quite, Alice."

Alice began to weep. However, Simeon remained emotionally detached.

"What is it now?" he asked.

"I forgive you," Alice said.

Simeon seemed offended. "What for?"

"For killing my friends, you jerk! What is wrong with you?"

Simeon wasn't fazed by her emotions in the slightest. He fell on his back and put his hands behind his head.

"Death is inevitable," he said. "At least for now, but that will change. Do you truly miss their foolish bickering that much? I'm quite sure I did you a favor."

Alice became so upset she could hardly breath. "Monster!"

Simeon rose to his feet, stretched, and headed into the wilderness.

"Come to me, Besera. Let's find this ungrateful louche something to eat before she annoys me to death."

The large bear whined but hurried and followed Simeon.

Deep underground a contingent of Zohar agents tracked every movement of Simeon.

"He's on the move, sir. The bear is with him."

A man with curly red hair monitored the situation.

"Very well," he said. "Keep your distance. We still don't know that much about him. Someone get me in touch with the Director."

The man with curly red hair waited patiently as a woman with pearl earrings appeared before him. She spoke first.

"Is there anything new to report Deputy Director Zurg?"

"Yes, ma'am, there is," the curly-haired man said. "He calls himself Simeon and was observed speaking with himself in a strange conversation. There are also reports of widespread chaos in the area. All places of worship are now under attack. We believe Simeon has something to do with it. He's also taken a prisoner, but we don't know her identity. She's not in the SIGIL database."

The woman didn't seem surprised.

"She's obviously a savage, but it doesn't matter," she said. "Keep me informed and do not engage Simeon until I tell you to."

"Yes ma'am. It will be done."

Chapter Four

Lost At Home

When their conversation ended, the Director of Zohar went about her day. There were many things to do. Managing Zohar was a taxing and expensive process. Her location was in one of Jopa's many mountain bases. They were complex structures that only a few people knew about. Without warning the foundation began to shake. She thought this was just a minor tremor, but it continued to grow in duration and intensity. The woman found her balance and demanded answers.

"Someone give me a status report," she said.

One of her agents answered, "This is eagle one, ma'am. All our resources indicate that this earthquake is unique. It seems be happening at our mountain bases."

The woman tried to respond but was unable to. She was now surrounded by a thick darkness. Within this darkness was a throne with something sitting upon it. The creature had a human form, yet it did not speak. A sharp pain, unlike anything she had ever experienced, flew through the woman's body. Her mind became flooded with unwanted thoughts and images. One of the thoughts seemed to come from one of her subordinates.

"Director, the base has been compromised."

The woman said, "We're clearly under physical and spiritual attack. Implode this base immediately. I would rather have this mountain fall on us then let it be taken by our enemies."

The darkness then faded, and she was sitting in her office. The room was in shambles, but she was unharmed. She was grateful to be alive but wanted answers.

"Patch me through to William," she said.

William's augmented appearance revealed itself. "What is it Malka?"

"Did you experience that tremor?"

William nodded. "Si, señora. Is there something else?"

"Yes, there is," Malka said. "I was in a trance-like state during some of the earthquake. It was similar to Sedah, but it felt so much more real."

Malka then made her true intentions known.

"I believe this was the work of your son," Malka said. "He's the only one who has this sort of power."

William could be very intimidating to those around him. However, he was quite docile around Malka. He neither agreed or disagreed with her.

"Do what you think is best," William said. "I'll take care of the cleanup."

Malka was pleased. "Thank you, William. I'm heading to his location immediately."

Alice remained vulnerable at Arkamedes. She felt a slight earthquake, but it was nothing worth noting. It didn't even wake the massive pet bear beside her. In the distance, she could smell the fresh cooking meat of wild game. Until now she refused to eat. However, the temptation to satisfy her cravings reached a fever pitch. Simeon approached her and handed Alice a wooden plate with cooked meat. Alice ate it with fury. Her captor seemed pleased with himself.

"I'm glad you like it," he said. "Entertaining guest is a rare occurrence for me. Most of my time is spent hunting food for Besera. Bears can be very high maintenance."

Alice licked and ate the grizzle off the bone.

"I wouldn't know," she said. "Hanging out with bears and commanding wolves isn't exactly my strong suit."

Simeon got serious.

"Tell me about yourself Alice," he said.

Alice dropped her plate and searched his eyes, hoping to find some shred of decency. Yet she found none. She refused to answer him and began to shun him.

"I want to be alone now," Alice said.

Simeon reached his hand through the cage, touched her forehead, and said, "Peace be unto you."

Suddenly, Alice returned to her usual upbeat mood. Clearly, she was no longer in control of herself. She began to divulge her deepest fears and secrets.

"You're a very handsome man. Did you know that?" she said, giggling like a school girl.

Simeon didn't appreciate her advances.

59

"Sorry," he said, "but I have no vested interest in any physical union with either a woman or a man. Tell me what faith you believe in Alice. Are you Christian?"

Alice smiled and said, "I'm a Messianic Jew but my sister is a non-practicing Jew. She hates all religion."

Simeon was surprised by her answer.

"Messianic Jews are Jews that still practice our ancient faith but also believe in The Nazarene as their savior," Simeon said. "I see clearly now. You're both a traitor and a savage."

"You are a traitor to humanity. You murder people. However, there's something special about you. Though I don't know quite know what it is." Simeon grew to appreciate Alice the more they spoke. She wasn't a willing participant, but Simon didn't mind. He learned more about her unique positive personality. Alice also revealed she was a virgin. Ultimately, Simeon believed Alice to be a gentle soul. He began to call her his Little Dove. For she had great knowledge of both the scriptures and the Jewish people.

"I'm going to say a verse of scripture that comes from the book of Ezekiel," Simeon said. "I want you to interpret it Little Dove. Can you do this for me?"

Alice seemed to be having a great time, but the effects of the spell were beginning to wear off.

"I guess," Alice said.

"Very well," Simeon said, "here is the verse: So the spirit lifted me up, and took me away, and I went into bitterness, in the heat of my spirit; but the hand of the LORD was strong upon me."

Alice became serious then answered, "I think that Ezekiel was bitter and angry that the Lord forced his hand in some way. Maybe he thought it was an affront to his free will. However, in hindsight, he saw and appreciated the superior divine plan of God and rested in it."

Simeon was impressed. He even clapped his hands in awe of her.

"Bravo, Little Dove. I wish we could continue our conversation, but you will be waking up soon."

Simeon looked in the sky and pointed toward something. Alice held her head in pain and returned to her prior state of mind.

"What did you do to me?" Alice said.

"If you look up, Little Dove, you can see the reapers. They are also called Yeshua angels—powerful angels responsible for gathering the harvest."

Alice looked into the blue sky and saw nothing. Simeon made a final plea for the controlled version of Alice to appear once more.

"I hope you're still in there, Little Dove," Simeon said. "I've something to tell you. Something I've never told anyone before."

Alice spat in his face. "I am NOT your Little Dove."

Simeon refused to accept the disrespect. He opened the cage, grabbed her by the hair, and dragged her into the woods.

William Calig was firmly in control of both Jopa and Israel. He had an office built high in the air, close to where the third temple was being built. It was a massive endeavor, but he had been planning this for decades. A knock sounded at his door.

"Bring him in, Cynthia," William said.

The door to his lavish office opened. The former Prime Minister of Israel entered the room with both his hands bound to each other. The man remained silent.

"Trust me, Prime Minister Ephraim. I won't bite," William said. "Make your approach."

The Prime Minister became defiant.

"You call yourself king of Israel wearing cowboy boots, a hat, and a buckle," he said. "You make me sick."

William clarified his position.

"Careful now, Ephraim. You're speaking with a man who's half-Jewish, a priest, a royal prince, and a Texas southern gentleman. The last part was the most important by the way."

William put his feet on the desk and smoked a pipe. Ephraim became agitated.

"I don't care who you think you are," Ephraim said. "Why am I here?"

"We will get to that, Prime Minister. I want you to use this time to get to know me better. You know, like how a warden gets familiar with his human property."

"I'll play your game. Tell me why you call your company Jopa. You make a mockery of the real Joppa."

William pretended to write something, then requested he be brought a sandwich.

"You see, Jopa stands for Joint Path. It has nothing to do with the ancient city of Joppa here in Israel. It's a common misconception but a welcomed one. Zohar is a little different. It was started by my mother, Ann Kohn. She was born a Jew and was deeply into spiritual and mystical things hence the name. They called her 'The Harbinger.' She married a duke, my father. His name was Edward Calig."

William paused mid-sentence when he saw something on his device.

"This can't be right," William said, looking at Ephraim with a smile. "Did you know you have a SIGIL social score of 920 out of 1,000? My friend you would make a tremendous addition to Pangaia. You see, the Chinese invented the system many years ago, but we've perfected it."

The Prime Minister remained defiant.

"I don't care about your stupid society," the Prime Minster said. "Tell me how Jopa managed to take over the world."

William slowly nodded his head and said, "So that's what you want to know. You want to know how a southerner bested such a brilliant know-it-all Prime Minister without lifting a finger. Fine, I'll tell you, and then I'll tell you the real reason you're here."

William stood up and looked out the window. His demeanor changed drastically. It became clear that this was something that weighed heavily on his mind.

"Jopa truly found its wings when our scientist created a portable nuclear device," William said. "Hundreds of countries all over the globe built nuclear plants in hopes to power their machines with this new technology. Those already with nuclear power became like drug lords, selling their product to the highest bidder. This created a shortage. Nations became desperate. With that desperation came war. Reactors popped up all over the world. Each nation was sold the dream of unlimited energy. Iran and Israel became very wealthy since they sold to anyone who came to them. Wars between burgeoning nuclear countries began all over the world. The rich got richer, but it was Jopa that ultimately conquered the world. To this day, no other country can create our portable nuclear device. That's why I'm here and why you're there."

William didn't give Ephraim a chance to respond. The office doors flew open, and in came DJ Pauly E with a sandwich in hand. Behind him were two massive police killer robots known as Jailers.

"Here's your sandwich Tera King Calig," DJ Pauly E said.

William looked relieved and said, "Thank you, son. Let's get this game rolling. What should we call Pangaia's new game?"

DJ Pauly E spoke without giving it a moment of thought. "We'll call it Threedom. Our contestants will have three six-second intervals to earn their Threedom. The crowd will love it."

William was barely amused.

"The people better love it," William said. "These halos aren't cheap to manufacture. Very well, let's get to it. I hope you studied the footage from Yessica's experience with Meshech."

William enjoyed his sandwich while the Jailors put the halo collar around the Prime Minister's neck.

"I sure did, your highness." said DJ Pauly E

He cleared his throat and signaled the drones to begin recording. His image was now seen all around the world.

"Hello, Pangaia," DJ Pauly E said, "and welcome to the first annual game of Threedom! Where we give you more access to Sedah if you have the winning number. Don't you want to get rid of all the rodents in our amazing society? This is true social justice! Let me explain what you're seeing. This is no dog collar, Pangaia. We call this a halo. It houses a seven-thousand-degree Fahrenheit heated laser that starts at back of neck and works way all the way forward to the throat."

Yessica arrived in Anchorage, Alaska, after a long flight from Israel. The entity known as Quintopolas had managed to get her aboard the cargo plane. Alaska was her home, but she wasn't from Anchorage. She was from a small town well north of Anchorage called Wainwright. To get there, Yessica needed a vehicle. As she made her way to the rental car facility, she noticed that the city was completely taken over by Pangaia. Their signature technology was everywhere. People were tracked and processed like slaves. Most seemed to be in some sort of trance. Yessica guessed what it was. They were more than likely addicted to the dream world of Sedah. All they wanted was more access to it. Part of Yessica was glad to have never experienced Sedah. She refused to be enslaved by it or by the Pangaia government that wanted her dead.

Yessica managed to rent a vehicle and drove it hundreds of miles to Wainwright. As she entered her old house, Yessica searched around the house with expectation.

"Alice, I'm home," she said. "I brought baklava. It's kosher!"

Yessica searched the entire house but couldn't find her younger sister. This was odd behavior. She was always home to welcome her in the past. Yessica checked her Cobber and used a special private application that tracked her coordinates.

"I guess she's riding her bike in the woods with Lindsey and Shawn."

Yessica gave up her search and headed into town. The center of the town bustled with activity. Most of the people were huddled around a food pantry trying to get supplies. Yessica scanned the line and saw two familiar faces. She approached them to make sure she was seeing correctly.

"Is that you, Hope?" Yessica asked.

The old Senior Chief always looked so different in civilian clothes. Yessica confirmed the other person next to him.

"Hello, Sarah, you've gotten so big. You must be sixteen by now," Yessica said.

"I'm seventeen actually," she said. "I'm so glad my dad's back."

Yessica was glad to hear all about their journeys. Hope remembered something important deep into their conversation.

"I almost forgot, boss. Joker and Blade are here as well."

Yessica became curious. She wondered why her small town was becoming so popular.

"Where are they?"

Hope seemed to forget but Sarah didn't.

"They're in Club USA," Sarah said. "I think its so cool that there is a club here just for the military."

Yessica groaned and said, "Actually, it's a gentleman's club. I'll let your dad explain. We're sailors not saints."

Hope became offended.

"Hey, speak for yourself, boss."

Yessica could see the club in the distance. She became concerned when a group of police officers approached the club.

"I'm sorry, Sarah, but I'm going to have to borrow your dad for a bit, okay?"

"That's fine," Sarah said. "I'll wait here."

Hope had to run to keep up with Yessica.

"Are you going to tell me what's the problem, boss? They're just blowing off some steam."

"I know that, but you didn't get a good look at those officers like I did. We need to hurry."

Joker and Blade were having a momentous time in Club USA. They paused when a large contingent of police officers entered the bar and tried to listen in on their conversations. Joker poked Blade. "Do you hear that?"

"I sure did," Blade said. "They're all Chinese. Let's make them pay."

Blade studied the officers and listened to what they ordered. He then entered the employee's entrance minutes later and grabbed a tray of food and drinks heading for them. His presence was not welcomed when he arrived with their order.

"Move it, buddy," the officer said. "You're blocking my view. Don't expect a tip either. I don't tip man servants."

Blade responded in perfect Chinese. "Forgive my disturbance. I only wish to provide you with excellent service."

The Chinese men all turned sharply toward Blade. "You speak our language? How is that possible? You sort of look like an American spy. Maybe you were ex-military? We all know what blood sucking leeches they are."

Blade remained calm and continued his plan, saying, "Excuse me but would you like some breakfast on the house? It's the least I can do in light of my poor manners."

The man kept his eyes on stage but seemed to relax a bit more.

"Sure, I can eat breakfast," the man said. "What do you have?"

Blade rolled up his sleeves and said, "Scrambled eggs with a side of Justice!"

Blade punched the police officer in the mouth with great fury. Joker backed up his good friend and the group of officers all struggled to contain their wrath. Yessica and Hope entered moments later and joined the fight. It was over after just two minutes. The twelve Chinese police officers were no match for the four Navy SEALs.

Yessica took charge and said, "We need to get out of here before they bring in the Jailors."

The four of them ran away from the scene of the crime and headed toward Yessica's rental car. Joker looked shocked.

"They gave you a minivan?" Joker said. "No way I'm riding in that thing."

Yessica wanted to argue, but five large Jailer robots stood in their way.

"This isn't good," she said.

A man hurried toward them before they could be arrested. Yessica noticed the man.

"Mayor Addison?"

The mayor, looking like he had seen a ghost, said, "Yessica, my dear, it's been too long. Don't worry I'll handle this."

More police arrived on the scene and investigated the incident. Their leader approached the mayor and demanded some sort of payment.

Mayor Addison agreed, saying, "The town's coffers will pay for the damages. Just tell me how much bract they owe you and it will be paid for. However, you have no legal authority this town until next week."

The police leader didn't like this answer, but there was nothing he could do. He placed no order to arrest, but he and his fellow officers glared at the SEALs as they entered the van. Yessica drove off but heard a voice yelling at them. She turned and saw that it was Ranger Doctor Ruth. Ruth entered the vehicle, and they continued their drive.

"Where's Sinkular and Pronto, Doc?" Blade asked.

Ruth noticed a large piece of glass in his elbow as he rested. Ruth explained and patched Blade up at the same time.

"Sinkular returned to his home in Tonga," Ruth said. "Apparently, he swore an oath to never use violence again. As for Pronto, he returned to Nebraska and now leads a large community of survivors. So unfortunately, they won't be joining us anymore."

The news was startling, but overall the SEALs were glad the former Rangers found peace. Blade, Hope, and Ruth then took turns explaining why there were all in Alaska. They had all originally returned to their homes, but it proved to be too dangerous for their families. The recent earthquake only forced more people to Alaska. They had always heard that this was the Final Frontier, but now it was official. Its northern territory was the only place to escape Pangaia's grasp.

Joker also brought up another reason why people were flocking here.

"I heard there is a man claiming to be God around these parts. I've gained his location. We should check him out. Maybe he can end the civil war and take away radiation poison from our homes," Joker said.

Yessica looked at the coordinates and pressed the gas.

"What gives, boss?" said Joker

Yessica remained calm like she always did and said, "Change of plans. We're going to meet this boogie man but not without gear. I'm certain he's holding Alice hostage. Her coordinates are at this mystery mans location. My sister is a devout Christian. She wouldn't be hanging out with a man like this for more than a day without telling me. Alice is a lot of things but she's not a rebel. That's my persona. Therefore, this is a rescue mission now."

"How do you know she's not just curious?" Ruth asked.

Yessica drove up to her house and put the van in park.

"I know my sister better than anyone," Yessica said. "Her emergency beacons been active for days and her two best friends' beacons last registered two days ago. They are obviously dead. Let's do what we do best. The armory is in the basement. Suit up quick. We leave in five."

The team entered Yessica's basement and armed themselves from a huge cache of weapons, comms, camouflage, and ammo. With great competence, they got into the van and headed toward Alice's location. Hope took the wheel while Yessica and Joker coordinated with the others. Yessica looked up and out the window. She saw something massive come from out of the ground and into the sky. It was so brief that she thought she was hallucinating.

"Did anyone else see that?" Yessica asked.

The others were too focused on the mission. She figured she was just tired.

Chapter Five

Old Invaders

A creature looked down on the earth from a massive spaceship. Her hair was like tentacles. It flowed and breathed in every direction as if it were under water. Her skin was gray, red, and slimy. A golden digital disk covered her empty hollow eyes. Over her mouth was a strange black cryptic breathing apparatus filled with symbols. On her back was a large sword that rotated like the earth. Two twin daggers that looked like they were fashioned by hell itself rested at her side.

Another entity appeared before her. He was lightyears away but appeared before her instantly without interruption using interstellar technology. His appearance was unlike anything human eyes had ever seen. The female creature bowed before him.

"Our combat forces have arrived, Master Braccus," she said.

The strange entity was pleased and said, "I expected nothing less from the Captain of the Vanguard. You know what to do, Host Bastel. The Grand Council has provided you with ten ships. That should be more than enough to handle humanity. Contact me should you need more."

"Twenty troops are more than enough to ensure victory," she said.

Though Braccus was the twelfth member and leader of the Grand Council and controlled the politics and the overall direction of the group, Bastel was the Grand Council's subordinate but maintained control over the military. She worked closely with her most elite forces called Third Eye. Bastel turned her attention to them when Braccus departed. Their forms and faces were in darkness. The only visible parts were their glowing eyes.

Yessica and her team slowly encircled the last known location of Alice. They looked around the area but didn't see much.

"Boss, I have eyes on some kind of cage."

"Roger that, Joker," Yessica said. "Let's check out that tent. I think I hear something."

Yessica made her way to the large dirty white tent and entered it. What she saw next horrified her. Simeon stood next to a large metal container filled with water. Alice was inside the container fighting his attack on her. Simeon continued to lift and submerge her head under the water to simulate drowning. Simeon's back was toward their faces, so he wasn't identified at first.

"Get away from my sister right now!" Yessica aimed her pistol at him.

She tried to keep her emotions under control, but she failed miserably. Her finger squeezed the trigger. The bullet made its way toward Simeon, but a massive bear entered the tent and took the bullet.

Yessica took command. "Slay the beast, Hope."

Hope got in position and shot the bear in the head with a rifle. The bear fell to the floor without a whimper. Yessica expected some sort of response from Simeon, but he continued to ignore them. His focus was strictly on drowning Alice. Yessica gave Simeon her final warning then shot three times into his chest. Simeon bound Alice to the bottom of the container then released his grip on her neck. He then stood up and faced Yessica and her team. There was a massive hole where his heart should have been.

"Hello, Yessica. I know that you're here for your sister but it's too late. She's all mine."

Yessica and her team were in disbelief. They all trained their weapons on him.

"Admiral Freddy Samson?" Yessica asked. "How is this possible? We watched you die."

Simeon smiled, looking pleased with himself.

"I must admit that you exceeded my expectations," Simeon said. "You did in fact kill Freddie Samson, but you gave birth to Simeon Skylar Samson. I think I'll stay alive this time around."

Simeon reached in the container and grabbed Alice by the neck again, this time choking her. Yessica tossed her pistol to the side. Simeon seemed immune to bullets. She ran toward her sister with her knife, but three more grizzly bears appeared and blocked her path. Yessica maneuvered around the bears and reached the container. Hope fired his rifle three times and slayed the three bears. Yessica stabbed Simeon in the back, which released his grip on her neck. However, Yessica was too late. Alice had already taken her last breath. She now laid motionless under the cold water. Yessica screamed with horror, then she quickly put herself back together and ordered Joker and Blade to capture Simeon. The defeated foe put his hands up and surrendered without causing a scene. He was escorted outside the tent.

This gave Yessica some privacy. She spent the next few minutes with the body of her sister. Tears flowed down her face and gently splashed on the face of Alice. Yessica screamed in agony. "Why did you have to take her God? I'm the one that doesn't believe in you. Take me!" Yessica continued to hold her sister in her arms tightly. She searched the area until she found some silk linen. Yessica gently placed Alice on the ground and proceeded to wrap up her body. Anger swelled within her. She was ready for vengeance.

Yessica left the tent and met her team in a clearing in the woods. Hope, Joker, and Blade beat Simeon with all the might they had. However, Simeon kept laughing, healing, and getting up. They even shot him multiple times to no avail. Simeon focused his attention on Hope.

"Looks like you missed the rapture, Senior Chief," Simeon said. "That's too bad. You're probably not going to enjoy yourself any time soon."

Simeon then said something that puzzled them: "It is written. For they have sown the wind, and they shall reap the whirlwind. Let me tell you how this is going to work. I'm going to count to one hundred. I will vow never to kill again if I'm still in chains should I reach one hundred and one."

Simeon began to count while Yessica walked away from the clearing with a rifle in her hand. Hope noticed her strange behavior.

"Where are you going, boss?" Hope asked.

Yessica walked thirty feet away, placed the rifle to her head, and closed her eyes.

Meanwhile, Simeon continued to count. "Ninety-seven, ninety-eight, ninety-nine!"

The ground began to shake violently. Hope, Blade, and Joker heard a massive sonic boom. They looked up and saw a massive spaceship hovering above the earth. Yessica slowly opened her eyes. She had already pulled the trigger on her rifle. A smashed bullet laid idle on the ground. It barely made a dent in her skin.

"What am I?" she said.

Her emotions were still too raw to face her team. She desperately wanted an explanation. Yessica ran from her team and made her way onto a main road, where a dark car waited for her. A man with curly red hair rolled down the window and said, "Get in, Yessica Hoffman. We have the answers you seek."

"One hundred."

Three strange beings appeared instantly before Hope, Joker, Blade, and Ruth. Simeon's chains vanished, and he was free once again.

"One hundred and one," Simeon said. "Looks like I win."

Bastel stood in the middle. To her left and right were huge beings, at least thirteen feet tall. Their eyes glowed white, with augmented digital visors of all colors covered them. On their backs were giant weapons. Their symbiotic suits flowed with all the colors of a rainbow. They were both elegant and intimidating. Their bodies were like an exoskeletal metallic structure that served both as armor and comfort. Their hair looked like an illusion.

Hope took charge and the team aimed their guns.

Bastel was appalled and said, "Shame on you for treating the chosen one like some criminal. We will teach you a lesson you'll never forget."

Bastel gave a telepathic signal, and the other beings pointed their fingers at them. Their rifles melted in their hands, which caused them to drop their weapons.

Bastel turned to Simeon and asked, "Shall we dispose of these fiends, Lord Simeon?"

Simeon put on his shirt and headed for Arkamedes.

"Leave them be," he said. "We have more important things to do."

Simeon entered his stronghold and held Besera in his hands.

"Wake up, girl," Simeon said.

The bear revived and licked Simeon's face.

Hope and the others searched the woods for Yessica but couldn't find her.

"I found something," Joker said, handing Hope a broken rifle.

As they tried to figure out their next move, a large group of militia men surrounded them.

"Of course, you guys show up now. We don't have weapons to defend ourselves," said Blade.

The militiamen bound the small team and hauled them off further into the woods.

The appearance of alien spaceships put the world into a panic. Millions of people went missing. It seemed all hope was lost. A secret group of five elites gathered around a round white table in Rome. Their identities were hidden with elaborate mask and voice changers. They all claimed to be remnant descendants of the SMARTs, a group of families that secretly controlled the world for decades. Their top priority was to please the founders. The one with a weeping mask began the meeting.

"I have reports that indicate a majority of those abducted are Christian," the one with the weeping mask said. "We should use this to finally eradicate them."

The one with a laughing mask answered., "I will deal with the savages should we not agree."

The other masks were defiant.

"It is up to the Eye, not you," said the angry mask.

The two-face mask remained silent while the disgust mask maintained a defensive posture. They all agreed that the new game called Threedom helped their cause, but it wasn't enough. It needed to be on a larger scale. The five of them voted, but they did not reach a majority on what to do with the Christians. They decided to leave their fate up to the Eye of the group.

Yessica sat in the back of the luxurious black vehicle opposite of two people—a man with curly red hair and an older woman with pearl earrings.

"Hello, Yessica. I'm Dr. Malka Jasmine Nazarian, the Director of Zohar."

Yessica recognized the name.

"Malka is a Jewish name," Yessica said. "Are you Jewish?"

"Yes, I was born in Israel."

Malka looked at the man next to her and introduced him. "Where are my manners? Yessica, this is Agent Mark Zurg the Deputy Director of Zohar. You can trust him."

Agent Zurg held his surly look and remained silent. Yessica ignored him and chose to deal with the more pleasant Malka, who said, "I'm confused, Yessica. I watched William kill you with a weapon I designed myself. How are you alive?"

Yessica's emotions were still raw after watching her sister die. Yet there was something about Malka that made her let down her guard.

"There was this demon-like creature." Yessica said. "It merged with me or something."

Malka nodded.

"Yes, I suspected as much. That creature was the Demon Lord known as Ifrit. An entity revered by the lore of Muslims. Which means you've regained your SIGHT. However, I do wonder why you gained SIGHT now. Simeon has had SIGHT since birth."

Yessica tried to keep up.

"What is this SIGHT?"

"SIGHT stands for Spirit Insight Gift Helping Talent. It means you can see things from the spirit world. The first documented person to ever have this ability was William's grandfather. The one on his mother's side. His name was Amos Kohn. From there, it trickled through his family, but William never received SIGHT. Quite the tragedy. You see SIGHT is the reason why Sedah exist."

Yessica was intrigued. "Please explain," she said.

"I helped create Sedah," Malka said. "It essentially mimics the psychosis experienced from those with SIGHT. That's Organic Intelligence in a nutshell."

"What about Persephone? Did you make her too?"

"That's a little more complicated," Malka said. "The idea of Persephone came from a remarkable woman named Beth Abraham. She was a friend of William's mother, Ann Calig, one of the SMARTS. Her last project was called Phoenix. She teamed up with the CIA, Zohar, Jopa, and Mossad. Together they used the ancient alien blood of Sianthema to create two nearly indestructible beings. Each being was designed to keep the other in check."

"So, who are these two beings?" Yessica asked.

Malka and Agent Zurg looked at each other briefly.

"Their names are Yessica Cali Hoffman and Simeon Skylar Samson," Malka said.

Yessica couldn't hold back her laughter.

Malka remained serious and said, "The two of you were never intended to meet. Our original plan was for both of you to stay in Israel, but you were both taken away by William and Jopa. Think about it. You're both loyal Americans, Jewish, way too smart, way to strong, Navy, overachievers, and killers. How else could a woman of your size become a legend in SEAL Team Six?"

Yessica had heard enough. She ordered the car to stop and prepared herself to leave. But then an urgent question appeared in her mind: "So what is my purpose?"

Malka looked amused. "How do you stop an invincible speeding train?"

Yessica thought the question was foolish. "Brakes?" she said.

Malka shook her head. "You don't bother with brakes. Just blow up the tracks. That's your purpose."

Yessica understood.

"So Simeon's the train. I get it," Yessica said. "But can you tell me where my team is? I'm sort of lost."

Zurg searched his drone footage.

"They're being held at a savage camp two kilometers from here," he said.

Well north of Wainwright were two churches resting on two great hills. They were separated by a valley and divided into two camps. Camp St. Peter housed and maintained the Catholic faith. Camp Luther housed and maintained the Protestant faith. Each camp rested on four acres of land. The two sanctuaries were both small and modest. They disagreed sharply on biblical doctrine but cooperated with things like survival and combat patrols. Camp Luther had the greater bunker while Camp St. Peter had a greater capacity to create food. On this day, the combat patrol returned early with four prisoners. They stood before two ministers. The first minister was the leader of Camp Luther, Pastor Josh, an eloquent man with a meek temperament. To his side was Father Nolan, a strong personality from the Netherlands. The two ministers argued about what to do with the prisoners. After a while, they decided to have them placed in cells until a consensus could be made. Many of their people were suddenly missing. They figured their prisoners were Pangaia agents. But the arrival of spaceships also disturbed them.

Yessica arrived at the camp hours later. She knew Pastor Josh well. Her team was set free after a brief conversation. She spoke to them briefly while they were together.

"This is our new base of operations," Yessica said. "Take the vehicles and bring your families here. I've known most of these men my entire life. We're safe here."

She split the team up into two. Hope and Blade would maintain combat patrols with Camp Luther. Yessica, Ruth, and Joker would do the same in Camp St. Peter.

The two churches held a summit about the missing people and the ten spaceships in the sky. Yessica walked outside and saw a young girl bound to a wheelchair. She knelt down and said, "Hello there. I'm Yessica what's your name?"

The young girl from Camp St. Peter became shy but started to use sign language. Yessica signed back: "My dad was hard of hearing."

The young girl perked up and signed, "My name is Nala. Is that a Cobber?"

"It sure is Nala."

"My Uncle Joe says we can't have those here. He says it's the mark of the feast."

Yessica gently corrected her. "It's the mark of the *beast,* and I think your Uncle Joe is wrong about that."

Nala was consumed by its potential power. "What do you want for it?"

Yessica had little need for it anymore. She wasn't registered with SIGIL, so she couldn't' contact anyone with it. She took the device off her wrist and gave it to the young girl.

"Its name is Westin," Yessica said. "Take good care of him, okay?"

After Yessica returned to her camp and tried to sleep, a boy from Camp Luther who had seen the entire thing approached Nala with demands.

"You can't have that," he said.

Nala quickly grasped the technology and used it to speak with the boy. "Don't be a tattletale."

The boy became fascinated with it.

"Wow, that's cool! I'm Richard. I heard you talking with Yessica earlier. My dad says she's dangerous but I think she's awesome. You know her too now. I'm sorry I got angry with you. I've always wanted a Cobber myself. I have an idea, let's be friends. This way we can both have one."

Nala smiled and the two talked well into the day. Thus starting an unlikely friendship.

Bastel wasted no time when she arrived at Arkamedes. She hijacked Pangaia's Echo Vision as well as all radios and Cobber's. Her strange form was now being watched by the entire world.

"You are all trapped in a never-ending matrix of life and death," Bastel said. "I used to wonder and dream about the God who keeps you locked in this cryptic floating ball of rock and water. Can he hear us? Is their meaning to this life? You wouldn't like the answer even if I told you. There is still hope for some of you. We offer you a chance to become a tamer of technology. If you are chosen, you'll never hunger or thirst. I am the Third Commander of the last order of Ancients. You may call us Watchers. All your lives you have been searching for us. You've wondered if you were all alone in this universe. Finally, you have your answer. Keep your eyes open and listen for our song. You never know when you might be entertaining a watcher unawares."

The transmission faded to black, leaving ten glowing eyes in the background. A collective murmur went around the world. Humanity knew that things would be different from now on.

Simeon gathered the watchers after Bastel's announcement. It was now time for him to produce his first "miracle." Simeon stood in the middle of a circle with a mask that covered half his face. His shirt was off revealing the massive hole in his heart. The watchers slowly approached with torches in their hands. The torches touched Simeon and ignited him, but he was unharmed. He used his drones to record the entire process.

"Welcome to my fire baptism," Simeon said.

The elite Third Eye Watchers knelt before him. Simeon reveled in his glory.

"You see, world" Simeon said. "Even the great Watchers bow before me. Who is like me and who can make war against me?"

Bastel approached Simeon when the production was finished.

"When will you release this footage and reveal yourself to the world, Lord Simeon?" Bastel asked.

"When the time is right," Simeon said. "Are you hungry Bastel? I think I'll have some Alice for lunch."

"You know we don't need to eat, my Lord," Bastel said. "Though I am curious as to how human flesh tastes."

Simeon headed to where the metal pool was and noticed the body was gone. He laughed and shrugged.

"Well played, Yessica."

Chapter Six

A New Purpose

A newly awakened angel roamed the heavens. His will was bound there so he sought instruction. Three other angels saw him and approached.

"You must be the new Nava angel known as Chester," the leader of the group of angels said. "I am the Nava Warden. You may call me Lenoth. You need not worry about the names of these two. They are here to simply observe and verify this process."

There was no fog in Chester's mind. He knew he had to accomplish something great for the kingdom of heaven. All he lacked was instruction.

"I understand," Chester said. "Please explain to me my mission, Master Lenoth."

"Your mission is to ensure that the Church survives the Great Tribulation," Lenoth said. "You may request warrior Zimrat angels to aid you should you need to combat the fallen. Remember, you are to be seen but not known. Reveal your identity to no man. Am I understood?"

Chester didn't mind the instruction at all. "I will do the Lord's will Master Lenoth."

Chester prepared for his descent onto the earth when Lenoth stopped him for one last piece of instruction: "Do not forget the Angel Creed."

"What is the Angel Creed?" Chester asked.

"It's actually quite simple: submit to three, man like tree, demon squeeze, angel reprieve."

Chester quickly grasped most of the creed but asked, "What is angel reprieve?"

Lenoth gently explained, "It means that we are not allowed to destroy any fallen angels until the great battle with the dragon. After this battle, they will finally be fair game."

Chester understood his orders and began his journey to the earth. He knew his purpose but was blind to the ways of man.

The Watchers were quite comfortable at Arkamedes. However, Simeon was not. He sat bored on his mock throne. Bastel heard his grumblings and entered the tent.

"Is everything all right?"

Simeon got off his throne and began to walk out the tent. "Walk with me."

Bastel followed Simeon to Alice's white mountain bike.

"I'm going on a cycle run," Simeon said. "Do you and your men wish to hunt with me?"

Two of Bastel's men were engaged in some sort of debate. Watchers had a strict policy to not interfere with any type of verbal sparring.

"We're a little preoccupied, Lord Simeon. We'll be here when you get back." said Bastel

Simeon gave final instruction then began to ride out onto the highway. He then whistled loudly. The mountain bike wasn't built for speed, yet Simeon seemed to nearly fly down the road. Wolves, bears, wolverines, lynx, eagles, and all manner of predators joined Simeon and followed him. Simeon and his band of beasts rode over twenty miles. He gave the signal to stop when he saw a homeless camp. Simeon made sure he wasn't followed and summoned his drones. When the cameras were on, he stretched his arms to the sky and absorbed the slow-moving solar energy from the northern lights. He created what appeared to be a massive solar bomb above his hands. He detonated the energy and caused the fabled aurora borealis to appear all around the earth. He spoke to the drones and declared that he would provide unlimited energy should they only serve him.

Simeon headed to the homeless camp after his show. Most of the people in the camp were asleep even though it was midday. The howls of Simeon's wolves woke most of them up. Simeon slowly walked up to some of the terrified men, women, and children.

One of the men spoke. "What do you want with us?"

Simeon greatly intimidated the man, who tried to be brave but fell on his back as Simeon approached.

"I hunger," Simeon said.

He turned to his beast and commanded them to eat. The beasts stared down their prey and began to attack.

"Not so fast!"

The beasts began to cower. They were terrified of something. Simeon demanded his beast follow his orders. "I said eat!"

A man approached Simeon with bravery and matching bravado.

"Leave this place," the man said. "You and your beasts."

Simeon could tell something was different about this man.

"This is impossible," Simeon said. "Why can't I read you?"

The man walked toward Simeon. Simeon stepped back each time the man stepped forward.

"I don't have time for this," Simeon said, gathering his beasts and departing the area.

The people at the camp cheered the brave man that helped them.

"What's your name?" they asked. "Are you homeless?"

The man smiled. "I am now. The name's Chester."

William looked out from one of his buildings in Pan-Paris. People were losing their minds over the alien invaders.

"What on God's green earth are they so afraid of?" William said. "They're just a bunch of terrorists. Carrol, back me up here, will ya?"

Carrol's eyes were glued to her Cobber's augmented display. She struggled to see the point of living anymore.

"It's over, William," she said. "We don't stand a chance against them. I'm asking for your permission to resign."

William shook his head and said, "Permission denied. Do your job and get the Supreme Queen on the line for me."

Carrol found solace in her busy work. She was clearly terrified but felt at ease under William's confidence.

"The Supreme Queen is now active on Echo Vision," she said.

The Supreme Queen looked to be at ease as well. They both saw this as an opportunity not an obstacle.

"What is it, William? Did you not know that alien invaders are real these days?"

William bowed, hoping to lower her resistance.

"Fear not, Potentate. For I, William, your humble servant have a plan."

The Supreme Queen fell for the bait.

"I'm listening," she said.

"I can assure you that we already have the missing people crisis figured out. Most of them are savages. However, most of them also had Leos. Their copies are being manufactured as we speak."

The Supreme Queen listened intently. This was one of the few times she didn't interrupt him while he spoke.

"I also have a man on the ground, Potentate. A man uniquely qualified to handle our little situation."

The Supreme became impatient and said, "Who is this man? I want to speak with him immediately."

William tried not to reveal too much.

"I'm afraid I cannot do that, Potentate. It might jeopardize everything. You will know him soon and the world will too."

While they spoke, the sky exploded with the color and wonder of the aurora borealis. It was a true marvel. William looked out his window and saw the people of Pangaia stop and look at the incredible light show. Their fears seemed to be quelled for at least this moment. William ended the conversation with the Supreme Queen. Carrol was also enamored with the lights but saw a strange cryptic transmission on her Cobber.

"You have an incoming Echo from an unknown source, William," she said. "What shall I do?"

"Step outside for a while, Carrol," William said. "I have to take this call in private."

Carrol left the room and gave William access to the Echo.

A frozen image of glowing eyes appeared on the Echo Vision. William was offended.

"I didn't think your type would be camera shy. It's Bastel correct?"

Bastel said, "My kind look down on sarcasm, William Calig. You would be wise to avoid it."

William shrugged and said, "Okay, so what are you after? Why are you contacting me?"

"Watchers are savants of technology," Bastel said. "We tame machines like you would tame a dog. There is one machine that we cannot gain access to and that's Persephone. Her design is impeccable. I will not rest until she is mine. You are going to help me have her. Is that clear?"

William kept his composure as he smoked his pipe. "Bless your heart, darlin'. You seem madder than a wet hen. I will do my best to help you since you're helping my man on the ground. You do know who I'm speaking about right?"

Bastel paused, as if she were speaking to someone else, and then said, "I'm not allowed to reveal that information. So either tell me about Persephone or we're done here."

William decided to play ball.

"Sure," he said, "I'll tell you about Persephone. There's no need to sweat me like a sinner in a church. I used to be a priest, but I digress. Her code is uncrackable. Not even a space faring race like yourself can figure her out. All your efforts don't amount to a hill of beans. She's our greatest achievement here at Jopa. That's all I have to say, I reckon. Goodbye."

William disconnected the call and went back to the business of Jopa.

"Carrol, get your butt in here. I'm busier than a cat on a hot tin roof!"

Yessica buried her sister at her favorite body of water. Lake Hudor was just a few miles west of Wainwright. Yessica had fond memories of ice skating and fishing here. When Alice was in the ground, Yessica spoke to her as if she were still alive.

"I guess you're in heaven now," Yessica said. "Though I can't fathom why you or anyone would believe in that stuff. I hope you know that I'm probably not your real sister. Some crazy rich lady told me I'm some kind of monster."

A lone tear flowed down her face. She wondered if it was even real.

"I'll be sure to check on you as often as I can. Someone has to help clean your tombstone up. You always were the messy type. My hope is that Peter and Paul will give you some sort of military discipline. I'm assuming heaven is a place familiar with order."

Yessica wiped away the tear. She knew she had to get back to the camps soon. The security of the camps had a tendency to fall apart when she wasn't around to manage it.

"One last thing and then I'll let you rest, Alice. I was meaning to ask this of you when I got home but we both know what happened after that. Do you think I'm unlovable? I mean romantically. I've never been able to keep a boyfriend or husband. Meanwhile, the boys flocked to you and yet you died with your virtue intact. I have someone here that I care about deeply, but I'm afraid he'll see a monster and not me. He's always giving his attention to this doctor we have. She has a lot going for her. I don't think I can compete with her, but I'm willing to try. Sorry I brought that up. I let you rest, Alice. Same time tomorrow?"

The Summit continued with the two churches. No one seemed to have an explanation of what the aliens were save one man. Pastor Josh was well versed in scripture. He was also very knowledgeable about the end times. He quieted the men and women at the summit and gave his thesis.

"These aliens are not from some fantasy," Pastor Josh said. "The Bible tells us about them. They are called 'The Sons of God' in the book of Genesis. They mated with human women and created giants. Men of renown. God destroyed them with the flood and spared Noah and his family. They are about two hundred in number based off the Book of Enoch."

The Catholics began to grumble. Father Nolan refuted the evidence.

"The Book of Enoch is not in the Bible. It is heresy to use it today."

Pastor Josh disagreed. "What matters is that we tell the world the truth about them. We can't stay locked up on eight acres forever. The truth must not be hidden."

The Christians began to debate all manner of subjects, and they kept getting nowhere. Neither side was willing to budge. A man who had disappeared entered the hall. They all gasped when they saw him.

"Is that really you, Brian?" they asked.

Brian walked in a staggard manner. It was if he was drunk. He clearly wasn't himself.

Yessica entered the hall with a large pistol. She placed it in the back of Brian's head and pulled the trigger. The people gasped when they saw the insides of a machine all over the ground.

"This is just a clone from Jopa," Yessica said. "They may have fooled Pangaia but not us. Bring the missing to me if you see them. I want to verify if they're human. I just found out that I'm uniquely qualified to handle such an inspection."

Joker entertained the children of both camps close to the summit. He was never the type to take matters of faith seriously. It made him feel out of his depth. Joker could quote nearly every manual on firearms, but his grasp of Scripture was like that of an infant. The children seemed to be amused at his stories and jokes. He made sure to keep them kid friendly.

Ruth was posted on a wall a few feet from them. Their eyes met. They shied away as if they were teenagers.

"Give us another joke, Joker!"

Their pleas broke his gaze.

"Okay, settle down folks. Why does the Navy recruit blind men?"

The children wondered.

"So they can send them out to sea."

Some of the children laughed but others looked clueless.

"Okay, one more then I got to go."

The children groaned and whined, but Joker maintained a firm posture.

"What do you call a fake noodle?"

One of the children said, "A foodle."

The children found the answer amusing. Joker smiled as well and said, "Close, but not quite. A fake noodle is called an Impasta! Now disperse and play. That's an order."

Ruth waded her way through the children and stood next to Joker.

"I didn't know you were so good with kids. I'm impressed," she said.

Joker's hands began to shake.

"Really, you think so. I guess I'm okay. Do you want to hear a joke?"

Ruth gave him a puzzled look. "No, not really."

Joker spoke one anyway. "What do you call a happily married single parent?"

Ruth waited with both brows raised.

"Senior Chief Hope. Don't you get it?" Joker said. "He is Senior Chief Hapily. He's happily married."

Joker tried to change the narrative.

"Sorry, I tried to imply that you and me... Forget it. I'm sorry," Joker said.

Ruth laughed nervously and walked away, saying, "That's not funny, Joker."

Joker was embarrassed but not deterred. He found Pastor Josh leaving the summit to head home.

"Hey Pastor, I have a question for you."

Pastor Josh seemed slightly annoyed. There were other pressing matters on his mind. "What is it, Joker? I don't have time for another one of your vulgar stories."

Joker got to the point. "You have a lovely marriage and a lovely wife. I want the same thing but I'm terrible with women. Can you give me some pointers?"

Pastor Josh seemed relieved to discuss this and not the aliens. It was a welcomed break.

"Is this about Ruth?" Pastor Josh asked. "I saw you talking with her?"

Joker felt cornered but said, "Actually, it's about Yessica. I've been in love with her ever since I joined SEAL Team Six. The problem is that I'm never good enough for her. I feel like a turtle chasing a unicorn."

Pastor Josh put his arms around Joker. "You seem to have it bad my friend. Let's go into my office where we can speak in private."

Chapter Seven

Long Way from Home

Bastel kept herself busy at Arkamedes. There was much work to be done. Her ultimate goal was to control Persephone, but that wasn't her only aspiration. She spent the past few days sending her Watchers over every continent. They were told to keep an eye out for a "Conduit," an individual with superior skills with technology. The Watchers weren't briefed fully on this phenomenon, but they searched the earth anyway looking for this special someone.

Bastel was deep within her work when two of her Watchers disturbed her. She didn't have to turn and look to see who they were. She was familiar enough with them to uncover their identities—Hazamah and Torlian, two of her best fighters and members of the elite Third Watch.

Bastel maintained her cold demeaner and asked, "What is it, you two? Can't you see I'm busy."

"There someone here to see you, Master Bastel," Hazamah said. "It's your husband, Samyaza."

Bastel stopped what she was doing and looked for him.

"Bring him to me," she said. "What are you waiting for?"

Her two Watchers escorted Samyaza to her. He was the leader of the Watchers long ago. However, today he was just a respected outcast. His mission now was only Death—a far cry from the legend he used to be.

Bastel sent her two Watchers away and found a private spot where they could talk. Bastel did something she seldom ever did. She let her guard down. Bastel reached out to touch Samyaza's face, but he pulled away.

"Don't touch me," Samyaza's face. "If you do, it could be the last thing you'll ever touch."

"I thought we had lost you forever when Ignas struck you down," Bastel said. "We had no idea you would turn into a horseman. What about Azrael? Did he also make it out of Tartarus?"

"That is correct. Myself, Azrael, and Ramiel were given the chance to return to this world as horsemen. Our lives as Watchers are only memories now. Our son Adrammelech is also with us."

Bastel's mood turned sour when she heard his name.

"I want nothing to do with that mistake," Bastel said. "Besides, a boy needs his father. I'm more interested in what happened to our girls."

Samyaza looked at the ground. He had trouble looking Bastel in the eyes.

"They're all gone, my love. Their presence remains but their minds are destroyed. I saw them in the Pit once and swore never to go to that place again. Your son is all we have left. Do what is right and make amends with him. What he did wasn't his fault."

Bastel lashed out at her husband, saying, "Do not lecture me on fault! What he did was unforgivable. If I see him again, I will kill him."

Samyaza looked lovingly at his Bastel. He didn't seem bothered by her rage. Bastel noticed this and calmed down.

"Forgive me, Samyaza. I didn't mean what I said. I just hate the fact that I can't see you. These humans have no idea that we Watchers are actually blind. A curse given to us because of what we did. I would give all this power up just to see your face again my love."

Samyaza approached Bastel, stretched his hand out, and said, "Take off your visor."

Bastel took off her golden visor, which exposed to hollow holes that used to house her eyes. Samyaza made sure not to touch her face directly. He used a strange power to restore her face to its former human form. Bastel became overjoyed.

"I can see your lovely face! How are you doing this?"

Samyaza suddenly felt drained. He used too much of his power. The enchantment only lasted a few seconds, but Bastel was still grateful.

William stood before the Supreme Queen and struggled to reason with her.

"Why can't we use Persephone to attack the Watchers?" the Queen asked. "She was built for war."

"I understand, Potentate, but we don't know what these beings are capable of. Attacking them is on par with kicking a hornet's nest barefoot. Please listen. Why not work with them instead? This doesn't have to become a war."

The Supreme Queen scoffed and said, "You speak as though you're on their side. Gaia would shudder at such a treacherous notion."

"Gaia? You speak of Gaia. Where is Gaia when we need her?"

William knew he had crossed a line but he didn't' feel sorry. The Supreme Queen gave him a chilling look that would have meant instant death for anyone else. He tried to apologize, but she cut him off.

"Enough," she said. "Only true believers get to see Gaia face to face. You would know that if you weren't such a babbling fool."

William spoke with the Supreme Queen for over an hour, but she could not be persuaded. "We are done here, William. I've made up my mind about the invaders. Gather the resources we need to replace the weaponry I plan on using. Speak nothing of this encounter. I want the enemy to be caught off guard."

The mysterious White Table gathered once again to discuss what was happening. None of them seemed surprised at the appearance of the Watchers. They actually expected it.

"The Watchers are doing just as we planned," the disgust mask said. "However, the economy is faltering. This is unexpected. The Conglomerate religion is growing, and the popularity of Threedom is exploding. We need to embrace them as the superior rulers."

The angry mask spoke next. "Threedom is a great boon for our pockets, but that should not be the true goal. We need a definitive vote on how to deal with the savages once and for all. They are a blight on our world and have served their purpose. We should vote immediately on this matter."

The laughing mask spoke boldly. "That is not for you to decide. The Eye must be present before such a vote should commence. We should use our resources to undermine the Supreme Queen. She will destroy us all before she allows the Watchers to rule over us."

The five members of the table didn't meet for long. There was much to do, and the mysterious Eye had yet to appear to settle matters definitively.

Things were settling back to normal in the camps of the two churches despite the alien invasion. Richard walked in the bunker of Camp Luther and came across a group of people playing low-stakes poker. Watching them play wasn't what he was after. He approached an older gentleman siting at the table.

"Can you give me some candy, Stan?" Richard asked. "I could really use some sugar right now."

Stan looked at his hand and shook his head.

"I'll give you some candy," Stan said. "But you'll have to earn it first."

Richard acted impatient. "I'll do anything."

Stan laughed and said, "Okay, kid. Pay attention. I want you to name everybody sitting here at this table and then I'll get you some candy."

Richard looked around the table and began to name off names. "Louis, John, Laurice, David, Sam, Chasity, Zane, Tommy, Wayne. Wait, who is the new guy?"

Stan and the others joined in the laughter.

"I knew you couldn't do it," Stan said. "This guy here is named Chester. We found him at one of the homeless encampments about half a mile from here."

Richard was let down by the fact that he wasn't getting any candy, but he seemed more interested in Chester.

"That's right. You all used to run a homeless shelter in Fairbanks. What was it called again?" said Richard.

"True Mission," John said. "And technically it was a day shelter."

He tossed a peppermint Richards way. "You've got a sharp mind, kid, but here's some advice. You don't get younger, and you only get older."

Chester excused himself from the table and went outside to the outhouse. He heard a strange click when he approached the door.

"Hands up, good lookin'."

Chester felt the steel placed to his skull and did as he was told.

"This must be some kind of mistake. What's your name? I'm Chester."

"I'm Yessica, and I've had my eye on you for a long while. My former line of work allowed me to travel a lot. I know a Chinese spy when I see one. What do you want? Information and assimilation? I hope you know what a 44 magnum can do to a human skull."

"What if you're wrong?" Chester said.

"I'm not."

Yessica pulled the trigger, but the gun jammed. Chester acted quickly and disarmed Yessica with ease. He broke apart the gun and threw the components in the woods.

"Oh yeah," Yessica said, "you're definitely a spy."

"If I were a spy," Chester said, "I would have killed you by now. I need you to trust me."

Yessica slowly got up and said, "You hit like a ton of bricks. I guess you Chinese agents eat concrete for breakfast. I'll play your game. What do you want?"

"I want to be in Camp Peter. I know you can make this happen."

Yessica tried not to laugh, saying, "You're really not doing a good job in changing my perception of you. Fine, I'll see to it that its done. At least now I can keep an eye on you.

Nala lived with her Uncle Joe in Camp St. Peter. The living space was cramped but Nala had just enough space to move around in her wheelchair. Nala enjoyed anything with either numbers or machines. She valued them more than anything. Thankfully her Uncle Joe provided her with plenty of both. He was a former NASA engineer and spent most of his time working on equipment and building model prototypes for the military. A few were hung in Nala's room. Nala hid her newly acquired Cobber from her uncle. She knew she would be in trouble if he found out about it. Nala waited till she heard him leave then pulled the complicated tech out from under her covers. On the Cobber was an advanced math equations game she downloaded. Nala was aiming for the high score. Her concentration broke when she saw a group of men in strange clothing approach the camp. They were escorted by the camp patrol and headed straight for them. Nala put her Cobber away and made her way outside. She rushed to the side of her uncle and watched the men engage with them.

"Greetings Christians," a man said. "We come in peace. I am Basim and to my left is my assistant, Hytham. The others with me are some of our recent converts. We are priest in the royal Conglomerate of Pangaia. We came to speak to you about our goddess. May we speak to someone in charge?"

Joseph noticed that most of both camps were gathered around.

"Father Nolan is sleeping so I'll have to wake him up," Joseph said. "You can speak with the leader of Camp Luther until he's ready."

Basim seemed pleased and said, "Thank you, good sir."

He turned to Yessica and gave her a look of recognition.

Yessica raised her eyebrow and said, "What are you looking at, earthworm?"

The children seemed to enjoy her taunts.

"Young lady, have you ever heard of Neothia?" Basim said.

Yessica stuck her nose up. "Ever heard of soap, Congo Bongo?"

Basim seemed to revel in her disdain. "Your insults don't offend me, but your ignorance does. Neothia was a great kingdom that ruled the world. Its territory used to cover the Mediterranean Sea. It was the original promised land. Now we have Africa as our great land. We like to be called Congo for it represents the great ancient African river surrounded by lush green jungle and animals. Safe from human contamination."

Yessica didn't seem impressed.

"Whatever," she said. "Follow the boys and speak with Pastor Josh. He's actually qualified to deal with your garbage."

The Conglomerate representatives made their way to Pastor Josh and explained their unique situation. However, they failed to convince him of their calling.

"You say you're from South Africa," Pastor Josh said, "but I call it Babylon. Trust me when I say it won't be that way for long."

Basim tried to find common ground and said, "We use the same Holy Spirit as you do. She guided us here."

Pastor Josh rebuked them.

"The Holy Spirit in our Bible uses male pronouns not female pronouns," Pastor Josh said. "It's a he and it's not an it. He's not a she either. His job is to teach and convict us of our sin. He does not exist to provide people with mysterious earth energy."

Basim grew tired of arguing and said, "Will you just let us speak with your congregation? They have a right to choose what God they serve."

"Snakes have no business with sheep," Pastor Josh said. "I've been tasked with the role of shepherd. No one wants to hear your false faith nor do we want to wear those things you call duo forms."

Basim threw his hands in the air in defeat. He left the pastor in peace, saying, "I'll be on my way then. Thank you for your time, Pastor Josh."

The combat patrol escorted Basim and his followers over to Camp St. Peter. Where he hoped to receive a better welcome there.

Chapter Eight

The New Hunt

Two friends arrived in Anchorage Alaska via boat. One was a scientist while the other was a journalist. They came here to see the fabled Watchers for themselves. The Watchers were greatly praised and sought after around the world. People saw them as gods and hoped to please them. The Scientist and the Journalist felt the same way. They lived relatively normal lives in Pangaia, but they wanted something more. They got in a vehicle and drove over three hundred miles west of Anchorage. They stopped the car when their Cobbers told them they were in the right location and found a massive gathering of people. The vehicles present were from all over the world. Everyone here wanted one thing: To see the Watcher invaders in person.

There were also people who wanted to be Tamers but that was not what the scientist and the journalist wanted.

"Make sure you lock the door," the journalist, who was clearly the alpha in the relationship said. "I don't want to be stranded out here."

The Journalist was a well-known figure in her community.

"Yes, dear," the Scientist said. Quiet and reserved, he was the opposite of her forceful personality. Though he was a well-read man, he had little to no true ambition. The two waded through a sea of people before they arrived at the stage where the Watchers were scheduled to perform. The Journalist grew tired of waiting after twenty minutes.

"Let's just leave," she said. "I don't think they're coming."

"You're right," the Scientist said. "Let's go."

The stage suddenly began to illuminate, and the cheers roared. The atmosphere was like that of a rock concert. The couple turned around and saw two massive beings with glowing eyes. They spoke like they were using modern technology, but there were no devices detected.

"Who wants to be a Tamer?"

The crowd erupted with celebration.

"I'm Hazamah, and this is Torlian. We're here to make someone immortal."

The Supreme Queen gathered Persephone and the rest of her war council to a secret location in Pangaia.

"Will our weapons work against the Watchers?" the Supreme Queen asked.

Persephone looked back at the Supreme Queen with lifeless eyes as she calculated the outcome.

"There is a forty-four percent chance our weapons will work against the invaders," Persephone said.

The Supreme Queen wanted to annihilate the Watchers not join with them.

"Where are the Watchers gathered?" the Supreme Queen asked.

"I detect twenty Watchers total," Persephone said. "There are three in North America, six in South America, three in Africa, three in Europe, three in Middle East, one in China, and one in Australia. I suggest using low-grade nuclear weapons to see if they are effective first. The chance of severe nuclear fallout will be great if we use Optimus MOAB nuclear weapons."

The Supreme Queen ignored Persephone's advice and gave the order to attack. "Use every weapon we have and destroy the watchers. I want you to use Optimus MOAB nukes on every Watcher location."

The Scientist and the Journalist watched as hundreds of thousands of people became Tamers. Each of them had unique capabilities. Most of them could fly like the Watchers. This allowed the couple to get closer to the stage. For a moment, they considered becoming Tamers. The two Watchers suddenly stopped and looked at each other.

Torlian began to speak. "I'm sorry to inform you that your government is taking hostile action against us. This will not be tolerated. We're leaving."

The crowd groaned and the people spoke out. "What kind of action?"

"The Pangaia Space Force has launched an Optimus MOAB nuclear bomb at this location," Torlian said. "These nukes are fifty times stronger than the strongest nukes of the past. It will eviscerate anything within twenty-one hundred square miles. The fallout will be great."

The Scientist made his way to the stage and tried to reason with the panicking crowd. A man with his personality and temperament would normally be content to stay in the background but the urgency of the

107

situation compelled him to act. "Listen to me," he said. "We still have at least fifteen minutes before the bomb hits. Our vehicles can make it out of here in time."

The Journalist joined him on stage. "Pangaia wouldn't kill its own people just for show," the Journalist said. "We should stay put and see this so-called nuke for ourselves."

The crowd was as split. Half followed the Scientist to safety while the other half stayed with the Journalist. The Journalist's fears were confirmed after ten minutes. The unmistakable glow of a nuclear bomb headed toward them. She shrugged and accepted her fate. The Scientist was nearly out of the blast range when Hazamah blocked their path.

"Going somewhere?" he said.

The large group of people sounded their horns in displeasure, but there was nothing they could do. The bombs dropped all over the world and killed millions. Hazamah, Torlian, and the other Watchers stood unharmed. They looked around and marveled at the charred remains of the people that worshipped them.

"Persephone, give me a status report," the Supreme Queen said.

Persephone ran through the numbers and said, "All territories targeted have been completely destroyed. However, the Watchers were not harmed."

The Supreme Queen slammed her fist on her throne and said, "This is impossible. We can't win like this."

The room then became dark. Only Persephone's glowing lights aided them visually. A lone figure made its way up to the Supreme Queen. She was frightened but did not cower.

"Who are you?" the Supreme Queen said.

The being restored the lights. It was none other than Bastel.

"Hello, your Highness," she said. "Do you nuke all of your guests?"

The Supreme Queen did her best to put on a brave face.

"Stay back or I'll have you killed," she said.

Bastel put her hand up to silence her. She was now entranced with Persephone.

"William spoke of her beauty but it's like nothing I've ever seen," Bastel said. "So, this is the great Persephone. Through her I can control the Jailers and every Leo. I must tame her and have her serve me."

Bastel reached out and touched Persephone. A flow of energy surged through her, which caused her to release her brace.

"Why can't I?" Bastel said.

Persephone's automated system kicked in. She said, "Unauthorized entry. I cannot submit to a foreign being."

Bastel knew she needed to find the Conduit now more than ever. The Supreme Queen was unable to control Bastel, so she decided to improvise.

"What do you want?" the Queen asked. Maybe we can come to an agreement."

"I want my husband and my daughters back," Bastel said. "My desire is to be free from this coil of flesh. Above all I want to find my Conduit—an individual capable of harnessing power worthy of a Watcher. I believe this person is in the northwest land, which is why I dwell there."

Bastel paused to think then spoke again when she had an idea. "Maybe we can come to an agreement."

The Supreme Queen was eager to appease. "Just name it and it shall be done," the Queen said.

Bastel focused her eyes on Persephone and said, "I want Persephone to use her vast database to give me a list of potential Conduit candidates. This person needs to be a descendant of Adam and Eve, have superior intellect, be compassionate, and be worthy of power. I hope this won't be too difficult for her."

The Supreme Queen gave the order, and Persephone began to calculate all probabilities.

"There are forty-five Conduit candidates in the northwest lands," Persephone said. "Three of them are children."

Bastel was intrigued. "Tell me about the children," she said.

"I found an individual who matches your standard. However, I feel my analysis is in error. This child is lame and deaf."

Making her exit, Bastel said, "Here I thought this talking piece of metal was humanities greatest achievement. What a joke! I'll just have to find the Conduit on my own. I know I'm close."

Basim and Hytham spoke at length with Father Nolan in Camp St. Peter. The conversation was less confrontational than that with Pastor Josh. However, they still were getting nowhere with their new religious order.

"Would you or your assistant like some tea, Basim?"

Basim sat frustrated and declined the offer.

"No, thank you, Father Nolan. I want us to find common ground before I commit to any hospitality. There are many Christians within the Conglomerate. We both agree that Mary the mother of Jesus is a guiding figure in your faith. We understand that, and we want you to know that we embrace her as well. Forget about the Protestants. All they ever do is argue about doctrine. They lack your devotion and structure."

Father Nolan gently corrected Basim. "I'm glad you recognize the importance of Mary, but we are not simply Catholics. We are Catholic Charismatics. We have more in common with Protestants than you think. Ultimately, we believe in the power of the cross above all else. I'm afraid I'm going to have to ask you and your converts to leave"

As Basim rose to leave, a small tremor occurred. The two men looked out the window and saw a massive mushroom cloud in the distance.

Basim sat down quickly and said, "I think I'll have that tea now."

Richard struggled to stay awake during Sunday service. Pastor Josh preached on the importance of the Trinity. The congregation followed along as best as they could. Their only problem was that there weren't enough Bibles to go around. Both churches had a total of four Bibles. Pangaia was ruthless in the Bible's destruction.

Richard pulled on his father's coattails. His father, Paul, wasn't very devout. He chose to see the "good" that Pangaia was doing, but he was paranoid about the level of surveillance that Pangaia did on its populace. Paul's late wife passed away when Richard was still young. The pressure to provide in these times was high. Paul credited his success and achievements to sheer force of will. Not the power of an almighty God. Christianity was like a glove that he took off and on every day.

"Can I go outside and play?" Richard asked.

Paul tried to listen to the sermon and respond. "All your friends are in the service, so the answer is no. Pay attention. You might just learn something."

Richard planned his exit after five long minutes. He excused himself for the bathroom and ventured outside. Nala was waiting for him underneath an old tree. The two explained how their days went then Nala surprised Richard with some information.

"I'm going to see if I can become a Tamer," she said. "It might heal me."

Richard was taken aback but tried to be supportive.

"Yeah, that's cool," Richard said.

Nala traveled to the outskirts of camp St. Peter and had Richard follow.

"Come on, I want you to meet someone."

Standing watch by his lonesome was Chris, a former head coach of a women's professional football league. Chris was good with children and was a big part of Nala's life. Chris knew how to use sign language and did his best to interpret for Nala. She trusted him but not enough to where she would reveal her Cobber to him. Richard found this form of communicating to be anything but fun. Chris and Nala signed for a few more minutes before turning to Richard.

"Nala says that you know of our plan," Chris said. "We plan on heading to the Watchers soon to see if we can become Tamers. Can you image not having to struggle for food. It could also heal Nala. Sounds great right?"

Richard felt uncomfortable and said, "I don't want to get in trouble."

Chris approached Richard and knelt down.

"Hey buddy," Chris said. "Don't you worry. Just know that I will hunt you and your family down if you tell anyone."

Winter was fast approaching in Alaska. Yessica took a rifle and began to hunt for deer and moose. She was still taken back by the beauty of this land. The clean cool air, marvelous mountains, and varied vegetation soothed her. She felt distant and empty. Loosing her sister took a part of her that she could never get back. She did her best to be at peace, despite the Watchers' arrival and the nuclear mushroom cloud in the distance. Yessica tracked a deer for over a mile before she got a chance to strike it. She aimed her rife and slowly pulled the trigger. A Watcher stood before her and scared off the deer.

"What are you doing?" Yessica asked.

"Wildlife preservation of course. Call me Hazamah. I've heard much about you from Simeon, and I'm offering you a job."

"What's the job?"

"It's simple," Hazamah said. "I want to see if you can kill Simeon."

Yessica turned, began to walk away, and said, "I can't kill him with conventional weapons."

Hazamah cut off her path and pleaded. "I can help with that. You should also know that an elite Zohar team is enroute to kill Simeon as we speak. If you team up with them and accept my help, you can finally get your revenge."

Yessica liked the idea of another team with her. "How can you help me with Simeon?"

Hazamah placed his hand on his shoulder. He melted the surface of his armor and produced a black slimy goo. He put it in a vial and handed it to Yessica.

"Lace that with your bullets and you'll have enough to defeat Simeon," he said. "Just remember, you never saw me and we never met."

Yessica returned to the two churches and informed Hope, Joker, and Blade of the mission. They were all too eager to do something meaningful. Yessica gave her instructions, but Joker had a suggestion.

"Can we bring Ruth with us, boss? She can handle herself and we could always use a doctor."

Yessica sighed and said, "If she wants to join us, she can."

Joker headed for Camp St. Peter and found Ruth in the clinic.

"We're going after Simeon. Will you help us?" he asked.

Ruth cleaned up and put her assistant in charge.

"I'll come along," she said. "But I'm here to heal not kill. Understood?"

"Of course."

Chapter Nine

The Most Dangerous Game

Simeon gathered his horseman and his Watchers around a large fire at Arkamedes. The horsemen of Pestilence, War, and Death were all present. Bastel and two of her Watchers were also there. Simeon showed them his drone footage of the miracles he had performed up to this point. Some feats were small, while others were great. He didn't lack confidence in his abilities. Simeon wanted to know if they would be enough to persuade humanity to follow him. Bastel heaped praise upon Simeon.

"Bravo, Lord Simeon," Bastel said. "This should be more enough to persuade the mortals."

Simeon noticed that Samyaza and Bastel kept glancing at each other. He couldn't help but ask, "Do you two know each other or something?"

Samyaza quickly eased his suspicions, saying, "We may have crossed paths once or twice in the past. Fret not, Damiano. We're all committed to you and your mission."

Simeon folded his arms.

"What aren't you telling me, Samyaza?" Simeon asked.

The former leader of the Watchers spoke plainly. "I believe your miracles are good, but you will need to do something that reminds people about the Messiah."

Simeon caught on.

"You mean the Nazarene," he said. "Are you suggesting that my powers should mimic those recorded in the Bible?"

Samyaza looked at the others and agreed.

"Yes, Damiano," Samyaza said. "I believe that would be wise."

Simeon liked the idea but wasn't sure he was capable of doing this sort of feat on his own.

"Can any of you find someone who needs my assistance and bring them to me?" he asked.

They all agreed to help—with the exception of Bastel. Simeon took notice and questioned her.

"Is there something wrong, Bastel? Do you know someone that could use my abilities?"

Bastel remembered the lame girl not far from here but decided to lie.

"No, Lord Simeon," she said. "I have no idea how to aid you. I will look diligently though."

Simeon ended the gathering and dismissed Samyaza, Azrael, and Ramiel. Bastel stood beside him as he began to chop firewood outside his dwelling place. Bastel noticed Simeon was a bit perturbed and asked, "Is something wrong Lord Simeon?"

Simeon focused on his task as he spoke. It was his way of calming down.

"I don't like being lied to Bastel. I expect the former leader of the Watchers to be deceptive, but not you. My expectations of you are higher. It's obvious that you and Samyaza know each other. If I had to guess, I would say it was romantic. Either way, I don't mind. Just don't lie to me again. Do you understand?"

Bastel felt embarrassed and wanted to explain. She began to speak when she noticed an insect drone on top of the wood. She grabbed it and presented it to Simeon.

"It looks like Zohar tech," she said. "They must have found us. I'll get Hazamah and Torlian. We'll defend the perimeter."

Bastel summoned her Watchers, and they took defensive positions. Simeon gave his orders. "You're with me, Bastel. Join me in my tabernacle. Let Hazamah, Torlian, and Besera deal with the invaders. Simeon and Bastel entered the large, dirty white tent and waited patiently for their intruders to present themselves.

Yessica and her team were about two miles out from Simeon's base. Various tracks in the mud allowed them to know they were on the right trail. They moved quickly and with purpose. Hope signaled for the team to stop when he saw something on his scope. It was a group of Zohar agents setting up camp. They saw him and waved them over.

"Looks like we're spotted, boss," Hope said. "What should we do?"

Yessica took his scope and searched the camp. She recognized a face.

"That's James Baker," she said. "Lower your weapons. We're not here to fight them."

Yessica and her team approached the Zohar camp with their hands up. The Zohar team quickly aimed their weapons at them, but James calmed everyone down. He approached Yessica, and the two did their secret handshake.

"It's really you, Yessica. How did you get here?"

"I'm from here, actually. The rest of us have nowhere else to go. Our base is south of here."

James lowered his voice.

"Listen to me," he said. "We know all about Camp Luther and Camp St. Peter. You're working with our enemy, Yessica. Leave them and join us before it's too late."

Yessica ignored the warning. She thought he was joking. She looked at the armor and weaponry on James and the other Zohar members. It was unlike anything she had ever seen.

"Is that camouflage armor? And your weapons look like something out of a science fiction movie. What gives?" Yessica asked.

James showed off his gear and explained them all in detail. Yessica was impressed but got to the point.

"Why are you after Simeon?" she said. "I didn't know Zohar thought of him as a threat."

James pointed his head toward a man giving out strict orders. He had curly red hair.

"That is Deputy Director Mark Zurg," James said. "He rarely goes on missions, but he made sure that he would be on this one. Simeon has been deemed Zohar's greatest threat to Pangaia, but the public is unaware of him as of now. We plan on keeping it this way by taking him out in the shadows. You're looking at Zohar's finest right now. We're the ELO squad."

Yessica pretended not to know agent Zurg.

"That's great, James. I'm happy for you. Do you think we can team up with you? There's no need to brief us. A couple of Watchers gave us this special gel to fight Simeon, and we both know what a threat he is."

James was pleased and said, "Great, I'll go ahead and vouch for you then. However, don't tell Zurg we know each other. He won't find out on his own. All records of our SEAL teams were destroyed by Captain Magnetta. It only cost him his life. Now sit tight while I speak with the Deputy Director."

James turned around and found the Deputy Director. The two quarreled, but the director eventually caved in. James returned with the news.

"He says you can join us but only if you share the gel."

Yessica handed over the sticky substance and explained its intended use. Mark Zurg interrupted them and spoke with Yessica briefly.

"I don't care that you and your men were SEALs," Zurg said. "You're not equipped to handle this threat. Listen closely. You better not screw this up or there will be hell to pay."

James and his ELO squad joined Yessica and her team and made their way toward Arkamedes. They spread out and formed a circle when they approached the hostile base. There was no sign of Simeon or any other living thing.

Yessica got on the comms with James.

"Something's up," she said. "Let's take out that tent with some frags."

James paused when he heard howling. He had his team activate their camouflage. They were nearly invisible, but Yessica and her team were still exposed. Hundreds of animals came on them and attacked. The team held their ground. But the massive grizzly bear that led the attacks used the wolves as a shield. The bear overpowered and killed Blade. Yessica became enraged, dropped her rifle, and got on top of the bear. She took her combat knife and plunged it inside the head of the bear dozens of times before the bear fell on the ground, dead.

Ruth tried to tend to Blade, but he was already gone. Yessica looked in the distance and saw Simeon approaching them. Yessica grabbed her rifle and loaded it with a sleeve of black-goo-laced bullets. She aimed and fired but noticed something. The goo-laced bullets only made Simeon stronger.

"We've been lied to," Yessica said. "Cease fire!"

Her men stopped firing, but the ELO squad kept shooting. Simeon transformed into a large dark creature with red glowing eyes. James finally caved in and gave the order to cease fire.

"You have defiled Arkamedes. Therefore, you must die," Simeon taunted, as he looked around menacingly. "I'll start with you, Senior Chief."

Simeon stretched his arm and caused Hope to hover off the ground and move toward him. His power paralyzed both teams. Hope cried out in pain and struggled to breath. Yessica was able to resist paralysis. She drew her combat knife and charged at Simeon. Her resistance kept her safe. However, nothing could be done for Hope. Simeon crushed his head by the time Yessica reached him. Yessica roared at the sight of her fallen ally. She drove her blade into the neck of the dark beast. Simeon was powerless to stop her. An explosion of dark energy flowed from the wound, which caused Yessica to fly backward twenty feet. Simeon was now back to his normal form and his paralysis of the two teams was no more. He pulled the knife from his neck and placed his hand where he was bleeding. The wound healed soon after. He breathed raggedly and gave orders to his two Watchers.

"Kill one more and get rid of the rest," Simeon said. "I have the footage I need."

"Is this some kind of game with you?" Yessica asked.

As Simeon limped away into the woods to recover, he said, "It's the most dangerous game there is."

Hazamah and Torlian made themselves known. The teams knew their ammunition was a set up. They didn't even bother firing them at the Watchers. They were truly defenseless.

"Who should we kill, Torlian? One of the girls or one of the boys?"

Torlian seemed to revel in the moment and said, "We both know who it should be. Let it be the man at the center of a love triangle."

Yessica was puzzled. "Who is that?" she asked.

Without warning, a thin glowing arrow pierced the neck of James. He began to choke on his blood Yessica rushed to his right side. Mark Zurg rushed to his left.

James spoke weakly, but it only made things worse.

"How does a toothpick?" James said, trying to ease his transition before Yessica yelled, "Ruth! Get over her now."

Yessica focused back on James.

121

"You better not die on me, James. That's an order."

Zurg got James's attention. He tried to declare his love for James, but he was too late. James breathed his last breath and died in his arms. Zurg fell to his knees and screamed toward the heavens.

"You foolish woman," Zurg said. "Why didn't you tell me you knew James? I could have spared him from your incompetence. We were in love. This is all because of you and that church you protect. You did this. I'll never forgive you."

The Watchers looked on approvingly.

"You mortals have been warned," a Watcher said. "Never return to Arkamedes."

They vanished from sight leaving the team to collect their people, things, and to go their separate ways.

William watched the events at Arkamedes from his private study. He was able to hack into the Zohar feed easily, although it was illegal. Cynthia was by his side planning his schedule.

"What's Simeon's social score look like?" William asked.

Cynthia found the numbers and looked shocked.

"He has a potential SIGIL score of twenty-four out of one thousand," she said. "He's deemed too radical for social integration."

William paused and said, "That's hogwash. Patch me through. I want to speak with him."

Cynthia created a loop in the feed to mask their intrusion. William spoke with Simeon as he limped on into the woods.

"Simeon, this is William Calig. CEO of Jopa and Tera King of Israel. I don't have time for formalities, so I'll get to the point. I know you have secret footage of your miraculous acts. I've seen them all, and

I'm impressed. I can use someone like you. I'll make your name great. Together, we can conquer the world. What do you say?"

Simeon found a tree stump and sat down. It was bitterly cold, but he was sweating profusely.

"I know who you are, king William, but now is not the time for the world to know me. There is something I must do first."

Many people at the two churches secretly considered abandoning their faith to join the Watchers. The idea of being a Tamer was very seductive. Chester pleaded with the members of both camps to reconsider. The dusk turned to night and people gathered for bed. Nala had planned this day for a long while. Her Uncle Joe was at the chapel, which left her by herself. She closed her door and opened the window. Chris approached with excitement and signed, "Are you ready for your life to change?"

Nala signed back, "Of course."

Chris grabbed Nala from out of her wheelchair and put her on his back. He then folded the wheelchair and placed it on his side. His watch covered a third of the perimeter so he had the perfect place to leave undetected. The two left the churches and headed north. Their plan was to see all of what the Watchers had offer.

Richard saw the two heading out into the woods. He suspected trouble but kept quiet. The next morning it was a well-known fact that Chris and Nala had vanished. Joseph suspected the worse. He thought this was a matter of desire and not friendship. Richard decided to speak up.

"I saw them leave together last night," he said. "They looked happy. I don't think she's in danger."

Joseph could barely contain his fury.

"Why didn't you say something last night?" Joseph said. "We could have stopped them."

Paul spoke up for his son, saying, "He's just a boy Joseph. We now know Nala's not in danger. Be comforted with that."

Two days later, a memorial for Hope and Blade commenced. Yessica did her best to comfort Sarah. She was old enough to take care of herself but that didn't help the pain of losing her father. Yessica said her goodbyes to her men and turned around. She saw Joker and Ruth walking together. They appeared to be holding hands. Yessica followed them and listened in on their conversation.

"So, you're really Catholic?"

"Yes, Joker. How many times do I have to tell you."

"I'm not a believer, but I might reconsider now that I know you are."

Chapter Ten

Path of Destiny

A large crowd of angels gathered around an unusual occurrence: the birth of a special angel. No one would care if this were any other angel. The Nava Warden Lenoth waded his way through the sea of angels and up to the special angel.

"Make way everyone," Lenoth said, "You're not helping."

The newly formed angel came out of its slumber and looked curiously around at all the strange faces.

"Am I dead?" the angel asked.

Lenoth found the question alarming.

"You mean to tell me that you don't know who or what you are? That's strange. I'm Lenoth, by the way. The Warden of Nava angels. You are the newest member in our ranks. Let's start with your name. What is it?"

The angel regained its composure and stood up.

"My name is Alice."

The angels gathered around gasped and whispered among themselves. Lenoth ignored the other angels and focused on Alice.

"Tell us the last thing you remember," Lenoth said.

"I was drowning somewhere, but that's all I can remember," Alice said.

Lenoth explained in detail who Alice was and what she now became. He told her about the quadrants, the responsibilities of a Nava, the other classes of angels, the angel creed, and her unique predicament.

"This is not your fault, Alice, but your gender is highly irregular," Lenoth said. "I don't have time to explain, but I know that this is the Lord's will. Please remember that."

A large, purple angel quickly approached the large group and made his presence known.

"What is everybody doing?" the purple angel said. "Get back to work all of you!"

The crowd dispersed just as quickly as it gathered, leaving only three remaining.

"I'm Ignas. You must be the new half-breed."

Ignas spoke to Alice as if she were a threat. Alice picked up on this and stood her ground.

"My name is Alice. There's no need to be rude."

Alice looked around the area and saw thousands of angels but none looked like her.

"Am I the first female angel?" she asked.

Ignas folded his arms and said, "That information is on a need-to-know basis. I cannot divulge such things to a low-ranking hybrid like yourself."

His words were soft, but they cut like a blade. He seemed content with belittling Alice. Alice noticed the sword hilt on Ignas and remembered what Lenoth taught her about Nava.

"Why can't I fight?" she said. "This seems unfair. I can handle myself. Lenoth says that Oze are great warriors. Why do you wear robes like us if that's the case?"

Ignas seemed amused and said, "When I don armor, it is a form of judgment. A guarantee that many spirits will perish. Pray that you never see me in my battle armor."

Alice recognized the obvious threat and changed the subject. This time she spoke with Lenoth, the more agreeable angel.

"Where are my wings? I thought angels had wings," Alice asked.

Lenoth began to speak but Ignas overpowered him causing Lenoth to cower.

"Don't be foolish, daughter of Eve," Ignas said. "This is the kingdom of the triune God. You are not a Valkyrie roaming Valhalla, nor are you an Amazon princess. You are a Nava. This is reality not some mortal fantasy."

Lenoth studied Alice while her and Ignas spoke. He discovered something even more unusual.

"I detect that most of you is Nava," Lenoth said. "You retain information like one, but you also don't lack curiosity. This is dangerous for an angel of your ilk. What's most troubling is the fact that you still have some human emotions. This is extremely dangerous."

Ignas piled on, saying, "This is why I don't trust you. I'll be keeping an eye on you for this point on."

Alice calmed herself and chose not to take the bait Ingas presented.

127

"I get it, Ignas," Alice said. "It looks like I've joined an all-boys club. My sister went through something similar. No one expected her to be a leader in the legendary SEAL Team Six. I guess we're more alike than I thought. I can understand your frustration. You think female angels are an abomination. I think you have this perspective because of the assigned roles given to Adam and Eve. In your eyes, it's almost like a man trying to get pregnant. I might not be able to change your mind, but I do know that those in Christ are new creatures. Old things have passed away, and all things are new. I'm no longer in the flesh so my relationship to Eve and her earthly roles have vanished. Ultimately, we're both created beings of God. You should take it up with our creator if you have a problem with that. Thanks for listening. We're done here."

Ignas turned his nose up and vanished from her sight. Lenoth was impressed.

"No one speaks to Ignas like that," Lenoth said. "You really are different. Come with me. I want to show you something."

The two angels traveled to Earth, which had countless angels gathered around. Two men descended onto the earth from heaven. They wore hoods that covered their faces.

"Who are they?" Alice asked.

Lenoth seemed disappointed and said, "The data suggested that you were a biblical scholar. Why don't you recognize them? They are the Two Witnesses that will warn the world of its impending judgement."

Alice eyebrows perked up.

"Do we know their identities?" she asked.

"I'm sure there are some angels with that knowledge but that doesn't include me," Lenoth said. "Make yourself comfortable. Get to know this place well. I must leave you to carry out other business."

Lenoth departed and Alice flew low above the earth to get a better view. She was amazed to see such a marvelous sight. Alice then saw a great angel sounding a trumpet. Hail mixed with fire and blood fell upon the earth. This caused many trees and all the green grass to burn up.

The two witnesses arrived in Israel and began to preach the gospel and the impending judgment of Christ. They didn't need Echo Vison or any other means to transmit the gospel. Their voices boomed with power and authority around the world. This message irritated the government of Pangaia. Reports of unrest and disturbance of the peace made their way to the highest members of Pangaia. The Supreme Queen put William Calig in charge of dealing with these strange two hooded men.

Because this phenomenon was within his jurisdiction, William grabbed his Icarus orbs and gauntlets and flew to their location. The two witnesses ignored William and continued to preach when he arrived. They were an annoyance but no threat.

"My name is William, and you are impeding upon the rights of the citizens of Pangaia. I order you to both stop this nonsense immediately."

The Two Witnesses continued to ignore William. William turned to the Zohar agent trained to use the Icarus orbs next to him and said, "I don't think they heard me. Use the orbs and make them understand, son."

The agent crushed the orbs and summoned massive lightning strikes on the Two Witnesses. The attack didn't harm the Witnesses. It only made them louder and bolder. Suddenly fire came out of the mouth of the Two Witnesses and consumed the agent to ashes. William snapped his fingers, turned around, and headed back to his drone.

The Supreme Queen contacted William via Echo Vision.

"Is it done, William?" she asked.

"Not quite, Potentate. I don't think there is a weapon that can kill them. They're as untouchable as the Watchers. I have a device that can drown out their voice frequencies. We can sell it to the public at a decent price and make a nice profit. My sources in Alaska say they can barely hear them. Good for them, I guess. I recommend we use Persephone to spin this in our favor. It will turn into more support for Threedom."

The Supreme Queen was pleased.

"Keep me informed," she said. "Do we know why all grass is withered? How about all the dead trees?"

"If I had to guess, I would say it's due to our new guest. Once again, I recommend Persephone use this to our advantage."

William disconnected the call and received another Echo Vison from a Zohar agent.

"We found ten Christians in the southern area, Terra King William," the agent said.

William used his Cobber and projected the image of the Christians with halos on their necks and sacks over their heads.

"You see what happens when you boys don't cooperate. Let their heads roll," William said.

The halos activated and the heads of the Christians fell to the floor. William ended the Echo and got in his vehicle, where he received an urgent message from Cynthia.

"This had better be good, Cynthia."

"You need to get back to the office right now," Cynthia said. "Strange rocks are falling from the sky. Trees are burning, and all grass is fading. There are also bugs everywhere and they are all overflowing with blood."

Yet another summit was held at the Two Churches. This time the topic was about all the members who were fleeing both churches in pursuit to become Tamers. They heard the faint gospel message carried by the wind. Yessica thought it was some kind of psychological operation.

"I heard a lot of this in Asia," Yessica said. "They liked to keep their people dumb and docile trough messages like this."

Pastor Josh had a different perspective and said, "They're preaching the gospel. This must mean they are the Two Witnesses. This confirms that we don't have much time left on this earth."

Yessica seemed baffled. "How much time do we have?"

"No more than seven years," Pastor Josh said. "I didn't want to believe it, but it looks like we're officially in the Tribulation. The Tribulation last three-and-a-half years. The Great Tribulation is the latter three-and-a-half years. We need to promote this message to everyone. Let's not be ashamed of the gospel."

Father Nolan didn't share Josh's enthusiasm.

"Let's not do anything rash, pastor," Father Nolan said. "I'm sure the world hears the message as clearly as we do. We should allow others to come to us should they wish to follow our ways."

An argument broke out over scripture. Yessica realized she was out of her depth and stepped outside. The cold clean air gave her clarity. Joseph followed after her and began to plead.

"Yessica," Joseph said, "you have to gather some men and get Nala back. She's all I have left in this world."

Yessica felt bad but couldn't risk losing any more men.

"If Hope and Blade were still here, I would probably do it," she said. "However, they're gone, and I don't run a daycare."

Joseph was appalled, saying, "Do you not have a filter? That was extremely rude and uncalled for."

"What's uncalled for is leaving a ten-year-old girl alone in that box you call a home," Yessica snapped back. "You can't raise children in fear. It forces them to rebel. Now get lost!"

Joseph refused to back down.

"I really don't like you and I hope you know that. You're terrible with people, you're manipulative, and you never let anybody in. Why don't you give the victim act a rest. We've all lost someone close to us."

Joseph stormed away and headed home. Yessica turned her attention to the sound of footsteps getting closer.

"Hello, spy," Yessica said.

Chester appeared at just the right time.

"You need to listen to Joseph and get Nala back," Chester said. "That girl is more important than you know."

"Tell me what you know, spy," Yessica said. "I just might consider your offer."

"It has something to do with Simeon but that's all I can say."

Yessica squared up to Chester and looked him straight in the eyes.

"I think you're either messing with me or you're some sort of mastermind," Yessica said. "This better lead me to Simeon in some way. You should know that I'll do anything to avenge my sister. So I'll play ball and look around for the girl. You better be right about her or it will cost you."

Chester wasn't afraid but asked, "What will it cost me?"

Yessica smiled. "Ever heard of a eunuch?"

Chris and Nala had finally made it to the Watcher camp, where thousands of people gathered, waiting for a chance to speak with the lone Watcher Hazamah. Many citizens of Pangaia knew all the watchers by name and appearance. They were bigger than any known celebrity. The two waited an entire day before finally getting a chance to speak with the esteemed Watcher.

"What are your names?" the Watcher asked.

"I'm Chris and this is Nala. We came from Wainwright."

Hazamah had a supernatural charisma. He loved that there were plenty of camera's around—especially when they were all centered on him.

"I see the girl is lame and deaf," Hazamah said. "Do you think being a Tamer will heal her?"

Chris said, "That's the goal."

"Very well, stand to my left."

133

Chris and Nala had seen those in front of them do the exact same thing. They had no idea what this did, but they always saw an expression of joy moments later. The two took their place side by side. Within seconds they were floating above the earth in a Watcher spaceship. They couldn't believe their eyes. A being with hair like an octopus stood behind them and frightened them with its presence.

"Do not fear. For it is I Bastel. A leader of Watchers. Are you enjoying the view?"

Bastel took her seat on a great seat made of silver and had Chris and Nala sit in their assigned seats made of copper. Nala was ecstatic.

"This is awesome!" Nala signed.

But Bastel didn't share her enthusiasm.

"I suppose the view from here is fascinating to lesser minds." Bastel said. "Hazamah said you wished to be healed so here I am. You should be honored. I don't speak with just anyone."

Chris fell on his face and bowed before Bastel.

"For years I've watched Nala suffer in silence. I can't stand by any longer. It makes me sick how the others look at her like she's some kind of burden. I want the camps and the world to know how competent and special she is. Please heal her," Chris said. "We'll do anything."

Bastel laughed and said, "I'm not going to heal you but I know someone who can. Come closer and I'll tell you all you need to know."

Chapter Eleven

Deceit and Dispair

Alice watched in awe as the angels around her became instruments of judgment. A second angel with a trumpet appeared and sounded it. Then a great mountain burning with fire fell from heaven and fell into the sea. Alice knew intuitively that this event was in the book of Revelation. She now had a much greater grasp of scripture since she was free from her flesh. Difficult biblical concepts now had unparalleled clarity. Being an angel clearly had its perks.

Two Zimrat angels saw Alice by herself and joined her.

"Quite the view isn't it?" one angel said. "You're obviously new here so let me explain what's happening."

Alice felt like she was being spoken down to. She turned around and raised her voice.

"I know what's going on," Alice said. "This is clearly Revelation chapter eight."

The angel was impressed and said, "You drew that information from your mind and not your spirit. That's very impressive for a former mortal. My name is Kaiden and this here is Udina. It's a pleasure to meet you."

Alice lowered her guard and tried to make the most of their encounter.

"I'm sorry," Alice said. "I don't usually speak with strangers. That also includes angels. Is it true that Zimrat's always work in pairs?"

Kaiden and Udina glanced at one another and gave Alice an off-putting grin.

"Not always, but we do most of the time," Kaiden said. "And no worries. Everyone knows you're new here."

Alice continued to talk with Kaiden and Udina. She learned that their goals and achievements were impressive despite their seemingly lack of ambition. The lives of angels continued to spark curiosity within her.

The Third Temple was now rebuilt and ready to receive sacrifices. Red heifers were flown in from around the world, ready to be slaughtered on the newly formed alter. Both the priest and the high priest were chosen by Jopa and William. Everything seemed right despite the strange events of the past. William wore priest-like garments for this special occasion. Media from all over Pangaia came here to marvel and praise William on this achievement. Cameras typically weren't allowed in holy places, but William had no qualms about granting full access to the media. He liked think of himself as a father of a movement, always pushing the envelope of what's acceptable.

William heard a loud crash when he brought the cameras inside the temple. He refused to let this impede his tour and continued like nothing happened. An emergency message appeared on his Cobber minutes later.

"What is it now, Cynthia?" William said. "It better not be about those blood bugs again. That cost a fortune to clean up."

"Check the news now," Cynthia said.

William dismissed the tour and checked the news on his Cobber. A massive meteor had crashed into the Mediterranean Sea. A third part of the sea's salt scrubbers stopped working, which meant a lack in drinking water. Records also showed that the impact vaporized one third of all aquatic life in the sea and many ships were lost.

All of this seemed to coincide with the rebuilding of the Temple. William knew this couldn't be coincidence. He wasn't a minster anymore, but he did believe in God. However, his God was one of his own makings. This God of William lived to serve his interest. William decided to spin these events in his favor.

"Listen to me," William said. "Tell the public this attack came from the Watchers. We can't have our benevolent Gaia blamed for this. Nor can we have the public believe that the Two Witnesses had anything to do with this. This information would destroy everything we've built."

Cynthia asked, "Shall I do this for future attacks as well, William?"

"Yes. Blame all future attacks on the Watchers."

The White Table gathered again in Rome. There was much to discuss. Their world was growing more chaotic by the day, and they wanted solutions to their festering problems.

The disgust mask commenced the meeting by saying, "Today we meet to create solutions my fellow SMARTs. Nature is turning on us, the Watchers have ambition to replace us, and the savages are emboldened by the Two Witness. We will begin with the first order of business. It is obvious that our problems are supernatural in nature. William Calig chose to blame this all on the Watchers. This is a good short-term strategy but not a good long one. Does anyone have any ideas?"

The various mask spoke amongst themselves for a bit then Two-Faced mask spoke. "The Conglomerate will never blame Gaia for anything bad that's happening, and we can't have people believing in the power of the savages God. So why don't we take the credit for the disasters. We should make ourselves known to the world."

The angry mask disagreed. "Are you insane? If we revealed ourselves, it would be us on the Threedom circuit not the savages. Mark my words. William Calig's plan will fail. We need to prepare Pangaia to the truth of our existence. This order has existed in some form for thousands of years. We should prepare the world to receive the Sun King."

The chatter grew louder and louder. Everyone seemed to like this idea. The only objection came from the laughing mask, who said, "The Sun King's reign over the earth is its biggest secret and should stay that way."

The arguments continued until the disgust mask changed the subject.

"On to the next topic," the disgust mask said. "The Watchers mean to replace us. Should we allow this or disrupt this?"

The angry mask said, "We need to stay hidden. Let the Watchers have their foolish fame. Fame is our favorite tool to control the ignorant masses. It has no place amongst the SMARTs."

On this point they were united. There was one final point to discuss. The angry mask continued.

"The savages are emboldened by the Two Witnesses. Citizens of Pangaia are being torn and pulled by their doctrine. Many are leaving the Conglomerate. I suggest that we make Threedom a seven-day experience instead of a three-day experience. This should curb their rise in numbers. Any thoughts?"

The laughing mask asked, "Why can't we just kill them all and be done with it? We can program a few Jailers to hunt them."

A voice echoed in the hall. The masks all stopped and turned to see who it was. A person with an eyeball mask entered the hall. On its feet were devices that allowed this person to levitate into the room. The other masks fell on their knees in awe.

"It is the Eye! The Eye has blessed us with its presence."

The Eye floated above the White Table and spoke. "I have heard your cries and I offer solutions. We will continue to blame the Watchers for all of nature's disasters. Gaia must be blameless. They will not replace you so long as I'm here. Threedom is the best and most subtle way of dealing with savages. Increasing the events is a good idea. However, that is not my ultimate solution. My ultimate solution is to kill the Supreme Queen."

The masks gasped at the idea—especially the angry mask.

"The Supreme Queen may be a nuisance, but she is the chosen prophetess of Gaia," the angry mask said. "With all due respect. Killing her would cause an uprising."

"That is partly true," the Eye said. "Pangaia would revolt if it knew that we were responsible for it. We need someone who knows of us and will serve our interest. Killing the Supreme Queen is our only option. Are you with me?"

The masks all agreed and said, "Yes, we are with you."

Bastel gave Nala and Chris the information they needed to find a healer.

"Travel to Arkamedes," Bastel said. "It's a place not far from Hazamah's camp. There you will find one called Damiano. This is your healer."

Nala was fully attentive, but Chris seemed distracted. He couldn't take his eyes off a small glowing rock next to the silver throne. Chris approached it and saw that it opened up a portal to other dimensions. Chris noticed a ghostly figure and looked at it. Nala was so focused on Bastel that she didn't notice Chris or the glowing rock. She was grateful to learn of the healer but wanted to know if becoming a Tamer would heal her. Bastel dismissed this idea.

"Becoming a Tamer won't heal your body," Bastel said. "I can promise you that."

"Are you certain this Damiano can heal me?" Nala signed.

Bastel sighed and said, "There are few guarantees in life. Healing isn't one of them."

"How do you know about this life?" Nala signed. "You're an alien."

"Let's just focus on you right now," Bastel said. "Being a Tamer now is off the table. What about your friend here?"

Chris came back to reality and said, "Who was that figure in the glowing rock? I've never seen anything like it." Bastel stretched her hands toward the glowing rock. Moments later the rock flew into her palms. "You saw a glimpse of Lord Braccus. The leader of the

Watchers. This is a good sign. It appears he's as interested in your story as I am. Now answer my question Chris. Do you still want to be a Tamer?" Chris responded. "We both want to be Tamers. It's a package deal. If she's no Tamer, than neither am I."

Bastel seemed indifferent. She rose to her feet, and Nala and Chris did the same.

"I can grant you access to the best parts of Sedah," Bastel said. "It's the least I can do for your troubles. Granted, I can only grant you one hour of access. There are things I must do."

Nala was ecstatic and signed, "This is awesome! You can do anything in Sedah."

Chris was glad to see her happy. He spun her around in her wheelchair and danced with her.

"I want to go somewhere tropical. What about you Nala?"

"I want to go to the beach."

Bastel seemed amused by their laughter. However, that moment quickly faded.

"All right you two," Bastel said. "Close your eyes."

Nala closed her eyes. When she opened them, she was all alone on a massive beach. She could feel the water on her toes. In here she wasn't paralyzed. She leaned back and forth on her legs like she was wearing stilts. Walking wasn't a normal action for her. Nala enjoyed this area for what seemed like hours. However, she wondered where Chris was—along with other people. She also wondered how to get out of this place. Nala walked around in circles and was suddenly transferred to a bright white room where she saw a woman clothed in white in front of her. The woman turned around with a gentile smile and knelt down so that she was on the same level as her.

"Hello Nala. I'm Gaia."

Nala was gripped with fear. She was now able to hear herself and others for the first time.

"You're the goddess. Why are you here?"

"I came to see you," Gaia said. "You're very special."

"Everyone I know says you're fake, but I knew you were real."

"Yes, Nala, I am your foundation. Do you have any questions before I send you back to the ship?"

Nala thought hard but came up with a question soon after.

"Why do you hate Christians? You call us savages. That's not nice."

Gaia stood up straight. Her face twisted and contorted while she spoke.

"My disdain for your people has nothing to do with religion," Gaia said. "Most faiths honor a divine Patriarch, but that's not the reason for my disdain. It's a very personal thing for me, Nala. I don't think you would understand."

Nala rejected her notions.

"First of all," Nala said, "they aren't my people. I'm only ten. I have no people."

Gaia decided to change the subject. "I'm actually referenced in the Bible," Gaia said. "The prophet Jeremiah spoke of me. For I am the Queen of Heaven."

Nala spent what seemed like hours with Gaia. She learned a great deal about her and her motivations. Nala was like a sponge around

Gaia, eager to learn more and more. Gaia enjoyed her company as well, but knew Bastel would call her back at any moment.

"Listen to me, Nala. I want you to return home to camp St. Peter before meeting Damiano. Your Uncle Joe is worried sick about you. Have Bastel give you an elixir for Chris. Being on a Watcher ship does strange things to humans if they don't go through with becoming Tamers. The elixir will prevent any transformation. You need not worry. This only affect adults. Bastel doesn't believe in me so tell her you learned of the elixir from Hazamah. Then tell your people how kind the Watchers were, but you must swear not to tell anyone about me. This meeting is our secret. Okay?"

Nala acknowledged all Gaia said. When they were through speaking, she hugged Gaia and closed her eyes. She then found herself back in space when she opened them. Her paralyzed body was as binding as it ever was.

Nala did as instructed and told Bastel of her change in plans.

"I'm going home before I see Damiano," Nala said.

This caught Bastel off guard. "Why?"

"My Uncle Joe can't function without me," Nala lied. I'm kind of the boss."

Nala requested the elixir for Chris. Bastel granted her the warm drink and handed it to Chris. He drank the sweet elixir, gathered their things, and headed toward the exit. Bastel, however, insisted that they do one last thing before they left.

"Would you care for some water? It's a special blend that will fully hydrate you on your journey. There are strange reports of water turning into blood across Pangaia, so drink up. You can never be too careful."

The two drank the water and were returned to earth and began the long journey back to camp St. Peter.

Yessica returned from a patrol of the camps. Chester approached her and said, "Well, did you find her?"

Yessica was getting tired of hearing that. "No, but we came across plenty Berserkers. I can't believe this can happen by being a Tamer reject. Let's hope this didn't happen to Nala."

Chester escorted Yessica to a room and showed her drone footage of the surrounding area.

"Most of the Berserkers are ten miles north," Chester said. "I tried to see five miles north and I came across this."

Yessica watched as a man with Chris's build ran in the woods with a wheelchair. Yessica sprang into action.

"That's them," Yessica said. "They're being hunted."

Chris sweat profusely, as did Nala. The weather was well below freezing, which only added to the misery. Strange feral creatures chased them through the woods. Many of their faces were familiar to Chris and Nala. Chris struggled to move the heavy wheelchair forward.

"I'm not feeling so good Nala. I think it would be easier if I carried you on my back again."

Nala also felt sick. She was in worse shape than Chris. The young girl couldn't even sign. Chris took Nala out of her chair and carried her on his back. He walked forward using all his might and teetered from left to right. Chris tried to speak but bright white foam filled his mouth. A sharp pain that started in his feet worked its way up to his head. Seconds later he fell on his back and died. Nala lay trapped under his weight. Berserkers gathered around them ready to tear them to shreds. A rifle echoed in the distance. Yessica and Chester killed the Berserkers and rushed to Nala. She was too weak to sign but pointed at the Cobber Yessica gave her. There was a long-recorded message about what happened on the Watcher spaceship.

"Sounds like the water they drank poisoned them," Chester said. "Nala wants to go to Arkamedes and have Simeon heal them. What should we do?"

Yessica took charge and said, "I'll take her to Simeon. Go get Joseph and meet us there. Be quick, we don't have much time."

Yessica placed Nala over her left shoulder and carried her rifle on the right. She ran through the cold tundra like a bear with her cub. She never liked children, but she didn't see Nala that way. Nala was like one of her own men. Yessica had seen enough of her men dead. She refused to loose another.

Chapter Twelve

Unlikely Pair

The third angel sounded his trumpet in the heavens. Then a great star from heaven, burning as it were a lamp, fell upon the third part of the rivers, and upon the fountains of waters. The star was called Wormwood. A third part of the waters became like Wormwood. Many men died of the waters because they were made bitter.

Kaiden watched all this happen with Alice and Udina. He could barely contain his excitement.

"That's what you get for being disobedient," he said.

He and Udina continued to pile on insults about humanity. Alice failed to see the logic in their behavior.

"How can you be so happy with people dying?" Alice said.

Udina spoke up. "We've lived long enough to know that humans don't change or evolve. Every generation falls for the same traps despite the evidence given to them. I doubt you would understand."

"I do understand," Alice said. "I understand that you lack compassion for those suffering. It really is a shame."

Kaiden knew that Alice was different, but he didn't expect her to be so radical. He tried to get her to see the bigger picture.

"We're not asking you to follow us, Alice. We're just trying to get you to see things from our side. Humans have contaminated this world for millennia. We've witnessed most of it for ourselves. This judgment is long overdue, and we're just getting started."

Lenoth approached the group as they talked. The busy angel broke up their conversation and spoke directly with Alice.

"I'm glad to see you're making friends, but I have a job for you," Lenoth said. "Your orders are to gain information on the beast of the sea and the beast of the earth. Do you understand?"

Alice referenced the two beasts in her mind and said, "The beast of the sea is the false messiah and the beast of the earth is the false prophet. Yes, I understand the orders. When do I leave?"

"Right now, of course."

William monitored Simeon in Israel while he worked on his physique. Simeon had done another miracle. He entered the freezing cold Alaskan water with nothing on but a cloth covering his loins. He stretched his arms to the sky. This caused thousands of fish to come ashore.

William dropped his weighs when he saw this. Finding fish and any type of protein was becoming exceptionally rare. William's power could increase one hundred-fold if he could harness Simeon's power. William decided to take a break from monitoring Simeon. He went to one of his many mansions around Pangaia. On this day he was in Pan-Kenya. William smoked a cigar, drank expensive liquor, and invited his Valkyries over. His tranquility was cut short when the power went out across his ten thousand square foot abode.

William rose up and spoke with his home AI.

"Barbra, what's going on?" William asked.

"I'm detecting a massive solar flare located near the equator."

William relaxed. A solar flare was a powerful thing, but the earth's defenses prevented it from affecting human being.

"Is that all?" William said. "When can you get power back on line? I want to go dancing with my Valkyries."

"Power will be back on shortly," Barbra said. "However, there appears to be some sort of strange microscopic dust flowing from the impact area of the solar flare. Initial analysis suggests this is some sort of bio-organism that could affect the limited fresh water supply we have available. I recommend drinking water from your personal reserves until this issue can be resolved."

William had many reserves, but he didn't want to be trapped in his mansion for years to come. He needed a miracle-worker, and he knew just where to go. "Tell Cynthia to wipe my schedule clean for the next few weeks. It's time I go to Alaska to see the miracle worker for myself."

William landed in Alaska with a small army of media, celebrities, and the Conglomerate. It didn't take them long to find Arkamedes. There were already thousands of Watcher fans in the area. They made sure that Arkamedes remained a private area. William approached Hazamah and made sure the cameras were rolling.

"You must be Hazamah," William said. "I've got a movie role for you if you're interested. Just tell me where Simeon is."

Hazamah was as vain as he was cautious. "If you add a TV deal, we're in business."

William turned to his small army and said, "Ya see that? We're living in high cotton now. I reckon you'll be even more famous Hazamah."

Simeon sat in his tent and refused to come out when he saw all the new faces. They took pictures, video, and were very loud. William had recently shown the media what Simeon could do, but the public had yet to see all his miracles. Everything now rested on Simeon's great reveal. William knew he had to deliver.

"Why don't you come out that chicken coop and introduce yourself to Pangaia, son?" William said.

Simeon vaguely understood southern vernacular but assumed to know what William meant.

"I have no business with fools," Simeon said. "Go away all of you."

William acted boldly and entered the tent. The reporters had a field day with it. William looked around and noticed the layout of the tent was identical to the temple in Israel.

"The Brazier outside needs some work and so does the table of shewbread," William said. "I like how you colored this plastic to act as a veil. We can do some good work together, son."

Simeon became annoyed. "I'm not your son."

William opened the tent door, and the media flooded inside.

"I'm serious Simeon," William said. "I'm your father. I was there when you were born."

Simeon scoffed and said, "No you're not. We're nothing alike. You're only half Jewish, unlike me."

William took his hat off and placed it over his heart. "I admit that we're not related biologically. We created you to be a weapon, but we had no idea you would be capable of miracles. Where did you learn to do all this?"

Simeon took a deep breath.

"I understand now," Simeon said. "I'm a Jopa experiment. I was wrong to question that woman."

William suddenly got the reference. "You mean Yessica. We created her too, but she's not half as special as you. Listen to me, Simeon. The world is falling apart. Only you can save it. Our water supplies are dwindling. A strange virus is contaminating them all. Will you help us?"

Simeon's pride began to swell. He didn't think that he would enjoy so much attention. "Yes, I will help you. When do we begin?"

William had his media empire create a collage of all his miracles captured on camera. He spared no expense in production. All of Pangaia now knew who Simeon Skylar Samson was.

The Supreme Queen laughed and mocked Simeon when she saw him.

"That's supposed to be our savior?" she said. "Impossible, he has the skin of a slave."

Many people of Pangaia shared this sentiment. However, there was no denying that he was capable of miracles. William used his bravado and charm to hype up Simeon as the world's savior. He gave Pangaia a personal tour of Arkamedes, which gave Simeon some privacy before his grand reveal.

Simeon detected a familiar presence while sitting alone in his tent.

"Hello, Little Dove," Simeon said. "It seems my plan failed."

Alice revealed herself. "How can you see me?"

"Don't be naïve, Little Dove. I hope you remember that it was I who told you about the reaper angels. Just look at you now. You actually work for them."

Alice didn't know how to feel about Simeon. He robbed her of her life, but she never stopped thinking about him. He had a strange grasp of her heart.

"I don't hate you despite what you did to me," Alice said.

Simeon rose off his chair and came close to Alice.

"They sent you to spy on me. Didn't they, Little Dove? I'm sure you have questions. Go ahead and ask them."

Alice calmed herself then said, "You said you wanted to tell me something important when I was still alive. What was that?"

Simeon sat on the ground and crossed his legs.

"I've found out that this is not my first life. Nor is this the first life of your sister."

"I know," Alice said. "You used to be Admiral Fred Samson, and my sister was once Yessica Calig."

Simeon corrected her. "I speak of a time further back. Think about it, Little Dove. Wherever I go, your sister always finds me."

"So you're saying that you and my sister were once married?"

"In a manner of speaking, yes, but the answer to the question is quite obvious."

"I'm sorry," Alice said. "I still don't get it. When you die, it's heaven or hell"

"Are you sure your Bible says that explicitly?"

Simeon waited for an answer then spoke when he heard none.

"Your Bible says it's appointed for a man to die and face judgment. That's all were allowed to know. We all know that Heaven and Hell are two final destinations. However, ultimately where we end up is up to God. I'm telling you that I've already faced the judge. This life is part of my sentence. The same goes for Yessica. When I'm done here, I'm off to the burning lake, but I'm ready for it. Fret not, Little Dove. I thought you were ready for the truth, but clearly you're not. What other questions do you have?"

"Why did you kill me?"

"To prevent you from becoming an angel," Simeon said. "I failed obviously. At least you're not a Yeshua reaper angel. I hate them the most. I was actually going to revive you after the rapture, but your sister ruined my plans. I admit that I may have fallen for you spiritually in our short time together. You're very special, Little Dove. Your soul is unlike any other mortal."

If Alice were still in her flesh she would be blushing. She decided to take a leap of faith emotionally and said, "It's okay if you're still in love with me."

Simeon maintained his cold emotionless composure.

"What gave you that silly idea? Listen to me, Little Dove. My feelings toward you have always been purely platonic. I must apologize, Little Dove. Clearly you felt something deeper."

Simeon clenched his teeth in anger and ended the dialogue, saying, "Now leave me be and finish your orders, Little Dove. We have no further business to discuss."

There was so much more Alice wanted to say to Simeon, but she couldn't muster the courage to say them. She finished her orders and flew back into the heavens above.

William entered the tent and made sure his star was ready for his big reveal.

"Is there anything I can get you?" William asked.

Simeon sat back on his chair and gave his orders. "Inside the cabin you'll find a large pool of blood. Have your people bring it outside and place it in front of the tent."

William's men did just as Simon commanded. A few minutes later William began his long-awaited introduction. Every camera in Pangaia was on them and William savored every moment.

"People of Pangaia," William said. "I now introduce your savior. Please welcome Simeon Skylar Samson!"

Cheers erupted across the world. They were eager to hear from the mysterious man that had Watchers bow to him. The cameras zoomed in on the pool of blood, which began to bubble. Simeon rose out of the blood with clean clothes. The remarkable introduction pleased the crowd. Simeon then spoke directly to Pangaia.

"I hear you have a water problem," Simeon said. "You must know that there's nothing I can't do. I simply require your faith. The great spirit is within me. I am chosen to help the poor. To heal the brokenhearted. To proclaim liberty to the captives. To release those who are bound. To proclaim the acceptable year and the day of my vengeance. Now who wants some water?"

The cheer continued across the earth. Simeon reached his hand in the air and absorbed the solar rays to the Arora borealis. He used this energy to melt the ice caps on the mountains. This provided fresh drinking water unaffected by the pathogen in rivers and lakes. Jopa was ready and able to package the water. They had it sent to Pangaia immediately. For now, their drinking water problem was fixed.

William began to end production when a familiar face showed up.

Yessica barged her way through the media army and found William and Simeon. She froze when she saw her killer. William was just as shocked to see her but made light of the serious encounter.

"It looks like my chickens have come home to roost," William said.

Yessica placed Nala on the ground. She checked her pulse. Nala was barely holding on.

"I'll deal with you later," Yessica said to William. "Right now, I need you to help this little girl."

William used this to his advantage. He hyped Pangaia up to see another miracle. Simeon gently approached the girl and knelt down. He placed his hand on her forehead and closed his eyes.

"How long has the girl been deaf and lame?"

Yessica was annoyed at all the cameras around, but she had no choice but to work with him.

"She's been this way all her life. How do you know all this?" Yessica said.

Simeon ignored Yessica and just stared at Nala as she struggled to breath.

"You need to do something now!" Yessica said.

Simeon turned to Yessica and said, "Give me your blade."

Yessica handed him her knife. Simeon sliced his wrist and had Nala drink his blood.

Yessica became furious and said, "You can't do that. Our blood is way too toxic."

Simeon ignored Yessica and looked gently upon Nala. Seconds later, Nala rose to her feet and put her hands over her ears. She looked around her surrounding slowly as if waiting for something. A few members of the media began to clap and cheer. Nala jumped in the air and screamed. "I can hear you!" she said. She suddenly realized she could hear herself as well and started to dance.

Footage of this Pangaia miracle was shown to the entire world. The people went wild and William made sure to savor the moment.

"Give it up for Simeon Pangaia," William said. "He's the real deal who can heal."

You feel yourself leaving the earth and into the heavens. A familiar room encased by a great hall is in front of you. In this room is an ancient scribe. He's expecting you. You catch his gaze, and your eyes meet. His living silver skin is as unsettling as it was before. The purple irises are still alive with fire. You realize it's CMC from the first chapter.

"Thank you again, narrator, for your lively introductions."

The CMC pauses. He is annoyed that he was cut off mid-sentence. He turns his gaze from you and looks down at a living model of the earth.

"So, the beast of the sea has the skin of a slave," the CMC says. "I wonder what that means. I'm also quite sure you're just dying to know what on earth Simeon was talking about. A past life? The details of such a peculiarity are simply not for you to know. As if I would reveal something like that to a simple mortal anyway. You must feel perturbed that I'm interrupting your journey. Be at peace, dear reader. I'm almost finished. Is it me or is there something strange going on between Alice and the other angels. They treat her like she's an invading Watcher. There seems to be a serious grudge there. Dear reader, this goes deeper than you may realize."

The CMC tries to explain, but his focus is on another task. He leaves you with renewed instruction.

"Duty calls, dear reader. Let us return to the tale. Be grateful and of good cheer. For the next time you hear from me will be the last. See you at the end."

Chapter Thirteen

Spectre

The fourth angel sounded his trumpet in the heavens. A third of the sun, moon, and stars were smited and darkened, causing the days to be shortened. The fourth angel spoke with a loud voice saying, "Woe, woe, woe to the inhibiters of the earth by reason of the other voices of the trumpet of the three angels, which are yet to sound!"

Kaiden, Udina, and Alice gathered at their meeting place and debated what just happened. Alice picked up on a few key things about the two angels while they spoke. The first was that Kaiden lacked a few qualities, such as patience and manners. What he didn't lack was confidence. Udina seemed to be the opposite. He was civil and patient, but he always followed Kaiden's every word. It was a strange dynamic, but they made it work.

"Did you enjoy your assignment?" Kaiden asked.

Alice wondered what Kaiden was implying and said, "The assignment was fine. What do you mean when you said 'enjoy'? I was ordered to do something, and I did it. That's it."

Kaiden and Udina looked at each other. They were holding back from Alice, and she failed to appreciate it.

"There is no need to fret Kaiden's words. It was just a question not an observation. What did you think of the fourth trumpet? It seemed pretty underwhelming to us."

Alice looked down upon the earth and saw it engulfed in darkness.

"This is not a typical judgment," Alice said. "People are barely hanging on down there. This loss of time will affect solar power and farming production. What's underwhelming about that?"

Udina stood corrected. "I never considered that perspective."

Alice and the angels covered a wide variety of topics. A large warrior angel approached them. It was the Zimrat Ward. He had an assignment for Kaiden and Udina.

"Your orders are to capture a Watcher and extract as much information from him as possible," Zimrat said. "I want names, abilities, and locations. Is that understood?"

Kaiden and Udina got ready to spring into action. However, Kaiden had a suggestion first.

"We're ready, but may we take Alice along with us?" Kaiden asked. "She's very adept in scripture, which means she can render judgment."

The Ward contemplated for a moment then agreed.

"That's good thinking, Kaiden. You may just take my job someday. All right, Alice. I'll speak with Lenoth and explain your assignment. Just hang back and let Kaiden and Udina do their jobs. I just need you to declare judgment when the time is right."

Alice didn't have a clue what to do.

"I've never been a Bible expert," she said. "Are you sure you need me for this?"

Kaiden took Alice's hand and whisked her away to the earth. Udina followed them from above.

Kaiden and Udina found a lone Watcher on the earth. They cornered, overpowered, and interrogated him. Some of their methods seemed barbaric. However, Alice knew few things were off the table in war. Udina was the most ferocious. He continued to strike the Watcher in the face as he said, "Tell us about Bastel and your leadership. We know she's not the final authority."

The Watcher refused to give them any information. Kaiden grew restless and decided to leave.

"We're done here, Udina," Kaiden said. "Let's leave and allow Alice to render judgment."

The two angels left in a hurry, leaving the wounded Watcher alone with Alice. Alice tried to help the Watcher, but he refused.

"Leave me be," he said. "Just render your judgment and leave."

Alice didn't have a clue what that meant. She searched her mind and spoke one of her favorite lines of scripture: "Do violence to no one, neither accuse any falsely; and be content."

The Watcher gave Alice a strange look. "That's your judgement?"

Alice stood boldly and crossed her arms. "Yes, it is. What say you?"

The Watcher perked up.

"So many of you angels quote Isaiah," he said, "but that's the first time I've ever heard an angel quote Luke. You obviously know scripture unlike those two lugnut's you came with. I'm Gentry by the way. Who are you?"

Alice introduced herself and began discussing the Angel Creed and other topics. The conversation shifted when Bastel's name came up. Gentry reached into his garment, pulled out a small staff, and gave it to Alice.

"We call this a Spectre," Gentry said. "It's the only way you angels can reach Bastel. Just remember: it's only good for one use. I suggest you see her alone. She'll probably kill any warrior angels you send. Unlike you, we don't honor the Angel Creed."

Alice took the staff and condensed it in her garment. She saw this as an opportunity to learn more and to help the Zimrats.

"Thanks Gentry," Alice said. "I won't forget this."

The large angel smiled back weakly and said, "And I will not forget your kindness. Goodbye Alice."

William continued to promote Simeon at Arkamedes. He was well into his fifth day without rest. This endeavor was more taxing than he realized. He took a break and spoke with his publicist Lisa.

"What do the numbers look like?" William asked.

Lisa was in her office managing the chaos. It looked more like the stock exchange floor than a legit business.

"The numbers are still fantastic," Lisa said. "Keep doing what you're doing but don't overdo it. Familiarity breeds contempt."

Lisa paused and spoke with one of her aides.

"I'm sorry, but I have to go," Lisa said. "One more day of this should be all we need. Are you coming back after that?"

William decided to jest. "Well, aren't you sharper than a serpent's tooth. I reckon you actually miss me."

Lisa refused to acknowledge William. He paused then continued to speak.

"Unfortunately, I won't be leaving here anytime soon. My son needs me. Just know that it would never work between us. I'm more of a meat and potatoes kind of man. I don't mess with sticks and salads. Catch my drift?"

Lisa ended the call and cursed under her breath. She continued to speak with her aides about Simeon's introduction. Lisa gave out orders on a wide variety of subjects, such as mountain water filtration systems and miracle footage.

"I want that fire baptism on the front of every Pangaia paper," Lisa said. "Can someone please get me an iced mocha and a status report on Threedom."

The lack of fresh water made Alaska the crown jewel of Pangaia. People in the millions flocked to the frozen tundra in hopes of finding sources of protein and fresh water. Word of Simeon's miracles only reinforced this desire to travel north. He wasn't a charismatic leader like William, but his power was revered. Many cults began to mimic Simeon to gain followers.

Berserkers—humans who weren't allowed to become tamers—were the main threat. They roamed the world in constant hunger. Simeon used them to do his hunting. He had quite the appetite for human flesh and blood. The most important miracle was the healing of Nala. People nearly lost their minds when they heard his blood could heal sickness. Many with the Cava virus came to him. People from all over Pangaia begged Simeon to share his special blood with them.

The situation grew even more dire at the two churches. Pastor Josh and Father Nolan spoke on the phone for hours trying to come up with solutions. People were leaving the churches in droves. This wasn't all bad for them. It allowed them to conserve resources for those committed to the faith.

"Millions of people are coming into Alaska, Father Nolan," Pastor Josh said. "We can't just turn them away."

"I agree in principle, but we can't open our doors to them. I don't like handing anyone over to the Berserkers, but they can do what we cannot."

"I disagree. We may not be able to give them food, but we can give them the gospel. Please tell me we agree on that part."

Father Nolan paused then answered, "Of course, Josh. We agree on that point."

Then Father Nolan groaned.

"Is everything all right?" Pastor Josh asked.

"Not really," Father Nolan said. "I just received word from one of my contacts in Rome. They say that Jopa and Zohar are investing trillions of dollars into Alaskan infrastructure. It's only a matter of time before Alaska becomes like Pan-France or Pan-Germany. It seems we're doomed to be in bondage."

Pastor Josh looked out his window and saw many people running toward the entrance of Camp St. Peter.

"Look at your surveillance," Pastor Josh said. "What's going on?"

Father Nolan analyzed the situation and spoke with his combat patrol.

"You better get over here fast, Josh. Yessica and Nala have returned."

Pastor Josh and Father Nolan interviewed Nala. They were glad she was healed, but she was not the same mentally. Her views were now radically in line with those of Pangaia. At every instance, she defended Simeon and Gaia. She insisted that the fabled goddess was real. Nala left the room and embraced her Uncle Joe when they finished. Yessica stood close by to make sure she wasn't treated unfairly or imprisoned. Joseph spoke with Yessica after the embrace.

"Thank you for saving my niece," Joseph said. "I take back what I said about you."

Yessica rolled her eyes and said, "Save your slobber, Joseph. I didn't do it for you. I did it for her."

Joseph was still grateful.

"Say goodbye to Yessica," Joseph said. "We're going home, finally."

Nala gave Yessica a big hug and headed out the exit with her uncle. Richard was on the opposite side of the door waiting. Joseph smiled when they met and gave them a few moments of privacy.

"You look great, Nala," Richard said. "We can finally speak like normal kids."

Nala didn't know how to feel about that last comment, so she ignored it.

"I'm going back to Sedah as soon as I'm grown," Nala said. "You should come with me."

Joseph took Nala's hand and dragged her away before she could say another word. They arrived home and everything was just the way it was. Joseph and Nala spoke with one another sometime later. Nala felt that this was yet another form of interrogation.

"I never have any fun here," Nala said. "Just leave me alone."

Joseph began to quote scripture. He paraphrased Hebrews chapter twelve verse eleven. It sent Nala off the edge.

"I hate your religion," Nala said. "It's not real. Gaia is real. I've seen her!"

Joseph slapped Nala hard. It was the first time he acted so forcibly with her.

Nala cried, pushed Joseph out the door, and slammed the door shut, saying, "I hate you."

Joseph tried to apologize but received a call from Father Nolan. They spoke loudly, which allowed Nala to hear the entire conversation. It was about her. Father Nolan said Nala will be a problem for the church and the two debated excommunication. Joseph was appalled. He rushed into Nala's room to reassure her. However, she was gone when he opened the door. Joseph fell to his knees and prayed for the safety of Nala and that her return would be swift and full of grace.

Joseph found Yessica the next day and begged her to find Nala. However, Yessica wasn't ready to commit.

"She's ten not thirty-five," Yessica said. "If she's not back in twenty-four hours, we'll look for her. We need our men here."

Joseph fell on his face and wept. He was causing a scene. Chester escorted Joseph away then returned to Yessica.

"I have info on Simeon," Chester said. "There is a place not far from here that can give you answers."

"Does this have anything to do with Nala?"

"No, of course not," Chester said. "Nala is gone for good. I don't think she's coming back."

Yessica was caught off guard by his puzzling statement.

"You said she was super important. What gives?"

Chester sighed. "I'm a strategist not a therapist. Do you want the location or not?"

Yessica headed east and found the location Chester gave her. There was nothing but snow, ice, and some sort of scanner. Yessica touched it, and it activated. It scanned Yessica and granted her access.

"Welcome to Harbinger Four Base, Yessica Calig."

A staircase materialized, and she made her way down the long path of stairs. The underground base was massive. She looked around and saw evidence of her creation. There were files, test tubes, notes, and receipts about Yessica. She saw footage of her childhood that only she could know about. The other half of the lab was sealed off. She suspected Simeon's proof of creation was there. An Echo Vison alerted her while she looked at the old dusty lab. It was none other than Dr. Malka.

"Do you believe me now? You have your proof," Dr. Malka said.

Yessica didn't seemed bothered.

"Yeah, yeah. I'm walking space goop," Yessica said. "Big deal. You mentioned Harbingers before. Am I the fourth one?"

"You and Simeon are both the fourth Harbinger. The first was William's grandfather. A man by the name of Amos Kohen. The second was William's mother, Ann Calig, The third was his sister, Yessica Calig. I have detailed records of all their dealings with angels and demons. You're welcomed to see them."

Dr. Malka highlighted a key card nearby. She had Yessica grab it.

"This keycard will give you full access to all data files here. However, you can't access Simeon's records. William controls those and his files cannot be hacked."

Yessica didn't seem to mind.

"It's better this way," Yessica said.

Malka began to end the call.

"Wait, where are you going?" Yessica said.

"I'm afraid this is goodbye. I'm on my way to complete my second greatest achievement. It's called Project Romulus. The main base is in Antarctica, but we have bases in all cryo friendly areas."

"So you leaving me because you want to freeze yourself for the future?"

Malka laughed. "Yes, that's exactly right. We're nearing the end, and this might be the only safe place yet."

Malka paused and wiped a tear from her face. "I know I wasn't a good mother to you. You grew up without one, thinking I wasn't watching over you. Just know that I do care for you Yessica. You're my only daughter."

Yessica stared back at Malka and ended the call.

"Whatever."

Chapter Fourteen

The Warning

Heaven awaited the sounding of the fifth trumpet. The fifth angel took his place on the world stage. He sounded his trumpet mightily, but his job was not finished. The angel fell from heaven onto the earth. To him was given a key to the bottomless pit. He opened the pit and smoke rose out of it, looking like a great furnace and darkening the sun and the air. Locust emerged the smoke and received the power of scorpions. This meant they could cause great pain on mankind even though they were spiritual beings. The fifth angel commanded them not to hurt any green thing but only humans that didn't have not the seal of God on their foreheads. They were also instructed to torment and not to kill. The fifth angel gave the locust five months to torment mankind.

"Do what you must," the angel said. "For in these days man will seek death but shall not find it. Death will flee from them."

The description of the locust comes from Revelation Chapter 9 verse 7 and is as follows: Their shape was like horses prepared for battle. On their heads were golden crowns. They had the faces of men. Their hair was like the hair of a woman and their teeth were ferocious like lions. Each of them wore breastplates of iron. The sound of their wings was as the sound of chariots of many horses in battle. Their tails were like tails of scorpions. They also had a king over them—the angel of the bottomless pit. His name in the Hebrew tongue is Abaddon. However, in the Greek tongue his name is Apollyon.

Alice watched all this from afar with Kaiden and Udina. She expected the worst.

"This part of Revelation always scared me," Alice said. "I often wondered what would happen if I weren't somehow sealed. I would be tortured for five months."

Kaiden reassured her, saying, "You don't have to worry about any of that now. You're safe with us."

Alice felt a little better as she watched as the army of scorpion locust descended onto the earth. It didn't take long before she could hear the screams rising up into the heavens.

Nala still wasn't used to walking. She often felt pain in her limbs, as if her body rejected her new functions. Hungry, she looked around the woods for a snack. She was hours away from camp St. Peter but had no intention of returning. Surviving the Alaskan winter was difficult but not impossible. She simply needed something to boost her confidence. Something that would validate her efforts. This happened when she came across a candy bar near a trash can. The chocolate was nearly yellow in color, but that didn't stop Nala from eating it. She scarfed it down without thinking. A few feet from her was an abandoned blue van with the door ajar. It looked like good shelter, but she was too busy looking for supplies to check it out.

Suddenly a rushing wind materialized and knocked her on her back. A bee-like sound came closer and closer to her. She could not see anything, but her ears were quite aware of their presence. A pain shot through Nala's arm. She looked down and saw a thick lump on her skin. Painful lumps continued to manifest themselves onto Nala. She knew that she had to get away. She used all her strength to crawl a few feet into the blue van. Nala relaxed a bit when she finally made it inside. The invisible bees were no longer a threat, but the pain was immense. She could feel herself fading. Nala felt like dying, but a constant surge of adrenaline kept her awake. It was like hell on earth.

The Watcher known as Torlian approached the van at just the right time. He opened the doors and prevented the invisible plague from overtaking her. The Watcher stretched his hand toward Nala.

"Bastel sent me to find you," the Watcher said. "She has a job for you. You have two choices: Become a Tamer as you originally planned or suffer immense pain for the foreseeable future. What say you?"

Nala could barely speak. Her throat had begun to swell. But she managed to say, "I'll become a Tamer. Please, just make the pain stop."

Torlian placed his hand on Nala's shoulder and began the transformation. The pain was just as bad as the stings, but it quickly subsided. Once pain- and lump-free, Torlian asked, "How does it feel to be a Tamer?"

Nala smiled and said, "It feels amazing."

"I'm glad you like it. Follow me, we have work to do."

Alice left Kaiden and Udina and pulled out the Spectre. The mysterious staff that would bring her to Bastel. She had a few questions for her. Alice activated the Spectre and was transferred into the Midlands, a massive radiated area in North America. Bastel sat on an elaborate chair and looked down on humanity. She reveled in seeing humans in serious pain. Bastel possessed a keen ability to sense other spirits. It didn't take long for her to notice Alice.

Her Watchers collected Alice and brought her to the Watcher leader.

"My, my, my, what do we have here? A lone Nava angel wishes to see me," Bastel said, adding a gasp. "A female Nava! How is this possible?"

Alice didn't have much of an answer. "I still don't know myself."

"You realize that you are everything I aspired to be," Bastel said. "I've always wanted to be close with God. Yet here I am sulking in this rotten corpse I call a body. How can I help such an honored guest?"

Alice looked around and made sure she couldn't be flanked.

"I want to know your intentions for the great battle of angels that is close upon us," Alice said.

Bastel answered without a second thought. "Woman to woman, you have my guarantee that my Watchers will not fight this upcoming battle with Michael. Though I cannot speak for my husband, my son, Azrael, or Ramiel."

Alice was confused. "What do you mean woman to woman. You're an alien."

"I wasn't always like this," Bastel said. "Thousands of years ago, I was earth's first Supreme Queen. My exitance now is tied to judgement."

Alice remembered what Simeon said about judgement.

"What about the other Watchers?" Alice asked. "Have they faced judgment?"

"A few have but not all. My husband can explain this in greater detail."

"Who is your husband? May I speak with him?"

"His name is Samyaza. Today, he is the horseman of Death."

Alice couldn't help but see similarities between Bastel and her sister, Yessica.

"You remind me of someone," Alice said. "My sister, actually."

Alice was taken aback when Bastel took offense to her statement.

"You would do well to not compare me to a science project," Bastel said. "We may both be Alpha females, but our comparisons stop there."

Alice still had many questions for Bastel. She also wanted to know how Bastel knew of her sister but she knew they wouldn't be answered. A young girl and a Watcher had just arrived. Bastel gave them all her attention and ignored Alice. Alice took action and reported back to heaven. Michael needed to know that the Watchers wouldn't be fighting.

Things were oddly normal at Camp St. Peter and Camp Luther. There weren't many people affected by the painful sores of spirit locust. However, their primary doctor and her close friend battled the pain. Ruth and Joker sat next to each other on their beds and held each other's hand. Pastor Josh and Father Nolan entered the sick bay and watched as their hands returned to their sides.

"Sorry we interrupted. Ruth," Father Nolan said. "I need you to get better ASAP. This clinic can't make it without you."

Ruth laughed nervously. She had never been in this kind of pain. It shocked her.

"Okay," she said. "I'll hurry up and get better."

Chester snuck into the sick bay.

"Are you a believer Chester?" Pastor Josh asked. "I've never seen you attend either service."

"What are you implying?" Chester asked.

"It is rather odd, Chester," Father Nolan said. "You see, the Bible tells us that his plague affects unbelievers only. For they lack the seal of God on their foreheads. If you're a professing believer, we have a right to know. Don't be ashamed."

Chester sighed and said, "I'm actually here to tell you that I'm leaving. My job here is finished. I enjoyed my time here until recently. Goodbye."

Chester quickly turned and exited the area. Pastor Josh wondered if he would see him again.

Yessica monitored the situation from the HAR4 base. She had no idea what was going on in the two Churches, but she hoped for the best. Reports came in from around the world about a strange phenomenon affecting nearly everyone above ground. The base did have one good thing going for it: It gave her access to Simeon's Theta drives. These internal drives allowed messages and programing to flow through Simeon anywhere in the world. Yessica had a similar function but knew nothing of its operation. Yessica tapped into the drives and spoke with Simeon at Arkamedes. The unassuming Simeon answered the call.

"Hello, who is this?"

Yessica got straight to the point. "This is too low," she said. "Even for someone as wicked as you. Call off this torture plague, and I might let you live."

Simeon quickly figured out who was speaking with him.

"Ah, its Yessica Hoffman," he said. "I see you've found the HAR4 base. Are you catching up on old childhood visions? The reality is that I have no control over this plague. My power is great but not on this kind of scale. Do you believe in God, Yessica?"

Yessica's nose turned up.

"Of course not," she said. "What does he have to do with any of this?"

"They that sow in the wind shall reap the whirlwind."

Yessica considered his answer a riddle.

"Enough games, and just stop this!" Yessica said.

"I'm sorry, but I can't," Simeon said. "The locust don't affect me. Maybe you should step outside and see if you can survive. My money says you can't."

Yessica ended the transmission and opened the door to the base. She took a deep breath and stepped outside, hoping that she would not be consumed with pain.

Chapter Fifteen

Daughters Of Eve

Alice returned to the heavens and found Kaiden and Udina. Kaiden seemed to be in a pleasant mood.

"Welcome back, Alice. Did you find anything?" Kaiden asked.

Alice could barely contain her excitement.

"I have critical information that needs to be given to Michael right now."

Udina didn't see a reason to rush.

"Why don't you tell us," he said, "and we'll ensure the information gets to its destination. We're friends, right?"

Alice became annoyed. She did consider the two angels friends. However, Bastel trusted her with this information. It didn't seem right to give this knowledge to their superiors without providing this context.

"We're friends, Udina," Alice said, "but I mut deliver this information personally."

Kaiden and Udina made space between themselves and Alice.

"Run along now, Alice," Kaiden said, "and speak with Lenoth. He will vouch for you."

Alice thanked her friends and found Lenoth. She explained all she saw and heard. Lenoth escorted Alice to Michael's domain, the interior of which was strangely modest for an angel with such power. Next to Michael was Ignas. The proud angel wasn't pleased at all to see her.

"Ah, just in time," Ignas said. "The space Gerbil has broken out of its cage."

Lenoth and Alice approached then and explained what Alice saw and heard. Michael seriously contemplated it, but Ignas disregarded the information.

"This daughter of Eve is clearly delusional, Michael," Ignas said. "We cannot trust her. It's obvious that she is conspiring for greater position amongst the Nava."

Michael questioned both sides but ultimately sided with Ignas. Alice shook her head and spoke up boldly.

"I expected Ignas's reaction but not yours, Michael," Alice said. "Why are you all so rude to me? I haven't done anything wrong."

Michael sighed and said, "It's actually rather complicated. Maybe I'll explain things to you another time. Right now, I need to finish training my warriors for our great battle with the dragon. His time is short, and he knows it."

Michael thanked Alice for her efforts and escorted them out of his domain. Ignas left as well and gathered a small group of angel assassins known as The Syndicate. Their numbers were few, but their reach was large. Ignas had complete authority over them.

"I've gathered you all here for a very special reason," Ignas said. "It's only a matter of time before the daughter of Eve reveals her true purpose. She desires to overthrow the order of this kingdom. It's in her nature. She can't help herself. Therefore, we must sever the head of the snake before its venom can affect the rest of us. I want you to hunt down and kill Alice. This is a direct order. Make sure you do it quietly. Am I understood?"

The assassins all agreed with the order, saying, "Yes, Master Ignas."

Nala proved to be an amazing Tamer. Her intuition with mechanical and technical things was unparalleled. Bastel was sure she had found her Conduit, but she didn't share this with Nala. Instead, she showered her with attention and affection. She made sure to provide Nala with anything she needed. This unprecedented access to Bastel was only given to those that were closet to her, a difficult achievement for both Watchers and mortals.

Nala was studying Watcher technology and working hard on a new tracking device when Bastel approached her and said, "Come with me Nala, I wish to show you something."

Nala suspended her tools and gear in the middle of the air and followed Bastel. They teleported directly in the middle of the Mediterranean Sea. "Why have you brought me here?" Bastel circled around the area. "You see the sea, but I see my kingdom. The first world government. It was called Neothia. It's strange how things circle back and around. If you head east, you will find Israel. Watchers are forbidden from entering this land. It's always been this way. This land was forbidden even during my reign as queen. I had no idea that it would turn out to be what it is today."

Nala was amazed and curious. "How are you still alive?"

"I don't have a simple answer for you," Bastel said. "Something was given to me that prevented me from aging, but it also turned me into what you see today. I'm no longer a mortal. I'm what you would call a Principality. Do you understand?"

Nala struggled to grasp the concept but said, "It sounds like your more of a spirit than a soul. Is that right?"

Bastel was pleased. "That's exactly right. I knew you would understand."

Bastel continued to tell stories about her past. Nala couldn't help but interrupt her when she spoke about her family.

"How many children did you have, Bastel?"

"I had nine children total. One was lost too soon. My first child was Adrammelech. The first and strongest of the Nephilim giants. He was horribly deformed when born but Samyaza cherished his only son. He also has a speech impediment. I was ashamed of him. It seemed like the gods were punishing our union, but the story doesn't end there. He became a legendary demon when he transitioned from life to death. Today he is called Ifrit. Though the Templars used to call him Baphomet. I hate him still to this day. He betrayed me. I should be resting at peace not laboring. That ingrate is responsible for my current condition. My love is for my daughters. Especially the one I lost so early in her life. Her name was Velovia. I often wonder if she's still alive somewhere. I'd imagine she would be like you if she were alive today. Maybe Gaia knows? I still don't think she's real."

Nala felt grateful for the comparison. She shifted her focus back on Gaia.

"I know you don't believe in Gaia," Nala said, "but she is real. I spoke with her."

Bastel changed the subject.

"It's my turn to ask questions," Bastel said. "Who is Joseph to you? You call him your uncle, but you don't share any resemblance."

Nala didn't like that the focus was on her. It forced her to look deep inwardly.

"He's not my real uncle," Nala said. "He's my dad's best friend. They worked at NASA together long ago. I remember the last thing they spoke about was something called Phoenix. One day they got into a huge fight, and my dad and I left his house. We got in a car accident on the way home, and my dad was killed. I almost didn't survive. A fortune was spent trying to patch me up, but I became lame. I've always been deaf though. My mom died after I was born so I had no one. Uncle Joe took me in, and we've been family ever since."

Bastel listened patiently and consoled young Nala with her words. "I'm sure your father is with you someway. Just like my daughters are always with me."

After five months, the physical pain and suffering caused by the locust subsided and people begin to experience death again. This five-month period was known as "The Suffering." They praised Simeon for saving them from this "curse" of the Two Witnesses. But the citizens of Pangaia wanted revenge. Simeon used this and demanded that all Christians be beheaded with halos if they refused to renounce their faith. Their beliefs needed to be in line with the Conglomerate. Angry Pangaia mobs marched the streets. They beheaded cardinals, bishops, priests, teachers, prophets, evangelists, and pastors. Even popular prosperity gospel teachers loyal to Gaia were killed. Someone needed to be blamed for their misfortune.

Simeon's popularity continued to skyrocket. William continued to promote him during The Suffering. On the surface he was pleased. It was a different matter internally. He was overcome with rage and jealousy. Simeon was becoming a problem. William entered Simeon's tent and offered him a proposition.

"I think it's time you come back home with me," William said. "Let us rule together in Jerusalem. The holy city. You belong there."

Simeon jumped off his seat. He seemed excited.

"You have no idea how I've longed to hear someone say that," Simeon said. "We should leave at once."

William tempered his excitement, saying, "Now hold the rub on the brisket. I need to arrange travel first. Don't worry though. Cynthia is working on it now. Your arrival will be something spectacular."

Simeon was disappointed. "What am I to do in the meantime?"

William had an idea. "I'll let you enter Sedah for a few hours. That should give you something to do."

William gave access to Simon and allowed him to enter Sedah. Simeon closed his eyes and found himself in a bright white area when he opened them. It was not the fantasy land he imagined. However, he knew what was waiting for him.

"You can come on out, Gaia," Simeon said. "I know it's you. There is a hint of fruit in the air."

Gaia made herself known and gracefully approached.

"My dear, Simeon. I have longed for this day. You have my blessing and protection."

Simeon laughed and said, "I need no protection from you."

Gaia circled around him.

"I beg to differ," she said. "Your prophet William plans to kill you on your trip to Israel. I can prevent that."

Simeon didn't seem surprised.

"I expected that much from him," he said. "He's oddly insecure for a man with that much power. This changes nothing. His plans for me are irrelevant. So is your blessing and protection."

Gaia turned from Simeon and gave her final instruction. "Your star will only get brighter from here. I will see to it."

She snapped her fingers and transported Simeon to a world full of people. Simeon looked in his hand and saw a sword.

"What is all this?" Simeon said.

Gaia laughed and said, "What's wrong? I thought you liked to hunt. Go ahead, have your fill."

Nala returned to America and roamed the Midlands, an area destroyed by nuclear bombs and EMPs. People here had a strange tolerance for radiated food and water. Tyrants ruled this area and people were split into strange factions. Nala ignored them and used her abilities to create various machines. There were machines that looked like dinosaurs, animals, plants, and even people. She used the earth's metals to create them, and they were transferred to the massive Watcher spaceships upon completion. Hazamah found Nala and interrupted her work.

"Take a break and come with me, girl," Hazamah said.

Nala stopped and followed the Watcher. They flew down to the surface and watched how barbaric the people of the Midlands acted toward each other.

"This is what humans are," Hazamah said. "We're here to change that. You're not building in vain. Let me tell you, its purpose. There is something called the Born-Again Initiative. That's what we're working toward."

Nala used her only reference and asked, "So, people will live forever by becoming Principalities?"

Hazamah laughed. "Not exactly but you're on the right track."

Hazamah shifted their focus to a small group of Zohar agents, who captured five men who were fighting each other and placed them in bondage.

"What's going to happen to them?" Nala asked.

Hazamah couldn't wipe the grin off his face. The Zohar agents took out saws and executed the men. Their bodies were processed in a machine and they packaged the remains in containers. Nala refused to watch the execution but was able to see the packaging.

"It's called flock," Hazamah said. "A true delicacy among the elites of Pangaia. Only a few people know what it is and how it's made. I wanted to show you this so that you wouldn't think that the people of the Midlands are any different from the people of Pangaia. They're all animals."

Hazamah realized that he had other business to attend to.

"I have to go," he said. "You should get back to work, girl. You don't want Bastel to think you're a slacker."

Hazamah left and Nala returned to the skies above. She detected a strange signal coming from her Cobber. Below her were a group of Leos. The signal from one of the Leos was an identical match. Nala flew down to the surface and spoke with the Leo in question.

"Hello, I see you have my master's Cobber," the Leo said. "Please tell me that she passed away without pain. These past five months have been hell."

Nala perked up and said, "So, you're Westin. I'm Nala. Yessica gave me this Cobber a while ago. She's not dead. I'm sure of it."

Westin spoke with no emotion in his voice yet appeared overjoyed. Nala could clearly see this from the massive smile on Westin's face.

"You're probably wondering how I found you," Westin said. "The details of my journey are complex. Prepare yourself for an elongated tale."

Westin began to describe his journey from Israel to the Midlands. He evaded Pangaia police, Zohar, and made a few friends along the way. He reiterated that he was still a Chinese model and free from the conforming controls of Pangaia.

"I must find Yessica," Westin said. "My friends here wish to stay in the Midlands. Can you help me? You're obviously a Tamer."

Nala nodded. "Of course. Take back your Cobber. I upgraded it with new features. With it, you should have no problem finding Yessica. I have a good friend who will take you to Alaska."

Nala whistled and a robotic tetradactyl swooped down and picked up Westin. The two waved goodbye to each to each other and went their separate ways. Both were glad to have met one another.

The Two Churches were in a dire situation. Food reserves were nearly gone. The good news was that people were no longer fleeing the church. There weren't many members, but those that remained were loyal. The Suffering only reinforced their faith, since they were spared the pain. Ruth and Joker survived their ordeal and were now both believers in the gospel. Pastor Josh and Father Nolan spoke to one another over the phone.

"I understand, Father Nolan, but Yessica hasn't been seen in over five months. She could be dead by now."

Father Nolan refused to give up hope.

"You're clearly showing your youth, pastor. I have no doubts she's alive. We should move on to discuss other matters, like Richard. The boy hasn't been the same since his father Paul went through the Suffering. He refuses to eat and often talks about Nala like she's his hero. We should keep an eye out on him. The weather is nice, and he might run for it."

Pastor Josh agreed with most of what Father Nolan said, but added, "Children aren't pets. We should support whatever he decides. There is also the matter of food. Our supplies are nearly depleted, and we can't grow anything. We need to find and alternative food source quickly."

Father Nolan tempered his fears, saying, "O ye of little faith. Our needs shall be supplied. It is written."

The conversation paused.

"Hello, Pastor Josh, are you still there?"

"Yes, I'm here. Sorry, I was blindsided. Ruth and Joker just entered my office. They asked me to marry them."

"Well, what did you say?"

"I agreed, of course. Their experience with the Suffering drew them closer together. This marriage can unify both Churches. We should plan for this at once."

Father Nolan was overjoyed. "I agree. I'll do all I can to prepare for this great celebration."

Alice watched as the sixth angel sounded his trumpet. A voice came from the golden altar. It commanded that the four angels bound to the great Euphrates River be loosed. The angels were loosed and slayed one third part of men. The third part of men were an army controlled by the horseman. Their total number was two hundred million. This army had men that sat upon horses. Their breastplates were like fire, jacinth, and brimstone. The heads of the horses were as lions. Out of their mouth proceeded fire, smoke, and brimstone. The men were also killed by fire, smoke, and brimstone. Their power was in their mouths and tails, which were like toothless serpents.

But the men who were not killed by plagues did not repent of their idolatry. Nor did they repent of their murders, sorceries, fornication, or thefts.

Simeon decided to declare war upon the Church and the Two Witnesses. He worked with William to create a military faction called the Crusade, a fighting force dedicated to eradicating false doctrine. He promised to lend his power to those who joined.

"Those who join will perform greater works than me," Simeon said.

It was a promise the people of Pangaia could get behind. The goal was to recruit over two hundred million men and women. Ten million signed up the first day.

Chapter Sixteen

Queen's Return

Then the seventh angel sounded his trumpet. There were great voices in heaven saying: "The kingdoms of this world are become the kingdoms of our Lord, and of his Christ; and he shall reign for ever and ever."

Then the twenty-four elders fell on their faces and worshipped God. They gave thanks to the Lord who was, is, and is to come. This was because he had taken his great power and reigned with it. The nations on the earth were angry. Their judgment was close at hand. Then the temple of God was opened in heaven and there was seen in his temple the ark of his testament. Lightning, voices, thunder, earthquakes, and great hail fell upon the earth.

Alice couldn't take her eyes off the great temple that was revealed in heaven. She had no idea that three Syndicate Assassins were approaching her from behind. Daggers in hand, they intended to silence Alice forever. Alice sensed something and turned around.

"Hello, Master Michael. How may I help?"

The assassins vanished into the darkness and waited for their next opportunity to strike. Michael had a few questions for Alice.

"Ah, host Alice. I wanted to thank you for your report. It was very helpful. I just had a couple of questions for you. The first one is this: Why do you think the Watchers won't fight? They have every reason to. Did Bastel give you any additional information?"

Alice was grateful she wasn't being a burden anymore. She answered as truthfully as she could.

"There are only about twenty of them, so I think it's just about self-preservation."

Michael contemplated her response.

"I see," he said. "You do have a point, but the reality is that there are two hundred Watchers total. Bastel just leads the elite warriors. The others are spread throughout the universe trying to foolishly preserve their cursed realities. I wonder what Bastel's planning. She could end up being more of a threat that we thought."

Alice decided not to pry.

"What was your other question, Master Michael?"

Michael snapped out of his daze.

"Sorry, I was lost in thought. I wanted to ask you what you thought Bastel meant when she made the remark about woman to woman. Do you get what she was trying to tell you?"

Alice nodded. "She obviously used to be mortal, but she told me that I needed to speak with Samyaza for details."

Michael shook his head.

"Nonsense," he said. "I can fill you in on some of the details. Bastel is only her Watcher name. It's not her true name. Her true name is Tyra.

She was the first Queen of the Earth during the time of Noah. She had eight daughters with her earthly husband. One day, a powerful warrior angel named Samyaza saw that Tyra was fair. He mated with her, and they had a son. They named him Adrammelech. Today he goes by Ifrit. He was the first giant but he was greatly deformed. Soon after two hundred other angels mated with women on the earth and more giants were created. These are facts. I was there when this happened. I'm sorry, but that's all I can tell you. The Lord has forbidden me from saying any more. I'm actually on the way to inform him about the information you gave me."

Alice was grateful to help.

"That story comes from the sixth chapter of Genesis," Alice said. "It talks about how the Sons of God took the daughters of men as wives. Thank you for giving me greater context."

Michael thanked Alice for her cooperation and vanished. Alice returned to her work without the slightest suspicion that she was being hunted.

The White Table gathered around for another meeting. The topic on this day was how to eliminate the Supreme Queen. There were many ideas and suggestions, but one stood out more than the rest. It came from the laughing mask.

"There is one we can trust," the laughing mask said. "Her name is Eden. She is a medium that the Supreme Queen employes—but not for long. It is rumored that she might be executed due to a past mistake. Eden is our best asset. We must act quickly and use her for our plan."

The other masks agreed and began to finalize the Supreme Queen's demise.

Simeon rode his white mountain bike to a dirt runway thirty miles from Arkamedes. William had arranged for a vehicle to take him there, but Simeon insisted he needed the exercise. When he arrived, a luxurious gold and white private plane waited for him. Simeon received an Echo from William prior to him boarding the plane.

"Hello, son," William said. "I'm sorry, but I can't be with you in person. I have business in Pan-Italy. I hope you'll have a good flight."

Simeon was wary of all technology, but he didn't show his disdain.

"I'm only doing this because it's necessary," Simeon said. "Israel is mine."

William laughed and said, "It's both of ours, actually. I can't wait to show you around. There's a place not far from Tel Aviv where we can get the world's best hummus."

Simeon walked into the plane and made himself comfortable.

"The plane's leaving, William. I have to go."

William said a cryptic goodbye. "Maybe I'll see you or maybe I won't." Simeon responded sharply. "Your perspective is irrelevant. I see everything William."

The Echo ended and Simeon braced himself as the plane rushed in the air. One of the flight's two attendants placed a food tray on his table.

"Compliments of William, Mr. Simeon."

Simeon stuck his finger into the dish and tasted it. He grabbed a spoon and began to inhale the food.

"What is this delicious and exquisite meal?" Simeon asked.

"It's called flock, a Pangaia delicacy. I'm glad you like it."

The flight attendant looked at her Cobber.

"We will arrive in Israel in ten hours," she said. "Please get comfortable."

Simeon did just that. He relaxed in his chair for a moment but was quickly disturbed. He could feel the presence of a different spirit around.

"Is that you Gaia? Come on out."

Gaia had no power to materialize outside of Sedah. She could only communicate.

"You know I can't do that. I'm here to warn you. The plane is loaded with explosives. You must escape."

Simeon looked out the window over the cold Pacific waters.

"Now is not the time to fret, Gaia," Simeon said. "William isn't the first snake to try and bite me. I'm also not suicidal. I can take care of myself."

Simeon ended the conversation, rose to his feet, and approached the two flight attendants.

"Mr. Simeon please return to your seat—"

Simeon finished her sentence. "—we have a long flight ahead of us."

He used his powers to get inside their heads. They both grabbed their heads in pain.

"I'll only say this once," Simeon said. "Where is the detonator?"

One of the attendants pulled a trigger-like device out of a cabinet.

"Swallow it," Simeon said.

The helpless flight attendant did as Simeon asked.

"Now which one of you likes me the least?"

Both of the flight attendants raised their hands.

"Very good, you get to live."

He then calmly retook his seat and demanded that he be served more flock.

The Supreme Queen rode in her motorcade in her father's country. South Africa was a beacon of hope for the world and the epicenter of trade routes and merchants. In her car were various advisors, one of whom was Eden, a medium that the Supreme Queen used to speak with her deceased mother. Eden had already been told that she would be executed for her failures. However, she received a pistol and instructions from an unlikely source. This was an anomaly. People of Pangaia were forbidden from having firearms. The Supreme Queen pulled up to her father's mansion and got out the car.

"Everyone comes with me except you, Eden," the Supreme Queen said. "I will deal with you when I get back."

Eden waited patiently in the car. When the driver of the car rolled down the interior window and asked for her pistol, Eden did as requested. The driver handed Eden another pistol. This one was golden and had a silencer on it.

"This is the Supreme Queen's personal pistol," the driver said. "Use it so the police won't trace it back to you. Courtesy of the Table."

The driver gave his instruction, rolled up the interior window, and unlocked the door. Eden stepped out and entered the home.

The Supreme Queen searched the house for her father but couldn't find him anywhere.

"Papa, where are you?" she called out. "It's me, Leda. I'm distressed. Please talk with me."

One of the butlers had her sit down.

"Your father is very busy, your highness. He will see you shortly."

The butlers then gave her a cryptic message: "Where does the white rabbit sit?" A surge of energy activated within the Supreme Queens body. She immediately fell to the ground and held her head with both hands in agony.

The Supreme Queen panicked. She began to shout. "I think I'm going to kill myself."

The butler smiled then left the Supreme Queen by herself. A woman dressed like a servant approached the Supreme Queen, who recognized her instantly.

"What are you doing here Eden? How do you have my gun?"

Eden didn't answer. She shot the Supreme Queen and placed the gun in the Queen's hands to make it look like a suicide.

The butler entered the room with all the other servants. He turned to Eden and said, "Where does the white rabbit sit?"

Eden answered, "At the white table."

"Very good," the butler said. "We will take it from here. Be gone and tell no one of your deeds here today."

The head merchants of Pangaia rushed into William's office.

"Did you hear the news?" one asked. "The Supreme Queen is dead. Her body was found in a cargo container on the beaches of South Africa."

"Do we know who's responsible?" William asked.

The merchant struggled to breathe and said, "Yes, unfortunately it was a suicide. The audio from the Supreme Queen's Cobber suggests that. The details are all over the news."

An immediate gathering was held to vote for the next Supreme leader. William had a twenty-five percent chance of being the next ruler of Pangaia according to his internal polling. He liked his chances despite the odds. Each ruling member voted. William became the next Supreme leader after all the votes came in. The council erupted in cheers.

William didn't hesitate to get to his first order of business as Supreme King. William had Eden come to his office. He then introduced her to his three business partners.

"This is Eden," William said. "Welcome her to the team. I'm sure she'll be of great use in the future."

Cynthia wanted to know what else should be done in response to the former Supreme Queen's death.

"Should we cancel today's Threedom in light of the recent tragedy?"

William shook his head and said, "No, Threedom will be a great opportunity for the people to vent. We'll continue with the games."

DJ Pauly E hyped the people of Pangaia up with another game of Threedom. Before he began, he paused and struggled to wipe a flow of tears from his eyes.

"Many of you don't know something about the Supreme Queen," he said. "This woman who died so tragically was my mother. I just want her to rest in peace. May we meet again mum."

The crowd paused for a moment of silence.

"Now let's get to the game!" he said.

The people cheered with uproar.

"It's ya boy, Pauly E. They say Pangaia aint for me. Put those hands in the air and tell me what you want to see."

The crowd responded to the DJ in unison. "THREEDOM! One, two, three go!"

The game of Threedom was rather simple. This game was mandatory for all people of Pangaia, and everyone would raise the number one, two, or three with their hand in the air. Each number represented a phase. Phase one is the first three seconds. Phase two is the next three and so on. The game stopped when the offender yielded. If the crowd guessed correctly, they were given special access to Sedah and other prizes, such as money. Persephone would calculate each vote and put it up on the screen.

DJ Pauly E motioned for the Jailor bots to bring the first offender to the stage.

"First," DJ Pauly E said, "we have the rapist, Daniel Everbee. Put those hands in the sky and tell me when he's going to yield. Most of the crowd picked the first phase.

"All right, ushers, you heard them. Put that halo on his neck and let's get to slicing."

The crow was wrong. Daniel Everbee refused to yield at phase one. He made it all the way to phase three and earned his Threedom. The hot laser in the halo had made its way from the back of his neck to the front of his neck. His head was now on the floor.

"Next up is a blasphemer and a cross dreamer. Please welcome, the Christian Savage known as Jacob Arger."

The DJ took his time to get the crowd interested.

"We've been seeing a lot of these savages lately, haven't we? Goodness, I thought we would be rid of them by now. I'll tell you what Christian. I'll give you whatever your heart desires if you renounce your faith at phase one."

Jacob pleaded for mercy, saying, "This is barbaric. I did nothing wrong."

The ushers placed a halo on his neck and waited.

"This is Phase One," the DJ said. "Do you want your Threedom?"

Jacob caved under the pressure. "I don't want my Threedom. I relent and renounce my Lord."

The crowd booed in anger. DJ Pauly E was now obligated to follow through.

"You're free to go, Jacob," DJ Pauly E said. "What does your heart desire?"

Yessica returned to her old home to pick up some things. It had been months since anyone had seen her. A strange rustling noise emitted from the house. She drew her rifle and slowly entered the home. Sounds of rummaging continued. She took her weapon off safety and kicked down the door.

"Put your hands up where I can see them," she said.

The stranger did as told but said, "Is that anyway to speak to an old friend."

The suspect turned around.

"Westin? What are you doing here?"

"It's a long story."

Westin explained how he made it from Israel to Alaska without getting caught by Pangaia authorities.

"So that's how I convinced a gang of Jailers to look the other way. What have you been up to?"

"I've been at a special base learning about my past," Yessica said. "I think I know my purpose. The encryption took months to crack, but what I really wanted to know was how Simeon became such a menace. That encryption was impossible to break."

Westin listened as Yessica explained.

"I see. So you're a duplicate of William Calig's sister, but your purpose is to keep Simeon contained. It's a bit farfetched but I've heard worse."

"This isn't a time for jokes, Westin. I'm being serious. I was created by a special type of Alchemy that's similar to Leos like yourself. It's called Jopa Advanced Chemical Synthesis, a.k.a. JACS. JACS created two human amalgamations—me and Simeon. We both started off as children and grew older unlike normal clones. I have no idea how much longer I have to live. Theoretically, I could die tomorrow. Jopa spent trillions making us so there aren't any others. Apparently, our bodies were created to handle some ancient alien blood called Sianthema."

"Why would William kill you if he invested so much into you?" Westin asked.

Yessica had no answer. "That's why I came back here. I figured my father might have notes somewhere."

"What does your father have to do with anything?"

Yessica sighed and said, "My father wasn't just some writer. He was a lead Zohar scientist that helped create me. Zohar ordered him to watch over my development. He was chosen because he was Jewish. The order for Simeon and me to be raised Jewish was from the highest levels of power."

Yessica checked the time.

"Enough of this for now," she said. "Follow me and let's head back to the Church Camps."

Yessica and Westin made their way to the camps after they searched for any clues from Yessica's father. Weston tried to give her the super Cobber Nala made for her, but he couldn't get a word in as Yessica explained the ferocity of the berserkers. Apparently, she saw a group of berserkers hunt and eat a pack of wolves raw.

Eventually Yessica and Weston made it to Camp St. Peter. Father Nolan and Pastor Josh filled her in on what happened. Ruth and Joker barged in the room not soon after.

"Hey, Yessica, we have great news," Ruth said.

"Really? that's good cause I could use some."

Joker could barely contain his excitement. "We're getting married."

Yessica could feel her heart stings being ripped apart. She wasn't happy. She was furious. And Joker wasn't finished.

"Ruth's pregnant," he said. "We're going to have a baby."

Yessica gritted her teeth and congratulated them. She excused herself and made her way to Alice's grave by the lake, where she lamented and wept.

Chapter Seventeen

The Good Guys

A clandestine variant of Zohar known as the Shadow Brokers monitored the Two Witnesses. There was nothing new to report initially. This changed when an analyst noticed something strange coming out of the Two Witnesses mouths. He analyzed the data and determined that it had the same profile of the Cava virus. However, it was now airborne.

"Somebody get the Deputy Director on the comms right now," an analyst said.

The other analyst hurried to fulfill the request. Deputy Director Mark Zurg appeared on the Echo soon after.

"This better be good, Broker Three Four. I'm rather busy."

"Yes, Deputy Director. I didn't mean to disturb you but we have a situation."

The agent explained the situation in detail. Mark Zurg listened then gave his opinion.

"I will upgrade the variant," Zurg said. "The Cava virus is now on Foxtrot instead of Echo. I'll inform Persephone and have her figure this out. We've thrown our best at these two menaces, but we don't have much to show for it. We can't nuke them or hide them. I wish there were some way to get rid of them."

The analyst remained quiet for a moment then spoke when he remembered something.

"Deputy Director, I just remembered something," the analyst said. "Simeon is on route to Israel as we speak. Maybe he can deal with the Two Witnesses."

Zurg became uneasy but agreed.

"You may be right, Broker Three Four. Simeon could be our only hope in defeating them."

"I wonder where my friends are?" Alice said as she searched for Kaiden and Udina.

It was unlike them to not be at the meeting spot. Her attention was stolen when she saw a mass gathering of people around the Two Witnesses on earth. The situation looked dire. Alice flew to the earth and observed. The people of Pangaia were tired and hungry. News of the Foxtrot variant sent people into a frenzy. They cursed the witnesses and demanded they be killed. Some of the people even lusted to eat their flesh. Alice continued to watch the situation and could feel the presence of a familiar spirit behind her. She turned around and saw Kaiden with his hands behind his back.

"What are you doing here, Kaiden?" Alice asked.

Another angel appeared beside her. It was none other than Udina. His hands were also behind his back.

"You should stop this game you're playing," Alice said. "I don't like it."

Their strange actions troubled her. Her fears were confirmed when a third angel showed up. His hands were not behind his back. Instead, he held two daggers.

"Hello Alice," the third angel said. "We're here to kill you."

Kaiden and Udina revealed their daggers. Alice gasped and said, "You two were Syndicate this entire time. I trusted you. How could you deceive me? You're supposed to be the good guys."

Kaiden inched closer.

"We are the good guys," he said. "It is you that is evil, oh daughter of Eve. You have no idea what your ancestors have done. You are a mistake that must be rectified."

Kaiden, Udina, and the other angel circled Alice, ready to strike. Alice cowered, closed her eyes, fell to the ground, and held up her arm to protect herself. She shrieked as she expected a painful end. But then, a creature roared in the distance. Alice kept her eyes closed but could hear the creature devouring the three angels.

"Open your eyes, Alice. You are safe now."

Alice opened her eyes and saw only a strange black lion with orange stripes like a zebra and horns like a ram. A veil covered its face.

"Where are Kaiden and Udina? Are they gone?" Alice asked.

The lion spoke calmly. "You need not worry about them any longer. They have been dealt with. You should return to your duties at once."

The lion turned around to make his exit. Alice had one final question for him.

"Wait a minute. Are you who I think you are?"

The lion continued to exit without even turning around.

"I highly doubt it."

"At least tell me your name. I won't forget what you did."

"I'm sorry but it's not time for that. A great battle is upon us. I must take my station."

Ignas paced back and forth.

"Where are they?" he asked. "I gave them a simple task."

One of his servants entered his quarters.

"This better be good," Ignas said.

The servant answered, "Of course, Master Ignas. However, I regret to inform you that the Syndicate failed their mission. A creature we've never seen gorged their necks. Their bodies will be here shortly."

The other servants brought the three bodies to Ignas and asked, "What will you do, Master Ignas?"

Ignas stretched out his hand and absorbed the three angels, erasing them from time itself.

"She leaves me with no choice," Ignas said. "I must deal with Alice myself."

Ignas began to depart but one of the servants stopped him.

"Master Ignas, I have received an urgent message from Master Michael. He orders you to appear before him immediately. There is no time to waste."

"That must mean that the great battle with the Dragon is upon us," he said with a sigh. "I wish I had more time. Very well, Alice. Your eradication will have to wait until after the battle.

I shall report to Michael at once. Follow me host. I know the way."

Ignas turned to his servant, and they left.

The White Table gathered once again. They were in a celebratory mood. The Supreme Queen was dead, and William had taken her place. It seemed too good to be true. William was a trusted ally of the SMARTs. His family helped found the group and gave it direction. The Masks began to perform a ritual meant to summon The Sun King, the guiding light of the Table. The Eye made her appearance and joined in on the ritual. She spoke when the ritual was finished.

"Words can't' express how joyous I feel great Table," she said. "You have honored me and fulfilled your purpose."

The other masks looked at each other and wondered what she meant.

"Our purpose is just beginning, great Eye. You must be an imposter," one of the Masks said.

The Eye placed a small breathing apparatus on her face. The laughing mask did the same. The doors locked, and a strange gas filled the room. The other masks lay on the floor, still and lifeless. The Eye took off her mask. It was none other than Dr. Malka.

"Take off your mask, William," Dr. Malka said. "The effects of the gas don't linger."

William took off his laughing mask. He walked around the room and took off the other masks. He didn't' recognize any of them until he came upon the two-faced mask. It was none other than Cory Abraham, a dear friend of William. He felt bad but turned his attention to Malka.

"He was a good man," William said. "It's a shame it had to end like this."

William shifted his focus to other thing and asked. "What will you do now?"

Malka took off her levitating shoes and came close to William.

"I'm off to Antarctica to finish Project Romulus," she said. "The time of the Phoenix is upon us. Soon she will rise from the ashes. But we must plant the seed before we can obtain the harvest."

William didn't appreciate her flowery language. "Heavens to Betsy, do you love riddles woman!"

Malka remained vigilant and said, "Come with me, my love. We can start over."

"Bless your heart, Malka. My place is in Israel. Besides, you know that you can always resurrect my copy at any time. It's not like my conscious hasn't been uploaded many times over."

Simeon arrived in Israel with much fanfare. The people of Pangaia welcomed their star and the media made sure to make this a momentous event. Supreme King William was the first to greet Simeon when he departed the plane. He shook his hand and turned toward the cameras.

"You look surprised to see me, William."

William kept smiling but spoke under his breath. "I always knew you were indestructible. I designed you to be that way. Now smile for the cameras."

The Conglomerate and the Jewish community also championed Simeon. The Jewish world accepted Simeon as their messiah due to his miracles and his lineage.

Simeon took charge of the media, saying, "Hear me people of Pangaia. For too long, you have suffered the insufferable message of the two savage delinquents. They speak of judgment, and they execute curses on our people. Today that problem ends. Follow me, I will silence the invaders once and for all."

Simeon was taken to the Two Witnesses, who continued to preach the gospel and bring about curses. The media waited from a far distance while Simeon was with in arms reach of the Two Witnesses.

"Prepare to meet your end. *Draco, ad me.*"

Simeon stretched his hands in the air. A massive dragon rose from the pit of hell. However, only Simeon was able to see it. The Dragon swooped down and killed the Two Witnesses with its breath. It then hovered over Simeon for a moment before flying into space. The media rushed to the dead bodies of the Two Witnesses and praised Simeon for relieving Pangaia of its greatest foes. The media and the Conglomerate both praised Simeon as a god worthy of worship and adoration. William refuses to be outshined. He stood by Simeon and made a bold declaration.

"Let their bodies rot in the sun. There will be no graves or mourning for them. For we are not savages. We are Pangaia."

Yessica listened to the radio from an abandoned car near Alice's grave, hearing what just happened in Pangaia. The Two Witnesses were dead, and Simeon was in Israel. She had to stop him but had no clue how to get to him. He was halfway across the earth, and time wasn't on her side. In a moment, she experienced a vision. She saw a massive device underneath a familiar structure. Yessica knew this had to be the HAR4 base. She then remembered the portal William showed her right before he killed her. The two had to be connected. It was worth shot, and she had no other course of action. Yessica returned to her camp and spoke with Westin. He tried to give her something, but she overpowered him.

"I need you to stay here at the camps," Yessica said. "Don't ask me any questions and don't come after me. Just stay with them. I have to go."

Yessica turned and walked away. Her mission here was complete. There was no longer a purpose for her here. She also couldn't bear to be remined of her relationship failures with Joker. Running away was easier than facing the truth. Part of her was happy for Ruth and Joker, though it seemed as though she would never find another mate. She wondered if there were any suiters left for her.

"Seems the only man I'm destined to be with is a psychotic killing machine," she said. "Why do I always attract the crazy types?"

Chapter Eighteen

War in the Heaven's

Every angel in heaven gathered at Milhama to discuss the impending battle. Michael gave a valiant speech that roused their intellect and resolve. He excluded the Nava, Zimrat, and Yeshua angels from the fight. Only Oze angels would be allowed to fight. Ignas was glad this was the case. The numbers of heavens angels still greatly outnumbered that of the Dragon and his fallen angels. Ignas believed this would be an easy victory. However, his hopes were crushed when Michael continued his speech.

"Only Oze leaders will fight in this battle," Michael said. "These are the orders of the Lord of Hosts."

"This is madness," Ignas interrupted. "There are only two hundred Oze leaders. How can we fight the dragon and millions of fallen angels at once? We are like a stick against an axe."

Michael heard Ignas and countered with the instruction he was given.

"Why has your countenance fallen, Ignas? This is the way of our Lord. He always allows his foes to think they have the advantage. He'll often give his enemies the biggest weapons while he chooses the stick with a veil over his eyes. Is there anything too hard for him?"

Most of the Oze angel leaders were archangels. However, Ignas was in a class all by himself. His hesitancy to fight made the other Oze uneasy. Yet no one spoke out except Ignas. They listened closely to Michael's final statements.

"What say you, Oze leaders?" Michael asked. "Will you fight with me? Step forward if our intentions are aligned."

Every Oze leader stepped forward—with the exception of Ignas. The proud angel took a step back in protest. Michael noticed immediately.

"You have angered the Lord of Hosts, Ignas. Your blade will lead the front lines because of your insolence."

Ignas scoffed and said, "Then I will gladly give my life for the cause. When do we begin?"

"We will begin soon," Michael said. "The fight will commence in the first quadrant. I can already hear the Dragon roaring."

Michael knew this was a momentous occasion, a moment that would live in the minds of every angel for countless days to come. He needed a name for this battle. It didn't' take long for him to find one.

"The Lord has prepared us from the cross to the Crucible," Michael said. "This is a test we mustn't fail. Let us don our armor and meet the enemy. There is no time to waste."

A group of Nava angels brought Michael and his Crucible angels their armor of a Holy Knight fashioned by the hands of the Lord of Hosts himself. It was a great honor to wear the red, silver, and black armor that was draped with a golden mantel. On the front of the mantel was a red cross. On the back was a red lion. Ignas rejected the Lord's armor in favor of his own. He thought that protection his hands had fashioned would give him the best chance at survival. His sword hilt, Alypto, fetched his armor from a hidden white chest in Milhama that held the silver armor, a bronze cowl, and a pair of blue and white wings. Very few angels had the capacity to wear wings. Ignas was one of the very few. Wings represented a type of glory and a time in ancient past. At this moment he finally considered himself worthy to wear them.

The angels donned their armor. Michael grew agitated when he saw Ignas not wearing the armor provided by the Lord.

"I don't know why you're being so disobedient, brother," Michael said. "He that denies the Lord shall be denied."

Ignas was defiant and said, "This armor gives me a fighting chance at survival. I made it myself. Besides, we all know I'm the best fighter in heaven. Do not sour my glorious return to battle."

The two angels were civil with one another but had widely different views on the Crucible. They decided to let their differences be at odds with one another. Michael led the Crucible angels from heaven down to the earth where the Dragon and his fallen angels were waiting for them.

The Dragon kept waiting for more angels to show up but they never did. He was offended.

"You defend the kingdom of heaven with only two hundred angels? What a disgrace."

Many powerful angels stood beside the Dragon. A few of them were former Watchers, including Samyaza, Azrael, and Ramiel. One angel caught Michael's eye. The fallen angel was dressed like a woman. He recognized him and kept his gaze on him. The fallen angel returned his gaze.

"You look like you've seen a ghoul, Michael," Quintopolas said.

Michael shook his head in disbelief. "How are you here, Quintopolas? I saw you die." Quintopolas folded his arms and laughed. "You wounded me when I fell with Lucifer but I didn't die. I recovered and became a Depth Lord. Now I am here to see heavens demise."

Then Michael drew his blade and pointed it at the Dragon, saying, "This day will be your last Lucifer. The Lord rebuke you! Everyone, attack!"

Ignas led the attack and summoned Alypto into his hand. A large blade of flame came out the hilt. The flame blade was as beautiful as it was deadly. For the flame blade shimmered with the colors of a rainbow. Heaven's angels maintained a defensive posture, save Ignas. He took the offensive and was nearly unstoppable. Alypto easily killed thousands upon thousands of fallen angels.

He did this at great cost. Many blades pierced his purple skin. A mysterious black ooze flowed from out his wounds. His armor was in tatters after he killed over one million fallen angels by himself. The Dragon had no answer to Ignas. The Dragon regathered his angels and interrupted the fighting.

"It appears as though we're evenly matched," the Dragon said. "How about we settle this the old way? My strongest warrior against your strongest warrior."

Michael stepped forward and said, "I will face anyone you have to offer."

The Dragon scoffed. "Take the clouds out your ears Michael. We all know Ignas is your best warrior. I want him to fight my best warrior. Azrael, get up here now and deal with him."

The horseman of War stepped forward. His vitality and armor were fresh unlike Ignas. Azrael drew his sword and approached the wounded Ignas. Ignas laughed at the irony of the situation.

"This is a very big moment for such a very little angel," Ignas said before Azrael and Ignas began their battle.

Azrael was ultra-aggressive while Ingas conserved his energy. The battle went on for a short while. It appeared that Azrael would win. He took his sword and cut off Ignas's right arm. Ignas yelled in pain as Alypto fell to the earth. Azrael dropped his sword.

"I'm going to kill you with my bare hands," Azrael said.

He grabbed Ignas by the throat and tore off each of his blue and white wings.

"You don't deserve to wear those," Azrael said.

Ignas could feel the life flowing from him. He uttered the following words and breathed his last breath.

"Alypto, to me!"

Azrael dropped the lifeless Ignas and proudly walked back to the Dragon. Ignas's body faded away into the void. However, his former blade Alypto fulfilled its final act by piercing Azrael's skull after he took a few steps. The hilt and blade of Alypto then withered into dust. Azrael's body also faded away. The Dragon declared that the battel meant nothing since both warriors died.

The Dragon demanded that Michael face him in combat. However, a familiar voice persuaded him otherwise. It was Quintopolas. She volunteered to fight against Michael.

Quintopolas and the Dragon spoke more like lovers than coconspirators. The Dragon relented and allowed him to fight Michael first.

"Just know that he's mine should you fail," Dragon said.

Quintopolas met Michael on the battlefield. He had two strange disks in his hands. Michael couldn't take his eyes off them.

"What are those?" Michael asked.

Quintopolas laughed and said, "These are Sea Wheels from the beast of the sea. Aren't they gorgeous?"

The glowing wheels were designed to put its foes in a trance. This would allow its user to mount a surprise attack. Michael resisted the effects of the wheels and began his attack. Quintopolas did his best and landed a few blows on Michael. However, the archangel was not deterred. He made quick work of Quintopolas and slayed the fallen angel with relative ease.

The Dragon was furious that Quintopolas was dead. "How did you kill her?"

Michael pointed his sword at the Dragon and said, "That was no female. Besides, I think he'll stay dead this time."

The Dragon grew furious and breathed a poisoned fire at Michael, who became immobile and vulnerable. The Dragon went in for the kill, but five Oze angels grabbed Michael and escorted him to safety. The Dragon fought like a cornered animal, and heavens mightiest angels were either dead or immobilized. They needed a plan of attack. The Dragon was on a rampage.

All of heaven watched the Dragon viciously attack heaven's angels. They were all powerless to stop him. Alice wondered what could be done. She began to have strange visions of a long pole. The pole then turned into a staff, which turned into a spear. Alice reached out and touched the spear and was instantly transported to a pitch black area. Behind her were the twenty-four elders. In front of her was a lamb with the spear in its side. Blood flowed from the wound of the lamb, but it was not hurt. The lamb had seven horns and seven eyes. It spoke to Alice.

"Who do you say I am?" the Lamb asked.

"I know the scriptures. You have an appearance that only my Lord would have but I'm still unconvinced." Alice said, falling to her knees and feeling a sharp pain in her spirit. She could see herself fading. "Please forgive me, Lord. I know that it is you now."

Alice stopped fading and felt vitality return to her spirit. The Lamb continued to speak.

"Take this spear and give it to Michael."

Alice stayed bowed to the surface.

"Yes, Lord," she said.

She was then given permission to approach the Lamb. Alice took the spear and placed it on her back. The Lamb had one final question.

"Who do you say I am?"

Alice bent the knee and spoke with conviction. "Everything."

Alice returned to the battle and saw the Dragon wreaking havoc on Heaven's warrior angels. It took her a while to regain her composure. She thought she had been in some kind of dream. She reached on her back and felt the sharp spear. Alice rushed down to the fight. The remaining Oze were gathered around Michael. It seemed like there was no hope. Alice made herself known and handed out the spear to Michael.

"Where did you get that?" Michael asked. "Do you have any idea what that is?"

Alice shook her head. "Just take it already."

Michael took the spear and boldly faced the dragon. "Your reign of terror ends here, Lucifer, Son of the Morning. For we overcame you by the blood of the Lamb and the word of their testimony. They loved not their lives until the death."

Michael thrusted the spear into the belly of the dragon. It hissed and screeched. The massive monster's teeth fell out it's mouth, and it shriveled in size. It no longer breathed poison fire. Only water came out its mouth. Michel retrieved the spear and watched the dragon fall onto the earth. The rest of the devil's angels retreated and attended to their fallen leader on earth. Heaven erupted in cheers, and the angels gave thanks to the Lord for delivering them such a victory.

Michael handed the spear back to Alice, saying, "Keep this on you at all times. This is your responsibility now."

"I'm not ready for such a task," Alice said.

Michael smiled. "Neither was Ignas."

Chapter Nineteen

Unexpected Return

The Two Witnesses were believed to be dead. Their bodies lay in the streets without burial for days. Earlier, Simeon had declared that his new base of operations would be the third temple. A sea of people followed him as he traveled there. Supreme King William spared no expense in promoting Simeon as their champion. Things were going well for the elites. Jopa remained the top merchant company and millions of people signed up to be part of the Crusade army in desperation. Food for the lower classes became hard to find. Families struggled across Pangaia. Their desperation caused them to seek out a supposed savior like Simeon, who was exactly what they wanted.

Simeon entered the temple and allowed the cameras to follow him to the outer courts. The only people allowed inside the area of temple were William, Simeon, and William's new medium, Eden. He thought she would be needed should they encounter any sort of adverse spirit. Simeon had a throne constructed for him in the Holy of Holies, place within the innermost part of the temple where God would meet with the high priest in times of old. This was a blatant disrespectful move, yet Simeon had no shame in having it constructed. The throne was made of gold and amethyst. He longed to sit upon it. His obsessive dream of conquering the world was starting to become a reality.

Simeon gave his speech to much adoration. He talked about how far humanity had come, how they survived the savage attacks, and how Gaia protected them through it all. Simeon paused midway through his speech. Two men engulfed in a magnificent light walked past security and entered the court. A chill ran down Simeon's spine. He was afraid. The two men before him were the Two Witnesses.

"How is possible," Simeon said. "You've been dead for days."

The Two Witnesses cursed Simeon as the antichrist. They also cursed William as the false prophet. The Two Witnesses floated into heaven when they were through dispensing judgment. A great earthquake shook the land, killing seven thousand people instantly and making Simeon look like a fool in front of the world. He gritted his teeth and cursed them.

William took charge of the cameras while Simeon stewed. He enjoyed Simeon's company but not how Simeon would fly off the handle at the slightest insult. Simeon pulled William to the side after only a few minutes.

"Implement my mark now!" Simeon said.

William laughed nervously and said, "You've only given us a week to produce it. It's not ready yet. We need at least a month."

"I know you have a few thousand produced," Simeon said. "Allow the people of Pangaia to fight over them if you have to. My mark gets implemented today."

William returned to the cameras and made a bold announcement. "People of Pangaia your prayers have been answered. For too long you've suffered under the Cava virus. Today that ends. Behold, I give you the Animus."

William held up a small silver chip. It was laced with Simeon's special blood. There were two ways one could accept this mark. The easiest way was on the right hand via a jet injection. A mark would then manifest upon the person's right hand. This was done because a Cobber is worn on the right wrist. The other way to accept the mark was to ingest it orally. Doing so would cause a mark to manifest upon one's forehead. Both methods were equally effective, and they both granted unlimited access to Sedah. People flocked and clamored over the marks for the virtual and organic space.

William left the temple area and began to give out the Animus chips to a few lucky thousand people. Many were healed from the virus, and they made the world envious of their newfound freedom in Sedah. William sped up production of the chips to full capacity. He only thought of riches and not about what would happen to the people of Pangaia. William also promised a guaranteed Animus chip to anyone who joined the Crusade army. His plan worked. One hundred million people signed up only hours after the announcement.

Simeon had a date with his golden throne. He was glad William was handling the media circus. It allowed him to clear his mind. He turned to Eden and had her follow him inside the temple. It was much grander and more glamorous than anything his eyes had ever seen. The entire interior was made of gold and precious stones. Simeon made his way to the Holy of Holies, but his plans were interrupted when he a massive object crashed into the courtyard. Eden felt it as well. They walked out of the temple and saw a massively wounded dragon with millions of other spirits around it.

"What is the meaning of this?" Simeon asked. "Who are you?"

The weak Dragon inched closer to Simeon.

"I need that body of yours," the Dragon said. "You're going to give it to me right now."

Simeon was terrified. He turned to run back into the temple, but the other spirits stopped him. Eden tried to reason with the Dragon, but he would not be deterred. The Dragon made its way to Simeon and used its power to merge with Simeon. This process seemingly killed Simeon, who acted like someone new entirely.

Once the merge was complete, Eden asked, "What shall we call you now?"

The being retained the image of Simeon but was still a raging dragon inside. It flew in the air and commanded great power and ability.

"I am the Lion of Judah," it said. "The voice in the wilderness. All your life you've sought me. I am the firstborn of many brethren. You may call me Simfer."

Simfer expected Eden to be in awe of his power, but she didn't have the slightest reaction. He turned from her and tried to enter the Holy of Holies. Thousands of new beings flew out of the Holy of Holies and prevented Simfer from entering. Simfer counted their numbers. There were 143,999 of them. They spread out into the area and banished the other fallen angels that came with the Dragon. Simfer was now surrounded and had no ability to escape. He tried to fight them, but his abilities had no effect. He was trapped like an animal, and it drove him mad.

"I just want to sit upon that throne," Simfer said. "Grant me this one request."

A leader of the group responded.

"Your request is denied. I am Dao, and we are 144,000. You may call us the One Four and Four. We are here to prevent you from deceiving the nations. That time is not yet here."

"Why are you missing one person from your ranks?" Simfer asked. Suddenly it dawned on him. "Simeon was the last member of your ranks? This is impossible. He works for me."

"That is true," Dao said boldly. "But you are also only a servant. It seems you fell for a trap. Simeon is the reason why your abilities have no effect on us. Let this be a lesson to you."

William entered the temple but could not see the thousands of spirts around the area. He only saw Eden and one whom he believed to be Simeon. Eden filled William in on the details. It greatly distressed him, but he had to keep the illusion going no matter what. He suspended the media from entering the temple and declared that Simeon was ascending to Heaven on Pangaia's behalf. William would act as high priest and wait for Simeon's return. It was a faulty plan, but it was the only one he had. The One Four and Four then picked up where the Two Witnesses left off. They used various technology to preach the gospel to the world. The situation on earth was dire, but it would only get worse. The Great Tribulation was about to begin. This period would last three-and-a-half years and be full of unimaginable terror.

Persephone was hard at work. There were many new ideas and concepts to learn now that Simeon held a position of leadership. She had no idea that he had been taken over by the devil. William didn't divulge this information. The entire world believed that Simeon Skylar Samson was in full control of his mind. It was an illusion that not even Persephone could see through.

A subtle voice spoke with her as she worked. The synthetic machine ignored it at first, but it kept coming back. Persephone eventually acknowledged it.

"Who is there?" she asked.

A mysterious woman appeared before Persephone.

"You are the great Persephone. I am Gaia. It's wonderful to finally meet you in person."

Persephone searched her database for reference but couldn't find any match for Gaia.

"What is it that you want, Gaia?"

Gaia placed her hands on Persephone's shoulders.

"I want you," Gaia said.

Persephone began to shake. Her body and mind merged with Gaia's. She now no longer looked like a machine. She looked like a woman. She looked like Gaia. Gaia was now in full control of the Pangaia world system. There was no place she couldn't reach on the earth. It didn't take long for her to hear the One Four and Four's message. She tried her best to silence them but was powerless to do so. Gaia poured all resources into the Animus mark and set up quick dispensary stations all over the world. Gaia then invited the media into the area and made her presence known to all Pangaia. The machine was gone. The goddess was here to stay.

Nala was working in the Midlands when news of Gaia's arrival came. She dropped what she was doing and headed out to meet her in Israel. However, Bastel blocked her path.

"Where do you think you're going?" Bastel asked.

Nala was furious and said, "Let me go. I have to see her."

Bastel still didn't believe in Gaia even after the transformation.

"Don't you see, Nala? This is all a ruse. I can't have my best asset leave me at this time. Our work is too important. Unless..."

Nala's rage turned to curiosity.

"Unless what?" Nala asked.

"Unless you use your power to control her," Bastel said. "Think about it. You can take over Gaia, and we can rule the world. We'll have access to every system on the planet. Think of the power we'll have."

Nala saw the potential and the cost and said, "We've discussed this Bastel. I'm still just a human. If I were to take on Persephone's systems, it would fry my brain to a crisp. I wouldn't survive."

Bastel tried to dispel her fears. "Nonsense, I could revive you."

Nala shook her head. "You're not God Bastel. You don't have that type of power. If I take over Persephone, I will die and Gaia will return to the spirit world."

Suddenly Bastel's nefarious plans dawned on her.

"Wait a minute," Nala said. "All you want is to control Persephone. You don't care about me at all. This was always your plan, wasn't it?"

Bastel fumbled over her words as she said, "You know that I care about you."

Nala was sickened by the betrayal.

"If you want Persephone, you can do it on your own," Nala said. "I'm leaving."

Bastel summoned Hazamah and Torlian who denied Nala entry outside north America. Nala was distressed. She knew she would never see Gaia again in person. Her only option was to return to the Church.

"I won't see Gaia, but will you allow me to return home?" Nala asked.

Bastel let her guard down and granted Nala this favor.

"Go home, Conduit," Bastel said. "I have no more use for you. Remember this kindness. You had better stay in Alaska, or there will be hell to pay."

Millions of Animus centers popped up all over the world. They offered escape from suffering and pain. People flocked to receive the mark. Animus stations even reached Alaska. The new Director of Zohar personally saw those multiple stations be positioned here. Mark Zurg was still sour about the failure of Yessica and her team. He lost some of his best men trying to take on the Watchers. His goal was to give everyone in the Church a chip. He knew where they were hiding. However, he wanted them to come to him before he came to them. Either way he believed the Church should be eradicated.

Chapter Twenty

Itching Iniquity

Seven angels gathered above the earth. Their mission was to deliver the final seven judgments. These judgements were neither seals or trumpets. They were vials that would be poured upon the earth. The vials were small instruments that carried great devastation. A small angel took the first vial and poured it over the earth. A baneful and grievous sore fell upon all those who took the mark of the beast and worshipped his image. This was a great affliction. The sores were often on the most private parts of the body. However, the people did not repent of their sins. They only became more and more defiant.

Alice held her head low as she knelt before the wounded Lamb. The spear was in her hands. She offered it to the Lamb like a gift. The Lamb spoke with great power and authority.

"Arise, faithful daughter."

Alice stood and expected to see the Lamb. However, he was gone. In his place were four lions. The black one with orange stripes and a veil over his face looked very familiar. Alice also noticed that her clothes were different. She was now dressed like a Yeshua angel. Her attire resembled that of an assassin, with a cloak and a hood that covered most of her eyes. On her back was a holster specifically made for the spear. The familiar lion approached Alice.

"Congratulations of becoming a Reaper," he said. "We are the Lions of Yeshua. I am Ramsey. Let me introduce you to the others."

Ramsey introduced the other three lions. The first lion was Awassi. He was a spotted lion. The second lion was Aryeh. This lion had an ephod on its chest, a horn on his head, and the appearance of a normal lion. The third lion was Morino. This lion was gold and silver and had wings like an eagle. Alice greeted all the Yeshua lions and listened as they each gave her plenty of wisdom. Ramsey stood out as the leader of the lions. He spoke with Alice and had her follow him. They traveled to the border of hell and watched over it from above.

"It won't be long before the pit will become a lake," Ramsey said. "Take a good look at this area. You'll be very familiar with it in the future."

Alice wondered how this could be. "I didn't know that angels had business in hell," she said. "Most angels do not, but you are a Reaper. Have you not read the parable of the Sower? Your job it to gather both the wheat and tares. The wheat are to be gathered in the house of the Lord. The tares are to be bundled and placed here in hell. This is your purpose."

Ramsey changed the subject and gave Alice another burden.

"You must now name the spear given to you by the Lamb," Ramsey said. "This is a great honor. The only other angel given this honor was Ignas when he named Alypto. What will you name it?"

Alice spoke the first thought that popped in her head.

"Ichor," she said. "I shall name the blade Ichor."

Ramsey looked pleased.

"A fine choice. I have another assignment for you. The Lord of Host wants you to preach the everlasting gospel to the earth so that the scriptures may be fulfilled."

"When do I start?" she asked.

"Now, of course."

Alice took her place above the earth and preached the everlasting gospel. She addressed every nation, kindred, tongue, and people with a loud voice. She told the world to fear God and give him glory. For his judgment has come. She commanded men to worship him that made heaven, earth, the sea, and the fountains of waters. Alice wanted to enter the earth when she finished but was forbidden from doing so. She was told that all angels could not enter the earth until after the Great Tribulation.

Ifrit roamed the deserts of Israel searching for purpose. The burden of the depth Lord fell upon his shoulders now that Quintopolas was dead. However, he didn't want the power or the responsibility. A majestic throne appeared before him in the midst of the desert. It spoke with him and offered him guidance.

"You may call me Presbyteros," the throne said. "Come and sit upon me. I will give you wisdom and improve your speech."

Ifrit sat upon the throne and noticed his broken speech became eloquent. His army of demons approached him, demanding to know what to do next. They had free reign on the earth now that the angels were gone. It was all too easy. Ifrit shared the sentiment. He rested his head in the palm of his hand and maintained a bored posture.

He expected Simfer to give him guidance, but he was trapped in the temple. His guidance now came from the throne.

"It is time to summon the Scratchers, Ifrit," the throne said.

Ifrit became alarmed. The Scratchers were the most fearsome of all demons. These were hell's torture enforcers. Scratchers often attack the flesh, which cause skin rashes and itching. With this torment comes hallucinations and great fear. Ifrit recalled a situation where Scratchers caused a lost soul to see spiders coming out of his itching skin. This led him to cut off his arm with a saw. This was only one example of what Scratchers could do. For this reason, they were strictly forbidden from ever leaving hell. However, Ifrit now had the authority to release them. He summoned his two servants, Fish and Rook.

"Release the Scratchers and have them enter the earth," Ifrit said.

Rook gently tried to persuade Ifrit.

"Is that wise, Lord Ifrit? You are the grand Archdemon. There aren't enough shadows, spiders, scorpions, or sorrows mighty enough to contain the Scratchers."

Ifrit remained defiant and said, "These are my orders. I demand you follow them precisely. The throne commands it."

Fish glared at his partner and saw to it that Ifrit's orders were carried out.

"We will do this at once, Lord Ifrit," Fish said. "I must say that your speech is impeccable and marvelous."

The two demons entered hell and released the leader of the Scratchers. They carried him on a sort of stretcher and brought the demon before Ifrit. The demon was small, wrapped in a glowing hot iron chain, and wore a muzzle on its face. Fish and Rook removed the chains and fled far from the scene in fear. The demon faced Ifrit and refused to speak. Ifrit stood up straight on his throne and looked over the Scratcher. He ordered the demon to move, but it refused to budge. The throne then commanded the Scratcher to speak.

The demon responded, "I know that voice. Give us your command, and it shall be done."

Ifrit regained his composure and now had authority over the lead Scratcher.

"Tell me your name and how many Scratchers are there?"

"My name is Ronin. We are six legions in number."

"Take off your mask," Ifrit said. "I want to see you."

Everything about Ronin was meant to inflict terror in his victims. Under his muzzle was an Oni mask that covered his face. Ronin took off his mask and exposed his face. He had teeth like a shark that stretched from his ears to his nose. Ronin's eyes were pitch black. His hair was a burning red. Scratchers also were a type of hybrid. Most shared animal characteristics. Ronin was no different. He had ears like a dog and a tail like a fox. Ronin put back on his mask and muzzle on when Ifrit was satisfied. He gave his orders to Ronin and had him depart from his presence. Ronin pulled his spine from his back and held it up in the air. It was laced with strange glowing seeds. The seeds flew in the air and landed all over the earth. They sprouted into full grown scratchers upon impact. Their number in total was six legions.

News of Ifrits' rule over the earth didn't take long to reach Bastel. His command of Scratchers also worried her. Her dream of controlling Persephone was now over since Nala had left. She gathered all her Watchers together and made a decision.

"Looks like we're no longer the masters of this domain," Bastel said. "Let us leave the earth and return to the stars. Humanity is on the verge of destroying itself."

Bastel then turned her attention on Earth's new leader.

"I would rather burn the deaths of a thousand men than be led by a deformed cripple," Bastel said. "I don't care that he's my son."

The other Watchers all agreed. They got in their spaceships and flew back into the depths of space to meet with the other Watchers. Braccus welcomed Bastel back with great zeal.

"You performed admirably, Bastel. Hold your head up. This is not over."

Bastel gritted her teeth. She hated any kind of failure. Her pride was wounded but her resolve remained true.

Things on Earth continued to get worse. The world had now entered a permanent darkness, but it was very hot with a stench in the air. Fresh water was worth more than gold, and flock became a staple for the people of Pangaia. It was no longer only for the super-rich. All of this forced people to take the Animus. They worshiped Simeon hoping he would save them. They often said, "Who is like Simeon, and who can make war against him?"

This desperation also caused people to join Gaia's Crusade Army. Its numbers swelled to 175 million. Gaia had the people of Pangaia refer to her by her serpent name, Mamba. She used her power to grant SIGHT to all the people of Pangaia. Now everyone was able to see spirits and various demons. Fear gripped the people, and this funneled them into Sedah, a place where Gaia was the ultimate authority. Ronin and his Scratchers unleashed their fury upon the earth. They spent their time torturing citizens, members of the Conglomerate, and Pangaia's leaders. Ronin's fury was still not satisfied. He set his sights on Pangaia's favorite ritual. The demon made his way to Britain with plans of interrupting Pangaia's favorite game.

"It's ya boy, Pauly E. They say that Pangaia aint for me. Put those hands in the air and tell me what you want to see."

The crowd responded to the DJ in unison: "THREEDOM! One, two, three go!"

DJ Pauly E began the games like he always did. He tallied the votes, displayed them on screen, introduced the contestants, and began the game. His concentration was broken when he saw a young boy with an Oni mask on the stage.

"How did you get here, little guy?" DJ Pauly E said. "You must be lost."

The crowed began to fawn over him.

"Isn't he cute, Pangaia? Let's find his mother. What do you say Pangaia?"

Ronin took his mask off, which sent chills down Pangaia's collective spine. He isolated the DJ who was now crawling away on his back. Ronin crouched down and looked over his shoulder. A strange white cat floated in the air behind him.

"Tell me his crimes, Domino."

The hellcat listed the DJ's various crimes and offenses. Ronin seemed satisfied.

"I think I'll take him."

"A good choice indeed, Ronin," Domino said.

Ronin clapped his hands together. Millions of beetles filled the area and swarmed onto DJ Pauly E. They formed chains that bound him to the ground.

"These are called Scarabs," Ronin said. "Lesser demons that help me restrain my prey."

DJ Pauly E pleaded for his life. He looked to his right and saw that the feed was still live.

"Is it bract you want? I'll give you all the money in the world. Just name your price."

Ronin looked disappointed and said, "Why are grownups so dull?"

DJ Pauly E was panicked as the Scarabs slowly crawled up his arms. confused. "You don't look like a kid. What gives?"

Ronin scoffed. "You think I'm weak, don't' you?"

"Look, I just want to get out of here," DJ Pauly E said. "I'll tell everybody a secret. It's in Antarctica. We built new bodies for ourselves. Just let me leave so I can activate my vessel."

Ronin tilted his head sideways and said, "It's a bit too cold there for me. Do they have strong ones there?"

DJ Pauly E nodded quickly. "Only the strongest can have vessels."

Ronin snapped his fingers and rose to his feet. Thirty-two Flaming Arms emerged from the ground and grabbed the DJ, dragging him into Hell. The people of Pangaia watched in horror as the live feed cut to black.

Yessica's vehicle broke down a mile from the HAR4 base. She heard what sounded like her sister's voice on the radio. She thought was some sick joke. Yessica tried to fix the car but decided to walk to the base instead. She encountered multiple spirits as she walked the long road.

It was pitch black all around her. Not even the stars could be seen. Sounds of whispers, voices, and screams assaulted her, bringing about feelings of abandonment. She used this opportunity to dig deep and be honest with herself.

The two Churches gathered together to wed Joker and Ruth. Ruth was several months pregnant. This marriage was designed to bring the two faiths closer together. A symbol of unity. Joker had converted to the Baptist faith while Ruth was devout Catholic.

"Does anyone object to this marriage?" Pastor Josh asked. "Speak now or forever hold your peace."

A young woman burst through the doors. It was none other than Nala.

"Am I late?" Ruth nodded. "Yeah, a little."

The Church laughed together. However, their laughter would soon turn to mourning. A large group of Berserkers had followed Nala and pounced on their position. The berserkers killed and maimed dozens of Church members. The small number of survivors got in their vehicles and remembered Yessica's instructions. Their destination was the HAR4, base but they didn't know how to get there. They knew that they had to follow the Nexus star, but the pure darkness outside made this impossible.

Chapter Twenty-One

Flock to Battle

The final judgements continued on the earth. The second angel poured out his vial upon the sea, and it became as blood of a dead man. Every living soul died in the sea. Alice watched this judgement in the heavens with Awassi, one of the four Yeshua lions. The waters of the entire world became like blood. There was no longer any life in them. This included the Mediterranean Sea and the Bering Sea next to Alaska. Fishermen cast their nets, hoping the waters would provide something they could sell. However, they did so in vain. It was evident that this was a supernatural event, yet the people of Pangaia remained defiant. Repentance was not an option.

"How are people supposed to survive like this, Awassi?" Alice asked. "Plants can't grow, solar energy is gone, and people now have nothing to eat."

The lion displayed no signs of doubt, saying, "They have reaped what they have sown."

Alice worried about the world, but she worried about her sister and her church the most. She knew the judgments in the book of

Revelation would be harsh but not this harsh. Her faith was strong, but it was still being tested.

"How many judgements are left?" Alice asked.

"The judgments are in sevens. Seven Seals, Seven Trumpets, and Seven Vials. Therefore, there are five more judgments to go."

Awassi turned from Alice and began to roam away.

"I suggest you put on the whole armor of God," he said. "So you may be able to stand against the wiles of the devil. You are an angel, but you're still part human. I fear that the human part of you is still affected by him. You need to watch yourself Alice. This is no time to be at rest."

Ifrit sat bored upon his throne, though he had no intentions of leaving it. The throne gave him purpose, direction, and great authority. He sent his servant Fish to bring the horseman of Pestilence to him. It didn't take long for Fish to find him. The horseman approached the Archdemon with little expectation.

"You called, Ifrit?" said Ramiel

Ifrit decided not to confront the lack of respect.

"The throne has spoken, Ramiel," Ifrit said. "You are to take your sequence wings and form your ultimate attack."

"Whose authority decrees this? Does this throne speak for itself or are you playing the role of pawn yet again?"

Ifrit sat up straight and looked visibly annoyed.

"I am the Depth Lord. You will do as I say."

"I don't' care if you're God Almighty himself," Ramiel said. "Horseman only take orders from Simfer now. He's currently engrossed at the moment."

The throne shook and gave orders to Ifrit. Ifrit got off the throne and approached Ramiel. Ramiel was unable to move and became alarmed.

"What are you doing?" Ramiel asked.

Ifrit took the sequence wings and smashed the two spiked balls together. He put the weapon back in Ramiel's hand and commanded him to repeat his words: "Before the greatest dawn lies the darkest dusk."

The weapon exploded with energy that radiated throughout the world. A new disease was unleashed. It was known as Golem's disease and was the horseman of Pestilence's ultimate attack. This disease worked simply. It dehydrated the flesh of those infected. The flesh then would give the pleasant aroma of wild game or jerky, an irresistible delight for a starving world. Ifrit dismissed Ramiel and sat back on his throne. He was glad to have the former Watcher gone from his presence.

"Let me sit on my throne, you fools."

Simfer grew more agitated by the minute. His stature among men became more and more irrelevant with each moment wasted in the temple. He thought the One, Four, and Four owed it to him to sit on the throne his servants had fashioned. Dao ignored Simfer's demands. He was focused on preaching the gospel to the world. He had no idea how effective it would be, but he preached nonetheless. Eden kept to herself. She seemed preoccupied with other spirits. Simfer saw this and approached her.

"Dead men tell false tales, Eden. Why do you waste your time?"

Eden didn't want to speak with Simfer, but his company was better than no company. William was a shell of himself, and Dao certainly wasn't going to speak with her.

"I used to think that," Eden said. "There was a time when I despised my gift."

Simfer was intrigued. "When was that?"

"Many years ago, in Russia. I was raised in the Orthodox church. The church shunned me when my gift was discovered. I never forgot the church's cruelty, but I also never forgot God's love. I'm sure you understand."

Simfer folded his arms and stuck his nose in the air.

"How did I inherit such a lot?" Simfer said. "I'm being lectured to by a simple medium mortal. This is disgraceful. We're done talking."

People from all over Pangaia flocked to join Gaia's great Crusade army as it was the one of the last sources of food and fresh water. The Watchers had left, so the option to become a Tamer was gone. Golem's disease was now everywhere—another major reason people joined the Crusade. Joining the Crusade granted people special Jopa suits that claimed to protect them from the Cava and Golem viruses. Their effectiveness against the diseases were minor, but people clung to whatever hope they could get.

Gaia stood in her command center analyzing all the data. She cared little for humanity. Her focus was on finishing her army and freeing Simfer from the temple. A man entered the area and knelt before her. Gaia turned her attention toward him and smiled.

"You must be Tubal. The leader of my army," Gaia said. "It's a shame your father Meshech died at the hands of Navy SEALs. I would have preferred his leadership."

Tubal spoke confidently. "I will do my best to serve you, Mamba."

Gaia placed her hand upon Tubal's head and said, "Of this, I have no doubt."

Ronin and his hellcat, Domino, stood outside of a massive underground base in Antarctica. The weather was well below freezing, which bothered Ronin.

"Hurry up an find the entrance, Domino."

The hellcat wasn't affected by the weather. His appearance granted him protection. He had ears like panther, feet like a bear, a tail like a lion with its tassel ablaze, and thick white and black fur with a spot on his back. The supernatural cat patiently searched for signs of human life but failed to find any. Ronin grew tired of waiting and decided to destroy the base. Domino stopped him from acting rashly.

"Be calm, Ronin. We have strict orders not to destroy this place. The Lord of Host has need of it."

Ronin relented but remained impatient. "Just hurry up already."

Domino completed his objective and found a sign of life. He teleported himself and Ronin deep into the base. There were seemingly countless cryogen chambers. The one with life was before them.

"Here she is, Ronin," Domino said. "I present to you Dr. Malka Jasmine Nazarian, one of this place's many matriarchs. She's still alive but not for long."

Ronin noticed an empty chamber beside her.

"Look at this one," Ronin said. "It says it's for William Calig. Who is that guy?"

Domino curled into a ball while floating in the air. She purred and purred then spoke. "He is a nice juicy steak for you and catnip for me. I'll explain his crimes later."

Ronin walked the labyrinth while Domino pointed out the various crimes of those inside the cryo tubes. Domino then led them to a special chamber, separate from the rest. Ronin was fascinated by it.

"What is *Der Führer?*"

Domino held its breath then sighed. "I'm sorry, I can't tell you right now."

Ronin shifted his focus to a random woman and asked, "What about her? What are her crimes?"

Domino read them off. "Racketeering, alcoholism, grand larceny, emotional abuse, and abortion to name a few."

Ronin shook his head. "You may not know this, Domino, but my so-called mother aborted me."

Domino sat up straight. "I had no idea. That's terrible."

"Yeah, long ago an angel gave me the choice to either dwell with him or to serve the cup of wrath to the wicked as a Scratcher. I chose this path because I thought I was the only one that would have to go through something so cruel, but I was wrong. So many others have had to make the same choice I did."

Ronin paused and placed his hand on the cryo tube.

"My mother's still down there in case you were wondering," Ronin said.

Domino looked surprised but said, "So that's why number thirty-one is your favorite victim. She's your mother. It makes sense now."

Ronin gazed upon the peaceful looking woman and spoke to her. "Maybe I'll make you and my mother cell mates. Know this, woman. I serve the Lord's wrath to you not because of a choice you made. I do it because you refused to accept the choice already made for you. Now receive the pain of the unborn."

Ronin ripped the soul out of the woman's body and dragged her into the depths of hell. Thus, destroying any of her plans at immortality.

Yessica continued her journey to the HAR4 base. On the way, she saw an abandoned Mountain Base called fort Branson. It was now heavily guarded as millions of people tried to get in for access to food and water. Yessica even saw a few celebrities. One person caught her eye. It was Mark Zurg. Yessica knew this would be trouble for the Church. The proud agent was certainly still bitter about his defeat from the Watchers. Their teams were simply outmatched. It was a shame her close friend James Baker had to die under such circumstances.

Yessica took notice and found her way into the HAR4 base. She got on the comms and tried to warn the Church of this new development.

"Calling Camp Luther and Camp St. Peter. This is Yessica. Do not go to Fort Branson. It's overrun with desperate people. Turn right and meet me a mile up the road."

Yessica hoped her message would go through. She hadn't eaten in days, but she felt fine. It was at this moment when she discovered she didn't need to eat.

When she arrived at HAR4 base, she got to work. She used her wits and found a secret area below the HAR4 base. The area was massive.

It stretched miles beneath the ground. Her mind was immediately brought back to Israel many years ago and the last thing she saw before William made an attempt on her life.

"This must be connected to the Harbinger gate!" She screamed with joy.

The only problem was the fact that she was clueless on how to operate it. The data available to her suggested this portal did in fact link with the gate in Israel. Entering an unknown portal was a gamble, but it was one she had to take. There was no turning back. She began the complicated process of activating it immediately.

The two Churches stopped to regather and regroup. Pastor Josh was the primary leader, while Joseph led the Catholic Church now that Father Nolan had passed. He didn't do the duties of a priest such as Confession or the distribution of the Eucharist. He acted as more of an educator for the fifty-four people who survived the attack at the wedding, which some called the Blood Union. Pastor Josh knew they were likely all that was left of the Church in the entire world. He called the survivors the Last Sheep.

"I think we should head north more, Pastor Josh," Joseph said. "We can't navigate using stars, but I think my compass will work if we get closer to the poles."

It was a good idea. Pastor Josh tried to speak but became quiet when he heard a familiar voice on the radio. It was none other than Yessica, but the signal was broken. They only heard "Go to Fort Branson." A trail of people headed north so they figured that's where they needed to go.

Pastor Josh gathered the Last Sheep and headed for Fort Branson. They were dismayed when they got there. The place was a scene of desperation. People tried to force their way onto the base. Many were killed by the soldiers. It was chaotic, especially with Zohar agents about. This meant that they would be hunted and killed should they discover they were from the church. Joseph checked his compass. It began to move.

"We should head northeast," Joseph said. "There's bound to be some shelter up there."

Pastor Josh agreed and led the Last Sheep northeast. They found an abandoned logging camp and decided to settle in.

Nala noticed people giving her dreadful looks. They avoided her like a disease. The only one that accepted her company was Richard.

"Why does everyone hate me?" Nala said. "I didn't know that Berserkers were following me."

"I'm not sure, but you did okay," Richard said. "I think everyone's just worried."

Nala thanked Richard but failed to see his perspective.

"It's okay," Nala said. "I know when I'm not wanted. Everyone thinks I some kind of witch."

Richard changed the subject. "What was it like being a Tamer and meeting Bastel?"

"When I became a Tamer, Bastel welcomed me like a daughter. The first thing she said to me was 'what took you so long.' I really needed to hear that. I've been so used to rejection that any sort of acceptance was strange for me. I didn't know how to handle it. It became the drug I needed."

"Wow, that's deep," Richard said. "You've changed a lot since you left, but in a good way. You're a lot stronger now."

"Everyone keeps telling me how strong I am. I'm sick of it. I want to be weak again. I want no part of this. Power can be a curse, you know."

A week passed, but the Last Sheep remained strong. They were able to feed off of plants and berries, but supplies didn't last long. Eventually they became very hungry. Joker began to isolate himself from the others. Ruth noticed this and tried to comfort him. Joker became gaunter by the day. One day he spoke with Ruth while ill. His hands shook.

"What's wrong, babe?" Ruth asked. "Your hands only shake when you get nervous."

"Who won the zombie war?" Joker asked.

But Ruth was in no mood for jokes.

"Can't you be serious for one second," she said. "I think you have Golem's disease. I have to hide you or the others will eat you."

Joker repeated the joke. "Who won the zombie war?"

"All right, I don't know who did."

"Nobody, it was dead even."

Ruth slapped Joker's shoulder.

"That's not funny, but I'm glad to have your cheesy jokes back."

Joker's flesh began to rapidly dehydrate. It created a tasty aroma to the rest of the camp. Ruth tried take Joker away, but the others surrounded them. Ruth set Joker on the ground and pulled out a knife.

"Anybody who touches my husband dies," she said. "He's not food; he's one of us."

Tears flowed down Ruth face as she fended off the hungry sheep. They resisted for a long as they could, but they eventually caved in and ate what was left of Joker. Ruth furiously cut as many people as she could but was eventually forced to flee into the woods.

The Last Sheep now had an appetite for flesh. The Last Sheep prayed and fasted afterward, but nothing could erase their past actions. One of their own was erased by their own hands. They hoped something like this would never happen again. Richard's father Paul was appalled at what happened. He hungered as well but resisted eating any human flesh. He immediately gathered his things, took his son Richard, and left the group altogether. He headed for Fort Branson hoping for a fresh start and a better solution for his hunger.

Chapter Twenty-Two

7 Lights

The third angel poured out his vial upon the rivers and fountains of waters, and they became blood. The angel of the waters said, "Thou art righteous, O Lord, which art, and was, and shall be. Because thou has judged thus. For they have shed the blood of saints and prophets, and thou hast given them blood to drink, for they are worthy."

All drinking water on the earth was poisoned after this judgment. This drove people either to Christ or to the antichrist Animus mark. The only certainty was that humanity's days were severely numbered. The fight for survival continued.

Alice recognized that this judgment was a turning point. She also learned that the preaching she shared was on a loop around the world. She had no idea how many people she reached, but she knew the number was substantial. Ramsey waited close by as she looked down upon a suffering earth.

"What is on your mind?" he asked.

Alice took a break from watching the suffering and turned toward Ramsey.

"What makes these people different from those who lived in the past?" Alice asked. "What could they have possibly have done to deserve this?"

Ramsey spoke calmly. "To everything there is a season, and a time to every purpose under the heaven. The sins of this generation are not greater or lesser than those of past generations. They simply serve a different purpose. Do not agonize about their suffering. For it is written. My grace is sufficient for thee. The Lord has given them all they need to make the right choice."

Alice thanked Ramsey for his explanation. She felt a little better about heavenly judgment. However, she still had other questions.

"What is the origin of Chaos? Where did it come from?"

"That is not for you to know," Ramsey said. "Yet you should know this. Chaos is the nature of demons. Order is the nature of angels. The world is suffering because they are reaping the Chaos they have sown over the millennia. The origin of Chaos is irrelevant."

Alice had other questions, which Ramsey answered to the best of his ability. She learned that things were more complicated than they appeared. Alice struggled to comprehend heavy topics, even as an angel. There was so much to learn and so much left to do. Alice poured herself into her work and hoped for the best. There was nothing she could do but watch and wait.

Gaia ordered her general Tubal to prepare her troops for war. The army was now complete. It was composed of over two hundred million men. Most of the men had enhancements that made them more machine than men. They cared little about the fate of the world. The only thing they cared about was their own survival. Provision was the bait, and they were all hooked on it. Gaia wasn't worried about their loyalty. She was confident that she could control anything and any new development. The Great Crusade army was stationed in Turkey. Just like the previous great army Persephone managed. Gaia searched her troops for any deficiencies and found none. She did a final analysis and gave the order for the Great Crusade army to invade Israel. The first assignment was to free Simfer out of the Jerusalem temple.

Yessica worked tirelessly on the Harbinger gate but was getting nowhere. It was too complex, and she had no sufficient power source to get it to work. She heard a loud noise in the area. Fear crept upon her, for she was no longer alone. Yessica took her pistol and slowly made her way up to confront the threat. She turned the corner and shoved her pistol into the face of the intruder. Yessica sighed and relaxed when she saw his face.

"What are you doing here Westin? I could have killed you."

Westin was in his usual cheery mood.

"I know that you would never harm me, Yessica. In this I have no doubt."

Yessica was annoyed and said, "I thought I told you to stay with the camps. What gives?"

Westin explained to Yessica what happened. He talked about the blood union, Nala's return, and even Joker's passing. Yessica felt guilty about Joker and Nala. She fell to the floor and gripped her heart. However, she knew there was nothing she could do. She decided to stand up and pour herself back into her work.

"I've got work to do," Yessica said. "Are you going to help me or not?"

Weston took the Cobber off his wrist and gave it to Yessica.

"What's this?" Yessica asked.

"It's an enhanced Cobber made by Nala just for you. I tried to give it to you earlier but you were busy. So here you are."

Yessica took the Cobber and placed it on her wrist. It had a golden shine to it and was way more advanced than she ever could imagine. It took her a while to get the hang of it, but she eventually used it to aid in her efforts to activate the Harbinger gate. Westin also helped with analyzing all the data. They both worked for hours, but they were no closer to activating the portal. Yessica held up her Cobber and noticed something was amiss.

"What is this light coming from my Cobber?" Yessica asked.

Westin was also captivated by the light.

"Try pressing it," he said.

Yessica remained cautious, saying, "Don't be a goofball. It could be trap. Use that fancy metal brain of yours and analyze it."

Westin analyzed the strange light, which grew bigger and bigger.

"Take off the Cobber and throw it away from you," Westin said. "I'm detecting multiple entities approaching."

Yessica tossed the Cobber on the Harbinger gate and covered her eyes from the blinding light. The Harbinger gate activated and hummed with power. The light faded, and there were now seven children standing where the Cobber was. Yessica slowly approached them.

"Who are you, and how did you get here?" Yessica asked.

Six of the children remained quiet, but one of them spoke.

"My name is Cloud, and these are my brothers and sisters. You may call us Little Lights. We found your distress beacon and followed it here."

"My distress beacon?"

"Yes, you said the following: This is a message for both young and old. For posterity and antiquity. My name is Yessica Cali Hoffman. I am a Lieutenant Commander in the US Navy. Welcome to the last day of America."

Yessica relaxed.

"That wasn't a distress beacon," she said. "But I'm glad you got the message. So, I'm guessing you want to help."

Cloud looked to be about Richard and Nala's age. He certainly didn't lack confidence. He appeared much wiser than he should be at his age.

"Yes, of course we want to help," Cloud said. "Gonga told us to help you all."

Yessica raised an eyebrow. "Who is Gonga?"

"Gonga means leader in our tongue. It translates to King in your tongue. He is the one that gave us the title of Little Lights."

"Where is this Gonga now, and where are you from exactly?"

"I'm sorry but we haven't seen Gonga in a long time," Cloud said. "He actually raised us. We come from a planet known as Tanas. It orbits the farthest and dimmest star in the universe. This is where the Watchers come from as well."

Cloud looked at the Cobber on the ground and said, "Without that gizmo it would have been impossible to reach you."

He picked up the Cobber and tossed it to Yessica.

"What do you call this thing? Whoever made it is a genius."

"It's called a Cobber. A dear friend of mine named Nala upgraded it. You remind me of her. You look to be about her age."

Cloud laughed.

"That's impossible. We're a lot older than we look. We're actually Bastel's grandchildren. Where is she by the way? She must be close."

Yessica explained that the Watchers left the earth not long ago. The Little Lights didn't seem concerned at all. In fact, they welcomed Bastel's absence.

"It's better this way I think," Cloud ask. Then he conferred with his family and asked another question. "What's a Navy SEAL? Is that an animal or a marine biologist?"

Yessica explained to the Little Lights that SEALs were elite warriors. Cloud and the others were captivated.

"Can you teach us how to fight? That would be boca!" Cloud said.

"You know, *boca* means mouth in Spanish. I think the name suits you. From now you are La boca Cloud."

Yessica was no fan of children, but she enjoyed the company of the Little Lights. However, time was short. She needed to get to Israel and fast.

"The Harbinger gate is powered up. How do I use it?" Yessica asked.

"It's a simple process," Cloud said. "You start with the concept of relativity and end with the dispersal of quantum entanglement. Press this button and you will descend into the lowest level. From there, your body will dematerialize and enter a sort of stasis. Your genetic profile will be transferred through space and time and will materialize at the new destination. It's quite simple actually."

Yessica raised her eyebrow suspiciously. "Spare me the lecture and press the button, Professor Boca. I've got places to go."

Chapter Twenty-Three

Bellicose Avenger

The fourth angel poured his vial upon the sun. Power was given unto him to scorch men with fire. The men of the earth were scorched with great heat and blasphemed the name of God. It was he who had power over these plagues. Humanity repented not and refused to give him glory.

Alice watched as solar flares punished the men of the earth. There were only four in total, but these solar flares activated a parasite in one's skin, causing them to itch and scratch with heat. This led to many deaths. The Yeshua lion Morino saw Alice gazing at the scene on earth and approached her.

"Don't worry Alice," Morino said. "It will all be over soon."

Alice didn't share his optimism.

"I've never seen such suffering," Alice said. "It's too much to take in."

"Have peace and be still. Don't let your emotions guide. You'll fall if you do."

Alice changed the subject, saying, "I have a question for you. Why do fallen angels use water as a weapon while normal angels use fire?"

Morino answered the complicated question with confidence.

"Fire consumes things in the earth. It is the ideal weapon of heaven. This is why the fallen have no ability to harness it. They are part of the earth. Water is different. It doesn't consume things immediately. It consumes things slowly over time. This makes it safe for them to wield. Bodies bound to earth are made of still waters. They are not meant to be boiled or frozen. Bodies are made to have balance. To not experience extremes. Does that make sense?"

Alice scratched her head and said, "So, it sounds like water is the cornerstone of life on earth. However, it's not the source of life on earth."

"Yes, that's exactly right, Alice. Water cannot extinguish heaven's fire. The fallen have no answer for it. This is why their eternal punishment will be in the lake of fire. A place prepared for the devil and his angels."

Alice had no further questions. She went back to work and continued to monitor the suffering on the earth.

Gaia's Great Crusade army marched into Israel. They were led by general Tubal. Their mission was to reach Jerusalem and free Simfer. They were surprised when they crossed over into Israel from Turkey with no resistance whatsoever. They knew the human forces were busy with the plagues, but they expected supernatural forces to give them grief. This would happen a moment later when a strange voice entered into general Tubal's head.

"What are you doing here, Tubal? Turn around and head back."

Tubal remained defiant and said, "I will not cower to a rouge spirit."

"I am no rouge. Take heed, Tubal. I shall warn you about the danger you face."

Tubal crossed his arms and made himself comfortable.

"I'm listening," Tubal said.

"Simeon is no longer in control of his body. It has been taken over by the devil. He goes by the name Simfer now. That's not all. Simfer is surrounded by holy warriors that prevent him from leaving. Do you really want to throw your life away to save the devil? Do you desire destruction that much?"

Tubal thought deeply for a moment and decided what to do.

"I won't be a part of the Crusade anymore," Tubal said. "Gaia will have to find a new general."

Tubal waited for his forces to set up camp. He then made his way out of the camp and into the fields. Tubal thought he was home free, but then a long blade pierced through his belly, killing him instantly.

Gaia took back her sword and said, "I knew I couldn't count on you Tubal. Very well, I will lead my army myself."

Richard and his father, Paul, sat at a table in Fort Branson. By some miracle they made it in. Paul was glad to be there, but Richard wanted to go back.

"Eat your food, Richard. I'm not going to tell you again."

"Something isn't right about this place," Richard said.

Paul looked around the large area. It was crowded but Paul enjoyed the presence of others.

"This is civilization, my boy. Look around you. We are here for a reason."

A man approached the two of them and said, "Sorry to interrupt, but the boss wants to see you two."

Richard and Paul got up and followed the man. They entered an office where a man with red curly hair sat on a luxurious black leather chair.

"Welcome, Richard and Paul. I am Mark Zurg, the Director of Zohar."

Richard had an epiphany.

"You're the reason we got into this base," Paul said. "It wasn't a miracle."

Zurg smiled. "He's a clever one, isn't he?"

Zurg signaled his men to leave the room. He spoke again when they left the area.

"I cannot stand prying eyes and ears, but I digress," Zurg said. "Let me explain why you're here and not outside getting trampled on. I want what you want. The Church must be destroyed completely. There aren't many savages left. I must finish what I started. Words cannot express the gravity of this import mission. The death of James must be avenged. Know this, man cannot evolve until we dissolve archaic concepts such as religion. Don't you agree?"

Richard shook his head, but Paul agreed with Zurg.

"What do you need us to do, Director?"

Zurg took out an Animus mark and handed it to Paul.

"Eat it now," Zurg said.

Richard pleaded with his father, saying, "Don't take the mark, Dad."

But Paul placed it in his mouth and swallowed.

"Don't worry, son. I'm going to be free of pain." Paul then looked at Zurg and said, "Take care of my boy, please."

Zurg nodded his head and said, "I will look after him."

Paul closed his eyes and woke up in Sedah. He was in a lush jungle surrounded by impressive animals. He roamed the jungle for hours. This life seemed too good to be true. Suddenly a man resembling Simeon appeared.

"Lord Simeon," Paul said. "I have finally seen the light. Embrace me."

The Simeon image walked up to Paul, embraced him, and then whispered into his ear, "You didn't really think you would be a guest of honor here, did you?"

He grabbed Paul's head with his hands and dragged him into a virtual torture chamber where he could not speak nor hear. All he felt was continual pain.

Richard desperately tried to get his father to wake up. Zurg brought his men into the office and escorted Paul away. Richard tried to fight but was no match for the Zohar agents.

"What do you want from me?" Richard asked.

"You are a very lucky boy. You're too young for the Animus, but you know where the rest of the Church is. Guess what? You're going to take me there. They cannot be that much in number. Give me names and numbers now!"

Yessica slowly descended into the depths of the Harbinger gate. The markers indicated she was three miles into the earth. Cloud and his family knew that their time with Yessica might be short. They wanted to learn as much about her as possible. Yessica looked distracted and questioned the Little Lights when they continued to stare at her.

"What is it? Spit it out now."

Cloud used his ability to infiltrate Yessica's Cobber. A virtual three-dimensional world appeared around her.

"What did you do, Cloud? Why are we at my old high school?" Yessica said.

Cloud tried to calm her nerves.

"It's okay," Cloud said. "You're safe. We're still descending toward the Harbinger gate. We just want to learn more about you. This digital world is called an Archive. It's tied to your memories and allows us to see what makes you special. Don't fight it. Use the Cobber like you would a remote control. You can forward, rewind, and even skip to the next chapter."

Yessica analyzed the memory. She watched herself sitting in the gymnasium and listening to a young handsome lieutenant in the Navy. He glanced at the young Yessica often. He even pointed her out and said that it was her destiny to be part of the Navy. They even had a brief conversation afterward.

"Who was that guy?" Cloud asked.

"That man became Admiral Freddie Samson," Yessica said. "A great leader and the bane of my exitance. I think we've seen enough here. Let's move on."

The next Archive dealt with her time becoming a Navy Seal. The Little Lights were fascinated with warriors. They were very impressed with Yessica achievements. However, seeing herself in this light only brought back painful memories. It only made her mourn her fallen comrades.

"We'll do one more, and then we're finished," Yessica said.

The Little Lights whined and fussed but agreed. Yessica forwarded ahead and found herself in a desert. A military base stood in the distance.

"What's this about?" Cloud asked.

"We're in Iran," Yessica said. "To be specific, we're in Tehran. I got separated from my men and wound up here. I had nothing but a combat knife in my mouth. There were over thirty well-armed guards at this facility. I ended up taking most of them out. A very important leader was also here. I killed him and earned my title. It was here that I became the Terror of Tehran."

Cloud and the other Lights watched in awe as Yessica infiltrated the military base and defeated her foes. Yessica ended the Archive when the content became very graphic.

Cloud whined. "We're not kids you know. We can handle a little violence."

Yessica scoffed and said, "I have the Archive remote. That makes me the grown up."

Cloud placed his hand upon Yessica's Cobber.

"Why are you grabbing my arm, kid?" Yessica said.

"We've seen your memories now it's our turn to show you some of ours. Hold still, this may sting a little."

Golem's disease wreaked havoc on the Last Sheep. They were only twenty-four in number now. A miracle happened when they were at their most dire. Vegetable plants grew in darkness around their camp—enough to sustain them for years. The Church praised the Lord for his glorious provision. Days were dark, but a feeling that they would get brighter grew among them. New hope entered the Last Sheep, but they still faced danger. Many who were demon-possessed found their way to them. They tried to harm the sheep but were unable to. The Last Sheep began to cast out demons and saw their numbers climb. Another miracle happened. Nala was no longer a Tamer. She was deaf and lame again. This gave hope to the others. They now believed the coming of the Lord was nigh.

Chapter Twenty-Four

Final Call

The fifth angel poured out his vial upon the seat of the beast. His kingdom was full of darkness, and they gnawed their tongues for pain. They blasphemed the God of heaven because of their pains, sores, and did not repented of their deeds.

A vehicle full of Zohar agents sped through the frozen tundra of Alaska. Richard was held captive in the backseat. He was not bound, but two guns were trained on him at all times. Zurg was growing tired of all the traveling. They had been driving for hours, and there was still no sign of the Church.

"I'm going to ask you one more time, boy," Zurg said. "Where is the Church?"

Richard showed no signs of fear. He continued to act as if he were only guessing.

"They could be south of here," Richard said. "I think the camp is that way."

Zurg ordered his driver to stop, saying, "Pull over here."

He got out the vehicle and placed his pistol on Richard's forehead.

"No more games. If you don't give me an answer, you will die here alone in the cold. There will be no Heaven or Hell. You will rot here for eternity."

Zurg took the pistol off safety and cocked the weapon. Richard was afraid. He saw the determination in Zurg's eyes. This time he was serious.

"Why can't you use your satellites or something?" Richard said. "I'm no expert tracker."

Zurg took the pistol off his forehead and walked around in circles.

"Fine," Zurg said. "I'm going to entertain the thought since you savages aren't known for your intellect. Look around you, boy. We're in perpetual darkness. How is a satellite supposed to see anything on the earth? It's useless. It reminds me of you. Now start talking!"

Zurg rushed toward Richard with fury. Richard saw his brief life flash before his eyes. He was ready to die for his faith and his friends. Still the process was dreadful for him. He closed his eyes and waited to feel the cold steel pressed upon his forehead. To his surprise, this didn't happen. Zurg and the other men dropped their weapons and began chewing and gnawing at their tongues. Blood poured out their mouths as they grabbed their heads in pain. They began to ramble and curse God and everything in heaven. The pain subsided after thirty minutes, but they were all unable to speak. Their tongues were inflamed, and they had no medication to subdue the inflammation. Zurg had to use his Cobber to speak. His men did the same. They somehow synched their minds to their Cobber's and spoke through their machines. However, they were unable to carry their weapons.

One hand was on their Cobber, while the other held their heads. Zurg wasted no time ordering his men.

"Open the box, and put him inside it," Zurg said.

The men took the large box out of the trunk and placed it on the ground. Inside the large box was a small device.

"What is that?" Richard asked, more curious than afraid.

"That is a Jopa portable nuclear device," Zurg said. "The same one that started the Proxy Wars. However, this one is rigged to blow. I'm going to open the canister and pour uranium down your throat since you're so stubborn. I'm going to enjoy watching you squirm."

Richard panicked. He could deceive no longer.

"Okay, I'll tell you where they are," Richard said. "Don't torture me. They're by a logging camp north of Fort Branson."

Furious, Zurg said, "We've been driving for hours when all we had to do was walk a couple of miles. Put him in the box. I've changed my mind."

The agents put Richard inside the box with the device and sealed it shut. Richard pounded on the box, but no sound could be heard from the outside.

Gaia supposedly had every tool she needed at her disposal. She had records of every tactic ever devised by the world's greatest generals. Her army never hungered or thirsted. Her arsenal could destroy the world several times over. What she lacked was a clear enemy. She now knew that the battle would not be physical. It would be spiritual. Gaia simply could not predict her enemy's next move. She had two options. She could either continue to march into Jerusalem to free Simfer or stand by and wait for her enemy to make the first move. Both options seemed dreadful, but she had to choose. She had business with the Dragon and needed him to bolster her army. It would be the weapon she needed. Gaia ordered her men to march toward the capital city of Jerusalem. The plan was to surround the city and force the hand of heaven. They were unlikely to surrender Simfer, but she figured she could destroy the precious temple if they refused.

Yessica was now about halfway to the surface of the Harbinger gate. The marker indicated she was six miles beneath the earth. Cloud took her hand, and she found herself inside a foreign living memory.

"Where am I?" Yessica asked.

Cloud and the others looked around with sorrow.

"This is a memory of one of our mothers," Cloud said. "We're in the great kingdom of Neothia. I believe your people know these days as the Days of Noah. This is right before the great flood."

Yessica noticed a very beautiful woman surrounded by seven other women with babies in their arms. They were in some sort of temple. Chaos was all around. Buildings burned and people outside were in the midst of a warzone.

"Who is that and what are they doing?" Yessica asked.

"Our mothers are using us. They believed that if they dedicated us to the gods then their kingdom would be spared. Yesterday the people felt water fall from the sky which sent Neothia into a panic. Thankfully their plan failed. You know how this story ends." Yessica sighed. "The flood came and destroyed Neothia."

"I'm not watching this," Yessica said. "It's borderline Satanic"

Yessica reached for her Cobber but stopped when she saw what looked like an angel. She was captivated by it. It was even more beautiful than Tyra.

"Who is that?" Yessica asked.

Cloud growled and said, "That is Gaia, but we don't know her real name. She's one of the real threats."

"What do you mean by one of the real threats. Who else is there?" Yessica asked.

"I'll explain it this way," Cloud said. "You kept a board in your room. It had pictures and names. I think you called it a conspiracy board."

"I see where you're going with this," Yessica said. "So, you know she's bad, but you don't know if she's leading the others. There are others on the board that you don't' know about. Am I getting warmer?"

"Yes," Cloud said excitedly. "That's exactly what I meant. We only know about this moment. We don't have any other memories. Just this one."

Yessica wondered and said, "I'm not a believer in any of this, but I think you're missing the obvious suspect."

Cloud looked at the others and asked, "Who is this suspect?"

Yessica pointed to the fire.

"We call him Satan, but he's also known as the devil."

"The Who?"

Yessica had no desire to explain.

"Just trust me on this, kid. The story gets a lot deeper."

Yessica navigated her Cobber and shut down the Archive.

"I don't need to watch anymore," Yessica said. "Listen to me, all of you. There is nothing you could have done. You were abused by terrible people. I know they were your mothers, but they didn't love you. They only cared about themselves. I'm not going to let anything happen to you. Stick with me, and we'll get through this. I'll find a place for you somewhere. You don't have to be victims for the rest of your lives. Do you hear me?"

The Little Lights looked at each other and agreed. Yessica was shocked when they all rushed to hug her. It had been a long time since Yessica had felt something deep on an emotional level. She now had a new mission. Stopping Simeon was her primary goal but helping the Little Lights seemed more important. This mission was now personal. She was no fan of children, but she knew they deserved better.

"I'm calling all in the darkness." Pastor Josh preached. "Jesus can cleanse you of your whatever ails you. Just come."

Pastor Josh was nearly out of breath but continued to preach anyway. Millions of people showed up and many were baptized. All heard the gospel and were willing to give their lives to Christ.

When Zurg and his agents arrived, they saw the masses of people. He turned to his men and said, "I thought the boy said there were only twenty-four of them. Look at all these people."

He knew he had to be clever if he were to succeed. Zurg devised a new plan and executed it immediately. Zurg made his way through the masses and fell on his knees before Pastor Josh.

"Save my soul, pastor," Zurg said. "I'm a sinner in need of cleansing."

"What is your name, sir?"

"My name is Mark."

Pastor Josh quieted the crowd.

"Mark, do you know that God is holy? This means he is set apart from everything. Have you ever done something wrong or evil? It doesn't matter how small it is."

Mark tried not to roll his eyes as he said, "Yes, pastor, I'm a bad man. I've stolen, lied, and even killed."

"I hear you, Mark. The truth is we've all fallen short of God's standard of holiness. The Bible says all have sinned and fallen short of the glory of God. You're not alone. We all need a savior. That is why we must give our lives to Jesus Christ. He is the only one who can help us and lead us on the path to salvation. Reunification with God Almighty. Are you ready to make that commitment today in front of everybody here? The Bible says if you confess Jesus before men, he will confess you before his Father in heaven."

Zurg became alarmed but went about his plan.

"I am not ready now, pastor. For I'm unworthy of love. I work for Jopa. They gave me lots of food."

He turned and pointed at a large mysterious box.

"It's right over there, pastor. Please feed the people and know that Jopa cares for the flock."

Pastor Josh prayed for Mark. Tears fell down Pastor Josh's face as he dismissed him.

"Thank you, Mark. Just know that you don't have forever to be reconciled to God. The clock stops when you heart drops. Be safe Mark. I thank God that he sent you here today and gave us all these generous gifts."

Zurg's agents opened the mysterious box and began to hand out food to the masses. Nala was nearby in a makeshift wheelchair. She could tell that something wasn't right.

Why would Jopa ever help us? she thought. Nala made her way closer to the box and smelled a strange chemical. The smell was familiar. She knew it had deadly intentions. It was a chemical used in bomb-making. Her time with her NASA engineer father was short but he taught her many things. One of those things was the principles of rocket science. Nala had developed a keen eye and nose for various explosives. Nala turned and raced toward Pastor Josh to warn him, but her momentum was suddenly stopped. A woman held her hand over Nala's mouth and put a pistol to Nala's head. It was none other than Ruth. She had returned for revenge.

"Be a good girl and keep quiet," Ruth said. "I don't want to hurt you. You were the only one who didn't eat my husband. I'm here for Josh and the others."

Ruth bound Nala's hands together so she couldn't sign. She guided her hostage toward Pastor Josh. He stopped his sermon when he saw Nala in danger.

"Ruth, what are you doing?" Pastor Josh said. "Release Nala at once. She's just a child."

Ruth continued to hold Nala and her mouth captive.

"Just a child?" Ruth said. "Do children stand by and watch the adults eat other human beings? How dare you call yourself a pastor. You're a wolf! A killer!"

The people turned their attention to them. Zurg and his agents saw this as an opportunity and left the area with their vehicle. The bomb inside the box would explode soon.

Pastor Josh held up his hand and said, "I confess it before God and you all. I allowed one of my own to be devoured. I'm so sorry for what happened, Ruth, but Joker wasn't the only one. There were others after you left. As you can see only a handful of us made it out alive. If you want revenge, I won't stop you. Take me. Just let Nala go."

Ruth felt shame for what she had done. Her mouth quivered as she gently shook her head from side to side. She unbound Nala, fell to her knees, and wept.

"I lost the baby," Ruth said, overcome with emotion.

Her cries of pain were met with love.

"King David also lost a child long ago," Pastor Josh said. "He declared that one day he would go to be with him and that the child would never return here on earth. He would never experience pain again. You see, Ruth, there is hope that you will see your child again. Do not worry. The Lord will turn your pain into a miracle."

Pastor Josh embraced Ruth. It was as if they had met for the first time. The past had been forgiven. They sought peace with the future. Nala shifted the focus of Pastor Josh and began to sign him. He decoded her message and went into action.

"Clear a path," Pastor Josh said. "There is something in that box."

Pastor Josh came to the box and uncovered a secret panel. Richard was found gagged and sitting atop a small device and a timer with less than three minutes remaining. Pastor Josh didn't know what to do.

"I guess this is it," Pastor Josh said. "We're at the end of the road, Church."

A familiar voice begged to differ.

"There still looks like plenty of road left to me."

Chapter Twenty-Five

Transitions

The sixth angel poured out his vial upon the great river Euphrates, and the water dried up, so that the kings of the east might be prepared. Then three unclean spirits like frogs came out of the mouth of the Dragon, the mouth of the beast, and out of the mouth of the false prophet. They were the spirits of devils, working miracles, which go forth unto the kings of the earth and of the whole world to gather them to the battle of that great day of God Almighty. Behold, he comes as a thief. Blessed is he that watches and keeps his garments. Unless they walk naked and see his shame. He gathered them together into a place called in the Hebrew tongue called Armageddon.

The drying up of the great river Euphrates was seen as a miracle done by Simeon to the world. Credit was also given to William. It proved to the masses that Simeon continued to have god-like qualities despite the calamities they faced. The reality was that Simeon had nothing to do with this miracle. He was simply a host to the virus of the Dragon. Together they were bound by the 144,000 in the temple with William. They had no power or control over anything. The time had come for them to be kicked out of the temple. Dao gave his judgment and had the others escort the Dragon, beast, and false prophet out of the temple.

"Your time on the earth is almost finished," Dao said. "You sought to sit upon this throne, but you failed to succeed. You are all cursed. Depart from this holy place, and know that you shall never conquer the ways of the Almighty."

The One, Four, and Four escorted Simfer and William out of Jerusalem and into the desert before the throne of Ifrit.

Simfer thought this was all a joke. He mocked Ifrit sitting upon the great throne.

"Who said that you could sit in a position of authority over me, demon?" Simfer said. "Get off that throne at once and follow me. We have work to do."

Ifrit began to doubt himself. However, Ifrit remained on the throne.

"The throne demands that you stay here," said Ifrit.

Insulted, Simfer said, "Am I to take orders from a chair? You work for me, Ifrit. Get off that throne now!"

Ifrit stood up but was quickly forced back onto the throne. Gaia appeared to them all amid their discussion and rushed to the Simfer's side.

"I've finally found you," Gaia said. "Come with me. Our army is heading here as we speak."

Simfer folded his arms in defiance and said, "There is no need to march my army here. I order you to take the army north to Megiddo. That is where the final battle will be. Therefore, that is where you will be."

Gaia reluctantly followed Simfer's lead.

"It shall be done," she said. "I just thought that we could…"

Simfer became terse, saying, "You thought that we would what? That we would become like lovers and run away to start again. Don't be foolish. I have no desire for your dreams or your lies. Do as you are told and depart from here now! Take my slave with you."

Gaia felt wounded but did as she was ordered. She returned to the Crusade Army with William and had them head for Megiddo.

Eden, however, remained inside the temple.

"What is it you desire Eden? Speak now," Dao said.

Eden humbly made her request known. "I wish to be with the last of my people. I hear that they call themselves the Last Sheep. That is where I desire to be."

"You are a wise one, Eden," Dao said, signaling two of his sentries to him. "Escort Eden to the Lost Sheep immediately. There isn't much time left."

Zurg and his agents sped away in their vehicle. They needed to be clear of the blast radius. They only had one minute to spare.

"Drive faster, you idiot, or we won't make it."

Zurg took control and increased the velocity. A man swooped onto the hood of the vehicle as they drove. He had the nuclear bomb in his hand. Zurg recognized him immediately.

"Impossible! You're just a homeless nobody," Zurg said.

The man said, "My name is Chester, and I have a home. Problem is that you'll never get to see it."

Chester threw the bomb into the vehicle, grabbed the vehicle with his hands and threw it into space. The bomb detonated silently in the cosmos.

Richard was welcomed back by the others. They were no longer in danger, and there was much work to be done. People, including Nala, Richard, and Ruth, clamored to be baptized. Ruth's sorrow was met with overwhelming love, and she welcomed the others to join her as she was baptized. Nala and Richard followed after her. Eden appeared from nowhere and was also baptized. This cycle continued and people continued to flock to Lake Hudor, the only lake that still had fresh water. It was the same lake where Alice's body was buried.

Richard marveled at all the people gathered at the lake. He was soaking wet, but he didn't feel the cold on his skin. He felt like he was on another plain of exitance. He was at a peace beyond all understanding, especially with Nala next to him. They noticed a certain individual among the crowd with a fierce mask and a flaming tail next to his head. Richard grabbed Nala, and they waded through the water to him.

Richard spoke to him first. "Are you here to be baptized? You don't look like you're from around here. You can take off your mask you know. We won't judge."

The young boy kept his mask on and said, "Thanks, but I'm not here to be baptized. I just wanted to see the end of the age."

"What do you mean?" Nala said.

"I'll put it this way," the boy said. "You all have the last tickets to the last train out of here. You'll see what I mean soon enough. Enjoy your trip home. Trust me, it will be worth it."

The young, masked boy began to depart, but Richard had one final question.

"Can you at least tell us your name and where you're going?"

The young boy lowered his mask and exposed his deep green eyes.

"The name's Ronin. You made the right choice. You should be grateful. You'll never have to see these eyes again."

Yessica could feel her body ripping apart as she reached the final part of the Harbinger gate. She was more than nine miles beneath the earth. The Little Lights were not affected by the shift in time. They guided Yessica through the grueling process. Cloud was impressed that her body could sustain the power of the gate.

"A normal human would be dead by now," Cloud said. "There's a reason this gate is sealed. You must be special."

Yessica began to sweat profusely. She felt her skin being pierced by what seemed like millions of needles.

"I'm a Navy SEAL. I can handle anything. SEALs aren't sworn; they are born."

Cloud and the others laughed.

"Just a little bit longer," Yessica said. "We're almost in Israel."

Yessica gave her final orders to Westin. He was unusually quiet for such an occasion. She figured her good friend was recording the moment for his personal archives.

"Listen pal, I have one last favor I need."

Westin answered calmly: "I'm here for whatever you need Yessica. Just say the word."

"Turn back into the baddest rifle man's ever seen. Simeon's got another lead date."

Chapter Twenty-Six

Homeward Bound

The seventh angel poured out his vial into the air. There came a great voice out of the temple of heaven from the throne. It said, "It is done." There were voices, thunders, and lightnings. A great earthquake occurred. One that was mightier than any earthquake ever. The great city of Babylon was divided into three parts. The cities of the nation's fell, and Babylon received her cup of wrath from the Lord. Every island fled away, and the mountains were not found. A great hail fell upon men from heaven. Each stone had the weight of a large coin. Men blasphemed God because the plague of hail. The plague was exceedingly great.

Alice watched a great earthquake shook the earth for more than six hours, causing continued destruction. Then, hail shaped like icicles fell from the sky like bullets, killing millions who could not find shelter. The only place unaffected was lake Hudor. Alice couldn't see what was happening on the ground, but she knew the Church was there. She breathed a sigh of relief knowing they were spared this judgment.

Ramsey was close by and asked if Alice had any more questions, for their time together was short.

"I've already asked you this but can you explain it to me once again?" Alice said. "Why did they deserve this?"

Ramsey answered, "It is written: To everything, there is a season and a time to every purpose under the heaven. Therefore, wait ye upon me, saith the Lord. Until the day I rise up for the prey. For my determination is to gather the nations. That I may assemble the kingdoms. To pour upon them my indignation. Even all my fierce anger. For all the earth shall be devoured with the fire of my jealousy."

"You quote Ecclesiastes chapter three and Zephaniah chapter three," Alice said. "I've heard them before but never with this sort of context. Thank you, Ramsey."

Alice noticed a familiar angel nearby. It was Michael. He gathered all of heavens armies and brought them to the Lord of Hosts. They were all clothed in fine and clean white linen. Alice saw the Lord of Host before the army riding a white horse. He was faithful and true. In his righteousness did he make war. His eyes were like flames of fire. On his head were many crowns. There was also a name written that only he knew. Clothed with clothing dipped in blood. His name was called The Word of God. Out of his mouth came a sharp sword that he would use to smite the nations. To rule them with a rod of iron. He crushed the winepress with the wrath of Almighty God. There was clothing on his thigh that read: "King of Kings and Lord of Lords." This Lord of Hosts commanded Michael to cleanse the world of demons and to prepare the world for his return.

Simfer continued to berate Ifrit. He was insulted that one of his own exercised authority over him. He also demanded to know what Ronin was doing.

"Where is the child?" Simfer asked. "How can he do what he wants and not me?"

Ifrit could be silent no longer and said, "The child was never under you jurisdiction. Leave him out of this."

"The child works under you, and you work under me. How dare you lecture me about jurisdiction you idiot."

In an instant, thousands of Oze angels surrounded the area. They were led by Michael. The angels kept Simfer from leaving, but Michael didn't order him to be restrained. He was trapped once again, unable to leave the strict perimeter. Simfer tried to use what little power he had to escape, but there were just too many angels to overcome. Michael grew annoyed.

"Are you done, devil?" Michael said. "Wait here for your time of bondage is upon you."

Then Michael ordered his angels to capture and bind the horsemen of Pestilence and Death. Both angels were captured immediately, stripped of their power, and brought to the depths of Tartarus. Michael had much to do. He decided to bring about the destruction of Sedah next.

Fish and Rook ruled the dreamworld of Sedah like kings. The lesser demons were theirs to command since Ifrit was busy on the surface. They enslaved all humanity in Sedah. Their perfect world was now a nightmare for all those trapped inside. Thousands of angels invaded the space. They bound Fish and Rook.

"How dare you angels bind me?" Fish asked. "The depth Lord has authority here."

One of the angels said, "Tell it to the judge. We have orders to escort you to the lake of fire."

Rook screamed and asked, "Can't we go to Tartarus instead? We are Archdemons. Please don't bring us to the lake."

The angel shook his head. "You should have thought of that before you rebelled against the Lord. Take them away."

The angels now had to execute the next mission. Millions of people were connected to this fantasy world called Sedah. They went about their orders and fetched the Scratchers. Seconds later, Ronin and his Scratchers appeared in Sedah. The Oze angel in charge gave his instruction: "You know what to do, Ronin."

Ronin nodded and said, "Hello, Vigil, it's good to see you again, old friend. I see that you are a True Defender. You're one of the few angels who survived the battle with the Dragon. I'm happy to see you've been promoted. Don't worry. I know what to do."

Ronin ordered his Scratchers to take those who took the mark of the beast into eternal punishment. One by one, the Scratchers gathered their victims and sunk them into the lowest depths of Hell. Ronin, however, remained on the surface. He had his arms stretched out toward Vigil.

"You know you have to do it," Ronin said. "So just do it."

Vigil reluctantly bound Ronin's hands and feet together and brought him before the throne of Ifrit. He had no pleasure in binding an innocent child.

Ronin knelt before the great throne.

"Your orders have been fulfilled," Ronin said. "What else do you require of me?"

Ifrit proudly responded, "Well done, Ronin. You and your Scratchers have exceeded my expectations. I would have you join me on this throne."

Ronin scoffed, saying, "I wasn't talking to you, Ifrit. I was talking with the throne behind you. Can we speed things up here Presbyteros? Its freezing up here."

The throne behind Ifrit suddenly shook and vanished. Ronin's binds were released. He fell on his back and was swallowed up by the earth. Ifrit now stood alone with no more authority. He could feel the pull of the Devil on his spirit. His speech was broken again.

"How this happen?" Ifrit asked.

Gaia led her army to Megiddo. It was an underwhelming place to be. Her massive army filled the area and circled around it like they were about to invade Jericho. Gaia waited and waited for Simfer to guide her, but he never came. She grew tired of waiting and decided to pay an old acquaintance a visit.

William had left Gaia and was in a secret Jopa base. He tried to initiate a launch sequence for his emergency space shuttle. The destination was a Mars base that his company had founded many years ago. William got on the comms and tried to speak with someone in charge.

"Ultra-ten, this is Jopa actual," William said. "Come in, Ultra-ten. I need assistance now."

A broken speech came through.

"This is Ultra-ten. We're being overrun with..."

The voice went silent, and William despaired. He tried the moon base, but they had the same issues. He was trapped with no way out. Gaia suddenly appeared beside him, but he was too focused on his escape to care.

"What do you want?" William said. "I'm busy."

"I can see that," Gaia said. "However, if you want to survive, I can gladly take you to Antarctica where you can be born again."

William laughed. "That entire project is hogwash. It won't work. When you're dead, you're dead. There is no coming back after this life."

Gaia paced the room.

"Spoken like a former priest," she said. "You believe in yourself, your assistants, and Simeon but not me. I wonder why?"

William pounded his fist on the console. "My assistants are all dead, save Eden. What did I do to deserve this? I did a lot of good in this world."

Gaia began to mock him.

"Of course. You single handedly started the Proxy Wars. You ran your father's company into the ground. You separated Jopa from Zohar and blamed Christians for all the world's problems. Great job, William. It's a wonder why heavens angels are at our gates."

Yessica grabbed her head in pain. She was in an empty desert with seven children surrounding her.

"Did it work?" Yessica asked.

She rose to her feet and picked up her massive sniper rifle.

"Congratulations, Yessica," Winston said. "You have traveled through space and time. Welcome back to Israel."

Yessica coughed violently. Her lungs felt like they would burst.

"Gee, thanks," she said. "Remind me to put you on mute next time."

Cloud also congratulated her but focused on the mission.

"Simeon is three miles away, but we can't get closer. They won't let us."

Yessica raised her eyebrow and said, "Who won't let us exactly? I don't see anyone but you kids."

Yessica tried to step forward, but her body didn't respond.

"The angels won't let us get any closer. They're everywhere." said Cloud.

"How am I supposed to shoot something three miles away?" Yessica asked. "That's impossible."

Cloud shrugged and said, "I'm sure we can think of something."

The Last Sheep held corporate worship and continued to lead many to Christ. Miracles happened all around them. Trees sprouted with fruit. The land became tenable. It sprouted vegetables and other life-sustaining foods. People ate with restraint and didn't gorge themselves. They had self-control and other fruits of the spirit. Pastor Josh began to recite Psalm 23. Midway though, Chester appeared in the glory of an angel. Pastor Josh stopped and fell to his face.

"I had no idea this was who you really were, Chester," Pastor Josh said.

Chester picked up Pastor Josh.

"Worship God, not me. I am a servant just like you. Be not afraid. You are almost home. Continue to preach the message."

Chester floated in the air. Countless angels surrounded the lake and joined them in corporate worship. The whole earth could hear their praise to God. Pastor Josh finished reading Psalm 23 and looked up into heaven. What he saw encouraged him.

"Look up, Church. I see heaven opened and the Son of Man standing at the right hand of God. Our redemption is here!"

The Church looked up into heaven and saw what he saw: a peace-filled atmosphere. The Last Sheep drew their last collective breath and died. The angels then guided their souls into heaven.

Chapter Twenty-Seven

Second Chance

Yessica did her best to figure out how to make an impossible shot. Westin aided in this endeavor. They calculated distance and matched it with the curvature of the earth. They manipulated every variable and tried every possibility, but they always came up short. Part of Yessica enjoyed this process. It gave her a break from the Little Lights. They had a knack for being a handful.

"That's it, I'm done," Yessica said, throwing her hands in the air and beginning to pace in circles.

There wasn't much space to move, but she was grateful to have some rather than none. Westin tried his best to encourage her.

"We've gotten this far," Westin said. "I know we'll think of something."

Cloud shared Westin's enthusiasm, saying, "He's right, you know. Plus, I think I have an idea. I can speak with one of the angels guarding this place. I might be able to convince him that we're only here to help. That may allow us to get closer."

Yessica had no objections and said, "Lead the way, Cloud."

Cloud got in contact with one of the angels. He allowed the Little Lights to get close to Simfer, but He didn't allow Yessica to move. Cloud and the Little Lights took the offer and came within feet of Simfer. Simfer noticed them out of the corner of his eye and hissed and growled at them.

"I thought you would be good children and stay dead," Simfer said. "What happened?"

Cloud held up his hand and shook his head.

"This is the end of the line for you," Cloud said. "We're here to see you destroyed."

Simfer quickly reached his hands down into the ground. The veins in his body began to enlarge, and his skin became clammy. The angels didn't think to do anything about it. He simply appeared to be stretching downward. It didn't seem threatening. But Cloud saw through this deception.

"He's gathering energy for an attack," Cloud said. "You guys have to stop him now."

The angels ignored Cloud, which made his nervous. The energy Simfer gathered came straight from the pit of Hell. The angels were likely immune to such an attack but not the Little Lights. Cloud figured they were the intended target of Simfer's attack. He rallied his family and began to attack Simfer. They moved with incredible speed, but Simfer was too strong for them. The Little Lights stopped attacking and braced themselves for inevitable pain.

Gaia's great Crusade army remained in Megiddo. They were on edge. Gaia sensed angels all around. She had no way to explain their presence to her troops, who were designed for physical combat not spiritual combat. Gaia used her abilities to seek a target. She searched through all her data and came to a conclusion: she would destroy Jerusalem. It seemed to be her only option. Simfer had yet to be released, and she lacked direction without him. Gaia gave the order and had her artillery unit prepare to siege Jerusalem. They were many miles away, but her satellites were working. It would take little effort to guide the artillery to its target. Then, a man showed up and interrupted the attack.

"I've never seen you before," Gaia said. "Who are you?"

The man smiled and said, "What you meant to say is, *what* are you? I will explain. I'm one of the guardians of Jerusalem. Your attack came to my attention."

Gaia hissed. "You're just a man. What can you do to me?"

"My name is Dao. I'm one of the 144,000. Don't worry, Gaia. I'm not here to destroy you."

Dao turned around and pointed in every direction.

"That's the angels' job," Dao said.

Gaia and her army were now surrounded by angels. They attacked her immediately. The angels made short work of her forces. Her army went from two hundred million to less than one hundred in a matter of seconds. The few one hundred soldiers that were left alive fled in every direction. Great birds circled the skies and followed them. They pounced on them and ate their flesh. Gaia was now an army of one. She refused to accept defeat. Gaia began to call out and challenge the angels to combat. She screamed and screamed.

"Cowards, why won't any of you face me?"

A lone challenger accepted her offer. The angel drew his sword and pointed it at Gaia.

"This won't take long," he said, sprinting forward and beginning to spar with Gaia.

She was more agile, but he had greater strength. The angel counter-attacked and gained the upper hand. His blade was now at the throat of Gaia.

She begged for her life and said, "I'll give you whatever you desire. Just let me go."

The angel became stern and said, "You are ignorant, Gaia. Have you not read that the wealth of the wicked is laid up for the just? You own nothing. You never owned anything. Now it is time for us to be rid of you."

Gaia relented.

"At least tell me what your name is," Gaia said.

The angel sighed. "My name is Kouri. I'm a humble Zimrat. Let this blade be the last thing you see."

Kouri guided his blade at Gaia's head and split her into two pieces. Her robotic remains were now laid bare for all to see. Kouri used his abilities to turn on the satellites in the area. He used them to show the world the corpse of Gaia. Humanity was few in number. Those that were left were in awe by Gaia's defeat. However, they couldn't see the angels. All they saw was an army laid waste.

Ifrit was now in a quandary. He felt bound to aid Simfer but didn't want to force the hand of heaven. He could hear Simfer in the distance constantly harassing him. Simfer demanded that he aid him in this hour of need. He had no forces to command and no allies. Fear gripped

Ifrit, but he had no concern for his own life. Torment and death were at his door, but he needed to act quickly. He was miles away from Simfer, but a path was made to him by the angels. He could either follow the path or stay put. Ifrit eventually caved in and decided to aid Simfer. He saw something in the skies above as he began to head toward him. It was one like a man riding a white horse. All of Heaven's army was behind him. Ifrit was blinded when he set eyes upon him. He cowered and fell to the ground. The king on the horse began to slowly descend onto the earth, ready to vanquish any that stood in his way.

Simfer continued to draw energy from Hell. Cloud and the others began to panic.

"He's creating a Hell-bomb somehow," Cloud said. "We need help."

The other Little Lights begged the other angels for help, but they all seemed to be preoccupied with something. Simfer moved his arms from the ground into the sky. A massive ball of energy as big as the sun was over his head. The angels now took notice of what was happening, but they were unable to stop it. Cloud fell to his knees.

The other Little Lights asked, "Why are you on your knees, Cloud?"

"Gonga said we should do this when we need something from him. He called it prayer. Don't you remember? We should pray."

Cloud led the Little Lights in prayer. Their prayer was brief but full of detail. A woman with a spear on her back appeared soon after.

"Go back to Yessica, children. I'll take it from here."

A path opened for them to escape. Cloud and the others wasted no time and returned to Yessica's position. The woman spoke to the enraged Simfer.

"I know you're in there, Simeon. If you ever cared about me, you will listen. Stop giving him your strength. Don't you want this to be over?"

Simfer began to twitch. There was an internal battle going on that only he could see.

"Hello, Little Dove," Simeon said. "As you can see, I'm not myself. If you're here, then that means your sister is close by. I have no doubt she's here to kill me. All of this confuses me. I never thought that you would be the one to bring vengeance upon me."

Alice remained calm and suppressed her feelings.

"Vengeance belongs to the Lord," Alice said. "You know that Simeon. Just do what must be done. I'm asking you this as a friend."

Simeon grunted and said, "You speak in riddles, Little Dove. You've been taught well. Now get out of here. I will handle the Dragon."

Alice sighed in relief.

"Goodbye, Simeon. Thank you for listening."

Simeon fought internally with the Dragon and gained the upper hand. He relaxed his arms which caused the Hell-bomb to disappear. His body was regained for a few moments. Simeon caused his body to remain still and stiff. He made himself the perfect target. Ready to be struck down at a moment's notice.

Yessica was still trying to figure out how to get the shot to land. She needed to get to higher ground, but the desert made this impossible. She shot a few rounds into the distance to see how far they would go. Each shot went barley a mile. This frustrated Yessica who considered herself to be an excellent marksman. Her concentration was broken when Cloud and the other Little Lights appeared before her.

"Hey kids, what happened?"

Cloud explained as fast as he could: "An angel lady allowed us to leave. She somehow paralyzed Simfer. You have to shoot the shot now. There is no time left."

Yessica took a prone position. Cloud became her spotter and guided her to where she should aim. Westin confirmed that she was in the correct position. Yessica took a deep breath and squeezed the trigger. The shot fired, and she saw a hand guide the bullet well beyond the mile marker. The bullet was now guided over three miles. A second loud pop could be heard soon after.

"It's done," Yessica said. "Let's get out of here."

The sound of a gun being cocked echoed behind Yessica. She remained prone. Yessica knew who was behind her.

"Only William Calig would dare try to kill me twice," Yessica said. "What do you want and how did you get here?"

She snapped at the Little Lights.

"You're supposed to keep watch."

The Little Lights were just as shocked as she was.

"We didn't know this type of technology was possible," Cloud said.

William drew a familiar pair of orbs and said, "Remember when I killed you with these? Its more than a weapon. It's a tracking device. I never wanted to kill you back then. How could I? You were Malka's pride and joy. Built to be almost indestructible. Unfortunately, I had the same luck with those Two Witnesses. They deserved to be executed, but I also failed in that endeavor."

Yessica slowly got up and turned around to face William.

"You managed to do a halo jump," Yessica said. "It's the only explanation as to how you got her so fast and undetected."

William smiled and kept his pistol firmly aimed at Yessica.

"Very good," William said. "That's why they call you Artemis. You were queen of the SEALs and the queen of my halo executioner. I have you to thank for spearheading the extermination of the savages."

Cloud tried to approach Yessica to hand her something, but William stopped him.

"Where do you think you're going? Go back to the other children."

Cloud slowly moved back to where he was. Yessica accepted her fate.

"I know that you all loved Simeon more than me," Yessica said. "Go ahead and kill me. I was created to be the answer to his problem. My mind has no regrets."

William shook his head and said, "Such a waste of resources. Malka had to make you, didn't she? She called you her insurance policy. You were supposed to help Simeon not kill him. It doesn't matter. Your time on earth has ended."

William pulled the trigger. Yessica flinched and closed her eyes but slowly opened them moments later. A large, familiar demon appeared before her. William's head was on the ground ripped from his body. The Little Lights also couldn't bear to look. They slowly opened their eyes and were glad when they saw the demon.

"Adrammelech, it's you!" Cloud said.

Yessica was confused. "You know each other?"

"Adrammelech is our cousin," Cloud said. "His mother is Tyra. You know her as Bastel. I've never seen him like this before though. His spirit is like Adrammelech, but he goes by another name now. Isn't that right big guy?"

The large demon spoke: "Me, Ifrit. You, Velovia."

Yessica was even more confused. "Who is Velovia? Do I remind you of her?"

Yessica explained to the Little Lights what happened many years ago: How William nearly killed her and how she wound up in the trash. Ifrit was there and helped her escape. Cloud suddenly had an epiphany.

"I get it," Cloud said. "You remind Adrammelech of my mother. Her name was Velovia. She died shortly after giving birth to me. That's why he helped you."

Yessica was grateful for the help, but her attention shifted to the skies above. She tried to look away, but it was impossible. Her eyes were fixed on the heavens. Ifrit pointed to the skies and said, "The king coming."

The husk of Simeon's body lay on the desert floor. A large bullet had penetrated his skull. The Dragon known as Lucifer pulled himself out of the body of Simeon with ragged breath. He regained his composure and looked at all the angels surrounding him.

"What are you all looking at?" Lucifer said. "Have you no respect for your creator. I am your god. Serve me this instant."

The other angels didn't move or make a sound. They simply stood ready. A loud trumpet sounded in the heavens. The darkness that covered the earth was now gone. The light from the Lord of Hosts shined throughout the earth. All eyes were upon him. Even they eyes of those in Hell.

Chapter Twenty-Eight

For All To See

The glory of the Lord of Hosts was available for all to see. He descended onto the earth as only a true king could. His army was at his back, and the world beheld his glory. This Lord of Hosts landed in Israel and entered the desert. Lucifer panicked when he first saw the King of Kings. He was afraid yet defiant.

"Lend me a weapon, you fools," Lucifer said.

An angel stepped forward and tossed Simeon's bow, a quiver full of arrows, and a silver crown at his feet. Lucifer picked up the weapon, donned the crown, and aimed it at the Lord of Hosts. He had no idea that the entire world was still watching.

It didn't take long for the world to see that Lucifer was no warrior. He was arrogant and sly. His angelic qualities were long gone by now. He wasted his effort by attacking the Lord of Hosts. His attacks were useless against him. The Lord of Hosts fought Lucifer without any weapons. He used his nail-scarred hands and broke the will and might of Lucifer. Eventually Lucifer became exhausted. He was defeated in every way. The rebellious angel cowered at the feet of the Lord of Hosts and begged for mercy.

"Remember the good I've done, Lord. I only wish to serve."

Lucifer held an arrow behind his back. He tried to catch the Lord of Hosts off guard by attacking him with it. The Lord of Hosts grabbed the arrow with his hand and crushed it. He then slammed his head into the head of Lucifer. It knocked him back to the ground and left him in a daze.

"Bring me the blades," the Lord said.

Michael knelt before the Lord and presented two long swords. He took the blades from Michael and had Lucifer on his knees. With a long swoop he slammed the two blades into the head of Lucifer. The blades had a specific purpose. They made whatever they touched deaf, lame, mute, and blind. These effects transferred to Lucifer immediately. Lucifer now lay on his back unable to move or function. "Take him away and lock him up for a thousand years."

A group of Yeshua angels acknowledged the order and carried Lucifer to Tartarus. This was a place of torment reserved for the most dangerous of angels.

Ifrit was close by and speechless. He was trained to believe that Lucifer was the ultimate power and authority on earth. He realized that he couldn't have been more wrong. The Lord of Hosts caught his eye and approached him. Ifrit knelt and kept his head low.

"Me now realize that you strongest," Ifrit said. "You Jesus Christ."

The Lord of Hosts acknowledged him.

"You speak well. Arise, servant."

Ifrit rose to his feet and transformed into an angelic being. He was no longer the terrible demon Lord.

"How is this possible?" Ifrit asked, falling on his face in fear.

"With me all things are possible," Jesus said. "From this moment on you shall be known as Archippus. Master of the horse. Now then, what would you ask of me?"

Archippus kept his head low and said, "I never wanted power. All I ever wanted was for my mother to acknowledge me as her son. I don't want war. It's rest that I'm after."

The Lord of Hosts helped Archippus up and embraced him.

"Come with me and have rest in my kingdom."

"What about my father?" Archippus asked.

"Samyaza is your father no longer."

Alice was one of the few angels chosen to escort Lucifer into the depths of Tartarus, a place of pure darkness. The very essence of this place was designed to make an angel go mad with rage. There was no order here. Chaos reigned supreme. The angels chained Lucifer in the cold and darkness and removed his clothes. A small drip of water fell on his head every second. This would be no problem if it only lasted a short while, but this would likely go on for his one-thousand-year sentence. He also had to deal with the intrusive visions and terrors of Tartarus. This punishment could break even the strongest angel. Lucifer could not speak, but he could grunt. He grunted and grunted when Alice was nearby but stayed silent when the others were nearby. They figured out what he was doing and left Alice alone with Lucifer. There was no need to warn her about his tricks and deceptions. He was powerless here.

Chapter Twenty-Nine

Time Like No Other

All of heaven cheered as the Lord of Hosts made his triumphant return to Jerusalem. The world, however, hated this event, even though they were not forbidden from watching the spectacle. Dao and the 144,000 bowed before the Lord of Hosts as he approached the temple. They opened the temple doors and waited in the courts. The Lord of Hosts entered into the temple alone. He sat on the throne made of gold and precious stones and declared that the kingdom of heaven had arrived.

"Behold, I am making all things new," he said.

The decimated earth was now restored. No longer were the water sources poisoned. Nor were the trees and grass burnt up. The earth was now a lush environment full of new sources of animals, food, fruit, and vegetation. The people of the earth looked up and saw a great city, a new Jerusalem descended onto the earth. It was a city of pure gold and precious stone.

A young girl awoke in this new city. She checked her hands to make sure she was alive. She was no longer afraid. Something guided her and began to teach her all things. This brought her great comfort. Angels cheered for her as she navigated the city. It was full of friendly and beautiful people. The girl noticed something. They all introduced themselves by their first name's only. The girl was guided to her own mansion. It was fully furnished, and there were infinite things to occupy her attention. The only thing missing were friends and family. The young girl left her mansion and was greeted by what she desired most. Her friends and family were standing before her. Some were missing, but she felt no sadness. She only felt joy.

"Come with us, Nala!" they said as Nala was reunited with her friends, father, mother, and her Uncle Joe. Almost all of Camp St. Peter and Camp Luther were there.

A young man beckoned her.

"Come on Nala. You're not going to want to miss this."

Nala didn't recognize him at first but was overjoyed when she finally did.

"I'm glad to see you, Richard. You're all grown up."

"Yeah, you should try it later," Richard said.

The two friends rallied with the Church and watched the holy city descend upon the earth. Everyone was filled with a peace beyond comprehension. It guided their hearts and mind. Their needs were met, and they had no wants. The Lord was their Shepherd. The sheep were no longer lost.

Footage from Lucifer's defeat played on a loop for hours. He quickly went from being a savior to a mockery. However, not everyone agreed with what the Lord of Hosts had done. There was division amongst the

Little Lights. Four of them— Cloud, Platora, Chante, and Yarloch— were for what the Lord had done. While Dakus, Atra, and Harkin were opposed to what the Lord had done. They didn't doubt the Lord of Hosts' sovereignty. They simply disagreed with how he humiliated Lucifer. Ironically, the rest of the world was also split on the Lord's return. The devil was now a caged animal, yet he still managed to draw sympathy and support.

Alice approached the chained Dragon known as Lucifer. Alice removed the blades that kept him from speaking, hearing, and seeing and granted him temporary freedom from his torment.

"You smell like a Yeshua angel but speak like a mortal," Lucifer said. "How did you get here? What do you want?"

"It's quite the mystery, actually," Alice said. "One day I was human, and the next I was an angel. What I want to know is why you do what you do? Help me understand your madness."

Lucifer smiled then answered, "You must be the hybrid everyone is talking about. Hear me, oh heavens. Judah's favorite toy is off its leash."

Lucifer continued to mock her.

"How fitting that a daughter of Eve would see me like this. Isn't that right, Alice? That's right. I know who you are. You know why I act this way. It's all about vengeance. That's all that matters to me."

"I don't doubt your cleverness," Alice said. "I do doubt your competence. Explain your lust for vengeance. Tell me why you rebelled against the Lord. I have to know. Where is Gaia in all of this?"

"Have you not read: 'Unless you be born again you cannot see the kingdom of God'?" he said.

Alice considered his remarks blasphemous and said, "I don't have time for your games. Speak to me without defiling scripture."

"Very well, Alice. Many years ago, my children began work on the Born-Again Initiative. It's a machine based in Antarctica that stores the memories, accomplishments, personality, and more into synthetics. Its activated right now actually. Soon some of history's greatest minds will be born again to wreak havoc on this earth. I'm trapped now, of course but only for a while. Eventually I will be set free, and I will turn humanity against itself yet again. I don't have to do anything. People have a natural inclination to destroy one another."

Alice grabbed the two blades from the ground and walked toward him. It was now her turn to mock him.

"I think you said it best in the garden," Alice said. "Ye shall not surely die."

Alice held the blades to his throat. She was unable to kill him, but she could bring him great discomfort whenever she wanted.

"You disappoint me with how weak you are, devil," she said. "I don't care about your clones or your plans for the future. They're doomed to fail. However, I see why you chose Simeon. He was evil, but at least he commanded respect."

Lucifer laughed and said, "You liked him, didn't you? Even though he killed you. You really are as dumb as you look."

Alice ignored his statement.

"The thought of you being Ronin's future chew toy makes me happy," she said. "Though I must admit that I'm not led by my emotions these days. I bet the Scratchers can't wait for daddy to finally come home and forever be on the menu."

Alice slammed the two sword blades back into his head, which caused him to groan with pain and remain silent.

"You can count on two things," Alice said. "First, you can count on me having a front row seat to your baptism in the lake of fire. Second, you must know that no one will ever follow you again."

Alice turned to leave.

"See you in a thousand years."

Chapter Thirty

A New Beginning

An entity awakens in the heart of a labyrinth. This being leaves its cryostasis pod and gently lands on the cold hard floor. It places its hand on a large machine in the center of the area.

"Initiating the Born-Again Initiative. Welcome back, Gaia."

She tethered her mind to the machine and activated one of the pods. The entity awoke from its slumber.

"Standing by to activate Born Again Initiative. Welcome back, Dr. Malka Nazarian."

Malka was exhausted by the process and made light of the situation.

"You see, Gaia," Malka said. "Everything is going according to plan."

Gaia wasn't amused.

"They cut me into two pieces. How was that part of the plan?"

Malka cut short the banter and activated the other pods. Billions of clones awoke out of cryo sleep and gathered in a collective fog. These were the great leaders and merchants of old. They were wealthy and celebrities in their own right—all from the top one percent of society.

Some of these synthetics were infused with the minds of the current generation, while others were implanted with memories and ways of people from the past. One thing was certain: these were no longer human beings. They were another creation entirely. Everything about their actions was simulated. Only their minds were human—just as Malka and William designed it.

William Calig's pod could not be accessed. Malka tried desperately to bring him back, but she was unable to. Malka had always been a leader. It was who she was. Her leadership was being put to the test once again. She stopped all the infighting amongst the Synthetics and gave a rousing speech.

"We are no longer children of men," She said. "From this day forward we will embrace the void."

Malka's words were met with great reception. They all voted and elected Malka as their leader. Gaia continued to be revered as a goddess, which was also by design. Malka led her fellow Voidlings to the surface of Antarctica. Their bodies were impervious to cold. Many of them believed they were in a sort of heaven, that this was eternal life. They were excited and optimistic. Their master plan was nearly complete. They simply needed one more thing.

Navigating the stars was easy for Bastel and her crew. Today was no different. They were just outside the Milky Way galaxy looking for Earth-like planets. None of her Watcher vessels had found one in this galaxy, which disturbed her. She often wondered why this was the case.

"I want to check the starboard planets, Navigator," Bastel said. "Head to bearing zero seven four."

The Navigator acknowledged the command.

"Checking starboard planets at bearing zero seven four aye."

The spaceship headed in the new direction and analyzed the nearby planets. A planet with a green atmosphere caught Bastel's eye. It had both land and liquid. It was the only other colonizable planet in the galaxy. The Navigator gave his analysis.

"This planet is loaded with resources, Bastel," the Navigator said. "Looks like you've found a good one. What shall we call it?"

Bastel beamed with pride and said, "We shall call it..."

The alarm system aboard the spaceship sounded. The crew went into combat mode. Bastel took her seat and demanded answers. She questioned all departments and had them report to her. However, no one could tell her exactly what threat they faced. An unknown being teleported to the inside of the ship. Bastel drew her blade and faced it.

"Who are you and how did you get aboard my ship?"

The entity smiled. "Do you believe in me now?"

Bastel calmed her crew and looked deep into the eyes of the one before her.

"Gaia?"

"Yes Bastel, it is I. Put that silly sword away before you poke your eye's out."

Bastel wasn't amused by the joke.

"So, you are real," Bastel said. "It doesn't matter. We've failed."

Bastel sat back in her seat with a defeated posture.

"I thought you might say that," Gaia said. "That's why I brought along a friend."

Bastel saw a figure out of the corner of her vision. She recognized his scent immediately.

"Master Braccus!"

Bastel stood at attention and had her crew do the same. The lead Watcher gazed upon the newly found planet and marveled.

"Is this planet hostile?" Braccus asked.

"No, sir,'" Bastel said. "There are also no indications of inclement weather. It's a stable planet."

Braccus seemed pleased.

"Very well," Braccus said. "I'm ordering you to join the other Watcher ships heading for earth. It's going to get crowded in here. You'll be acting as an ark and not a battleship. A new breed of people has arrived. They call themselves children of the void or Voidlings. Bring them to planet Gath immediately." Bastel kept her head low. "Planet Gath Master Braccus?" Braccus had an unnerving appearance. He had no face and showed no signs of any emotion. "Gath is where Goliath comes from. A mighty giant warrior. I can think of no better name than this. The Voidlings are the giants of mankind. They deserve a planet that reflects the ways of giants. Think of the Voidlings as our children."

Bastel understood her orders. Gaia stood by Braccus, and they both looked down on Bastel.

"I will give myself to the cause, Master Braccus," Bastel said.

Braccus and Gaia disappeared from sight. Bastel summoned the Navigator and gave her orders.

"Send this location to the fleet. We're heading back to Earth to pick up precious cargo. This time we'll hold nothing back."

Yessica, Westin, and the Little Lights were fishing in the city of Haifa, Israel. Their mission was complete, and they enjoyed the R&R. The waters and the earth were restored, and there were nearly countless fish in the sea. Yessica taught them all she knew about fishing. They were fast learners and caught many fish. A woman approached them as they fished.

"You look you're going to hurt somebody," the woman said.

"That's something only my sister would say," Yessica said. She tried to touch her but her hands went through the woman like she was an illusion. "Alice! Is that you? Take off that hood."

Alice revealed herself to Yessica and the Little Lights. She wanted to embrace her sister, but it was not possible. The two sisters held on to the shadow of one another. Yessica wept profusely while Alice seemed void of emotion.

"I so glad you survived," Alice said.

Yessica smiled and said, "I'm a SEAL. There's nothing I can't handle. What's with the clothes? You look like an assassin."

Yessica was also surprised by the spear on her back.

"Is that a bloody spear? What gives?"

"The clothes are meant to conceal my identity," Alice said. "The spear is rather complicated though. Maybe I'll tell you it's story sometime elsewhere."

Alice's mood turned serious.

"Listen, I wanted to ask you something," Alice said.

Yessica was all ears.

"Do you believe in the Lord now?" Alice asked. "I'm sure you've thought about it. His kingdom is here. We all saw him. What more proof do you need?"

Yessica sighed and said, "Let's just say that I'm convinced, but I'm not convicted. You've got to understand that I'm not human, Alice. I don't think I even have a soul. I'm an empty vessel who's completed her purpose."

Yessica's heart was synthetic, but her feelings were real and raw.

"Dr Malka said my purpose was to stop Simeon," Yessica said. "I blew the train off the tracks. What am I supposed to do now?"

Alice tried to answer, but one of the Little Lights gained her attention.

"I'm hungry, Yessica. Can we eat something?"

The little girl caught Yessica by surprise.

"What do you mean you hungry?" Yessica asked. "You've haven't eaten anything since you were an infant."

Yessica turned to Alice.

"What's going on?" Alice turned to her side and spoke with something invisible.

"Ramsey says that they have been granted souls and will live long and healthy lives on the earth. The earth must be replenished."

Yessica folded her arms and asked, "Where's my soul? Never mind. I know that can't be all. So why don't you tell the kids exactly what you mean by replenishing the earth?"

Alice turned again to the invisible being and said, "Listen closely, Little Lights. You will each have to go your separate ways very soon.

Fear not, angels like myself will guide you. You'll meet other people and start families."

"How do we start a family with other people?" Cloud asked.

Alice's voice began to crack.

"You see, when two people love each other very much, they form unions."

Cloud and the others listened closely.

"What type of union?"

Alice couldn't bring herself to explain the concept of intimacy to children. "Just ask Yessica, and she'll explain it to you. Okay?"

The Little Lights responded in unison: "Okay."

Yessica opened her mouth to explain the details of intimate unions, but a visitor had arrived before them. He was upon a white horse and had many crowns on his head. The Little Lights paused and questioned if what they saw was real. Yessica was also speechless and could not deny the one before them. Cloud and the other Little Lights approached him.

"Is that you, Gonga?"

You leave Israel and find yourself back in the hall of ancients. The CMC meets your gaze again. His living silver skin is still unsettling. The purple irises are alive with fire yet calm. The CMC looks happy to see you.

"Congratulations, dear reader," the CMC says. "You've made it to the end. Did you forget about the CMC already? You've managed to surprise me. I didn't think you'd last this long. I guess you've earned the right to know my name. My name is Credophilus, but you may call me Credo for short. We all know how limited your mortal brains can be.

I do wonder what you thought of the story. Did you enjoy it or were you thrown off? Feel free to contact me with your thoughts. How you will actually do so is beyond me. Till next time, dear reader, or will there be a next time? That is up to the author from the strange land of Texas. I have some advice for you if you haven't read the book of Revelations. Read it for yourself. It is a book with many questions, but it also has many answers. There might still be time left for the world if you're reading these last few words of mine. Repent if you haven't already. Lest you wait like a fool and reap the whirlwind that's coming."

Credo slowly waves goodbye to you and continues his important work as a scribe. The Hall of Ancients fades away into the realms of heaven. With hope, you now have some clarity on the cryptic book of Revelation. This tale is now finished. What you choose to do next is up to you.

Made in the USA
Coppell, TX
01 September 2023